OH DEAR, MARIA!

DEDICATION

I'm not sure I could fit here the names of all the people who I feel are owed thanks for the part they have played in my publishing this novel, to those of you who have supported and encouraged me in this very time consuming hobby, a thousand thank-yous. A thousand thank-yous also to those kind souls (to whom I am heavily indebted) for helping me polish, perfect and proofread this novel (and its forgotten forefathers). An eye for detail – something of which I am not in possession – is a valuable thing indeed.

With special thanks for the support of my fellow writers at Fosseway. And, of course, to my wonderful husband and son.

For Grandad B (The Creative Soul) — I wish you could read this. I am a relentless daydreamer and book lover — always with one foot reluctantly in reality and the other in a story — and I need not look very far to understand why.

For Grandad Penguin (The Industrious Spirit) — I'm not sure you much liked novels, but if it were not for your tenacious desire to provide for your family the opportunities taken from you, I am sure I should never have written this one.

I hate spoilers, but for those who might wish to be prewarned of any unpleasant themes in a story, you will find a few hints at the end of this book.

TABLE OF CONTENTS

CHAPTER ONE

CONSISTING OF TWO PARAGRAPHS.

Mr Fielding once reminded me of the value in laying the menu of one's literary offerings before a reader. I shall endeavour to summarise something from which you may judge what is to come. Of the world in which this tale takes place, I will say that I pictured it as a polyester-clad 1960s reimagining of the Regency Era. Indeed, if you look closely enough, you might notice Maria's ruby and diamond wedding ring was cast from none other than the finest plastic. As to the writing, you will find many archaisms of spelling, language and style. For that, I have no better explanation than it being the manner in which the words fell from my head onto the page. I shall say nothing of the characters; take them as you will. Gilly was always my favourite of the Jackson brothers, if you care to know. With that all said, l hope you have as much fun reading this as I had writing it. And now enters the stage our heroine, or as Gilly would name her, MARIA DIVINE:

For Maria Harrington, there was no greater satisfaction than that which could be found in her own misery. It had always been the way, and there was no explaining it, at least not by the lady herself; misery was her oldest, most-beloved friend, and she was forever in search of this companion. Only the saddest and most dispiriting of songs would satisfy. Only tales of the most abject sorrow could be read with any real enjoyment. Long had been acquired the language of those crestfallen heroines she so much admired, and not a day could go by without this young lady at least once declaring herself the most unhappy creature in the entire world. In what daily occurrence could not conflict and despondency be found? What great fortune – or what great misfortune – that the same trial of her most beloved heroine would shortly be hers.

CHAPTER TWO

IN WHICH MARIA AND MR KING ARE REACQUAINTED.

'Oh, Pearly, my dear, what fantastic news! Mr Jackson has written to confirm his attendance on Saturday evening,' Mr Harrington said to the woman he called his wife, though the law would disagree with him on that count.

'Oh, that is wonderful news, sir!' Pearl could not remember who Mr Jackson was or why this should excite Mr Harrington so, but she was delighted nonetheless.

'I had worried myself believing that he might consider the invitation an impertinence after such a short period of acquaintance. Oh, but what a cordial reply he has sent. Though, I would expect no less from such a well-bred gentleman, to be sure!'

'Oh, no less indeed, sir.'

'You must take Maria to buy new things this morning. She is to look exquisite! It is perhaps too late for a new gown to be made. But new ribbons, shoe roses, and gloves, these can all surely be found before Saturday?'

'Oh, well yes, sir. It is likely too little time for a new gown. But any gown can be considered anew with the addition of some diverting ornaments.'

Ignoring Pearl's response, Mr Harrington continued his thought, 'Though, should not enough money have her a new gown expeditiously made? Three days is no short length of time, is it not, dear?'

'Oh,' Pearl answered with an agreeable smile, 'to be sure, sir. Three days is ample time to have a new gown made if the payment is to be sufficient.'

To Mr Harrington's mind, there was not a single problem that could not be resolved by the tactical deployment of money. Maria cared very little for her father's money, or anyone else's for that matter. While her father and Pearl were deciding upon the design of this gown in the breakfast parlour, she avoided their ridiculous and infuriating company, taking a moment to disturb one of the young housemaids going about her work in the yard. The young housemaid thought Maria to be no less infuriating nor ridiculous than the master or mistress of this home.

An elderly gentleman named Mr Foston was their immediate neighbour, and, having nobody but his servants to keep him in regular company, he was often to be found hanging his head from the window of his study to converse with anybody across whom he might happen. Mr Foston was as content distracting the Harrington servants as Miss Harrington was herself. Though each of their conversations was nigh the same as the last, Maria was always pleased to happen across this pipe-toting gentleman.

'Ah, hello there! Mrs Harrington, how are you, dear?'

Maria replied to remind him she was not *Mrs* Harrington, but being rather deaf, he heard nothing of it, though pretended as if he did.

'How pleased I am to hear it! Indeed, I am quite well, madam. How are your husband and Miss Harrington?'

'It is I, Mr Foston. *I* am Miss Harrington!' Maria stood herself upon the housemaid's stool and cried her reply as loudly as her voice could muster.

'Ah, Miss Harrington, I beg your pardon. My eyes are not what they were. And how are you, my dear? And your father and mother, are they well?'

Pearl looked not a day over twenty. Still, Mr Foston had it fixed in his mind that she was Maria's mother, and nobody had ever bothered to correct him. This elderly gentleman was the only person Maria would allow to mistake Pearl for her mother, so she simply replied:

'They are both very well, sir. I am informed that you will be attending our party this Saturday, is it so?'

After Maria had repeated this question two more times, Mr Foston confirmed that he would be in attendance. Maria was glad for it and told him so in an obscene near-shout, inspiring an unseen arched brow from the housemaid. That would at least be one guest who the lady would be happy to see.

Every year her father held a party on the last Saturday before Christmas. The attendees typically consisted of his business acquaintances and some gentlemen of inherited means – friends he collected in his attempts to climb a little further up that well-greased social ladder. Maria would satisfy herself with the company of Pearl and Mr Foston. She cared nothing to converse with the inhabitants of her father's social sphere.

At length, Maria came down from her room on Saturday evening, after her father had sent for her on no less than three occasions; never did she like to do as he asked after only one request. The party, as she had anticipated, consisted chiefly of dull older gentlemen and their young, solemn wives. Upon arrival in the drawing-room, her father was engaged in conversation with a gentleman who appeared far younger than the rest of the crowd, though this was an assumption made only upon the appearance of the back of his head. Mr Harrington beckoned his daughter in his direction, and – being not so insolent as to ignore her father's bellowed instructions in a room filled with his acquaintances – Maria did as he asked. Mr Harrington cried joyfully at her appearance and loudly began introducing his daughter – naming her the prettiest girl in London – to Mr Jackson before Maria had so much as caught sight of his face.

The young man effused his pleasure at making the lady's acquaintance and was subsequently himself introduced. '*The Honourable*?' A curious smile crept upon her face. 'Am I to understand then, sir, that you are a member of Parliament?'

'Indeed,' her father interrupted, 'and this fine gentleman is not just *any* politician. Mr Jackson's father was an MP for thirty years before being made the Governor-General of Bengal – now is that not something, indeed? And his eldest brother, well, the gentleman is presently Home Secretary.' He made certain to impart those pieces of information very loudly. 'Mr Jackson here made his way to the House at the election this

August last. Aye, we are to expect great things from this young gentleman, to be sure we are!'

'All in good time, sir,' Mr Jackson replied with a faint smile.

It was a good thing Mr Harrington had a great talent for making conversation with people who had little desire to be conversed with because Maria had nothing more to say, and Mr Jackson was quite started into silence. The young lady had poorly disguised her shock at being presented to the charming man she had come to know some months before this day. Only then he was known to her as Mr King. She recognised his elegant features and his very charming voice. In every other conceivable way, he appeared to be an entirely different man.

Mr Harrington had made sure to notify everybody of Mr Jackson's influence, and thus the attention of this gentleman was desired by every highsighted social climber in the room. Maria's father, taking his duties as an efficacious host most earnestly, went about attending his other guests, leaving Maria in the solitary company of his lover. Pearl was just one year older than Maria at twenty-three, a kindly and mild-mannered lady who agreed with everything Maria's father said with a childlike malleability. Mr Harrington had a most preferred type of woman. It was fortunate that he was a benevolent-enough man who had no real malice in his intentions towards Pearl.

'He seems a nice gentleman, do you not think, Maria?' Pearl asked with her perpetual voice of slight confusion and concomitant watering eyes.

Maria quickly found a suitable lie. 'Mr Jackson? I know nothing of him that could suggest his being either nice or unpleasant. At present, I think nothing of him.'

'Well, your father believes that he is a nice man, and *he* is never wrong about these things.'

For much of that evening, Maria was held in conversation with Pearl, listening to the repetitions of observations Mr Harrington had made only an hour earlier. Pearl was a tolerable companion and was the preference of Maria above speaking with anyone else in the room. Tiring of the string of constant retellings of her father's thoughts, at length, Maria acted to disrupt the flow of Pearl's conversation and instead admired her pretty hairstyle. The ploy was fruitless:

'Oh, do you really believe so? That is very kind of you to say, Maria. Though, I cannot take credit for the design of it – that is your father's doing. When we visited the assembly rooms at Cheltenham when we were gone abroad, he had pointed out a young lady with hair precisely as I have mine this evening, and he said to me what a fine hairstyle it was and that he believed it would look infinitely more becoming on me because my face shape would be much better suited to it. On Monday, he declared that there was nothing that should make him happier than to see me wear the style at our upcoming party. Well, I could hardly scheme to get in the way of his happiness by ignoring such a declaration as that, and so I have had Hannah practice it with me all week. It is very much to your father's liking, I can assure you.'

'Oh, how glad I am to hear that, Pearl. I would be beside myself with grief should I learn that my papa did not like your hair after all your efforts to please him.'

Insensible to Maria's sarcasm, Pearl smiled and began to tell Maria how she could achieve such a style herself.

Maria's father had not aged poorly for his forty-four years. He bore a striking resemblance to Pearl's own father, Mr Foley, who Maria considered spoke to his only daughter like a beloved lapdog. Mr Foley seemed wholly unconcerned with her taking up residence with a gentleman almost twice her age and to whom she was not married. On his occasional visits to the Harrington household in Bedford Square, Mr Foley could be found perpetually remarking at what a fine home, furnishings and situation Pearl had happened upon. Mr Harrington and Mr Foley had both been born to families of lower middling circles, but the former had substantially improved his fortune and situation.

Maria and Pearl were prevailed upon to play at Casino with a table of young ladies, and though she little enjoyed cards, Maria was obliged by her companion, who could do nothing alone. Much of her time was spent observing Mr Jackson. He did not, though, return her glances and appeared perfectly insensible to her being in the room. Strange; there had once been a time he had declared himself unable to restrain his gaze from her eyes. *'Beautiful, mournful eyes,'* is how he had described them. In perfect contrast, he had said, with the constant presence of a disarming smile on her face. Maria had never noticed such things about herself. With his loud and permeating voice, it was impossible for Maria not to overhear her father

7

profess her beauty to Mr Jackson on two subsequent occasions. The young gentleman responded to these avowments with no discernable alteration to his countenance. Well she could guess the design of her father's conversation: with her comely appearance and Mr Harrington's *Midas touch*, there was every expectation the young lady would marry above her present station.

After some time, Maria found herself in conversation with Mr Foston, who had, for no insignificant period, been slumbering upon one of the sofas next to the fireplace. Bored with the discussion at the card table, she made her way to join him when he, at last, awoke. The old gentleman complimented her pretty gown, which had been produced at the expense of a great deal of money and the poor nerves of the seamstress.

'Aye, it is a good thing you decided upon such a fine gown, for I believe your father has Mr Jackson in his sights for you.'

'I believe you are not wrong, sir.'

'Ah, you need not sound so downcast at the design of your father's plans. He is a handsome fellow this Mr Jackson, is not he?'

'I could not swear against it.'

'Aye – although, I hear that he is the youngest brother of three and has little in the way of fortune. But that is of no consequence to a young woman such as yourself.'

'No, I suppose it is not.'

Maria cared nothing for Mr Jackson's being a gentleman of a small inheritance, nor for his being handsome; she had long been acquainted with both truths. Many more times she would cast her glances towards him that evening. He conducted himself with such a convincing indifference. Dear Maria could not help but colour and avert her gaze each time this gentleman arrested her eyes in his own.

CHAPTER THREE

IN WHICH MARIA AND MR JACKSON ARE REACQUAINTED.

Mr Jackson was, we cannot already have forgotten, one of those good servants of the people. The location of the constituents to whom he was such a faithful servant was of as much interest to me as it was to Mr Jackson himself, and for that reason, I cannot at all remember the name of the place. Aside from this little neglect or indifference – whatever we shall call it – Mr Jackson was a politician of great passion. Some mornings after the party, Mr Harrington was reading the particulars of an argument that had occurred in Parliament between Mr Jackson and another MP who had been feeling similarly bored with the lack of activity in the House one day in November. An abundance of '*sirs*' with a few '*honourables*' thrown in for good measure – pithy sarcasm – the coffins of respectable careers – objections being worth not a straw – one mention of horse excrement – and an absurd reference to treacle etc. etc. etc. It was apparently something about prison reforms.

'By Jove! It goes on and on and becomes even more scathing, if you can believe it. What a speech for a young man to give! Ah, I like him very much already. There is great value in a young man who has no fear in sharing his true opinions. I can see already he is determined to make a great name beyond the shadow of his brother and his father. What a fine match such a young man would make!'

Mr Harrington was so keen for his daughter to marry Mr Jackson that he took every opportunity to communicate the gentleman's character to Maria. What a keen interest in politics Mr Harrington had stumbled upon in this decade of life. And what a lot there was to be found in the papers. There seemed to be few honourable men too well established in their influence that it could prevent a challenge from the youngest Mr Jackson.

'Oh, indeed, sir. There is great value to be found in young gentlemen of such character,' Pearl replied.

Mr Harrington answered his lady with nothing but the condescension of a nod and pressed his daughter for her thoughts on the speech.

'I care nothing for his speech. His tone was far too proud and arrogant for my liking.'

'Oh, dear girl, that is simply how gentlemen converse in Parliament. They all speak in such a way. You must not allow his sarcasm in a little speech to colour your good opinion of him!'

'And who is to say that my good opinion of him is not already long coloured?' Of course, such a thought must remain in the confines of solely her own knowledge, and Maria replied to say that Mr Jackson's speech made no alteration to her opinion of him. Which was not untrue, although a jot deceptive.

'Oh, I am glad to hear it! For I have just this morning written to invite him to join us for a family dinner. And I am greatly inclined to believe he shall accept.'

Mr Jackson did accept this invitation and was to be a dinner guest at Bedford Square almost immediately. Maria attempted in vain to put the thought of this young villain from her mind before his visit, but her father was certain to discuss him at every available opportunity. Even in her many hours alone, it was not to be done; nothing could distract our young heroine from the collision of her present indignation and the remembrances of their former, flaming acquaintance. Mr King, who she reminded herself to know now as Mr Jackson, had made such an impression upon the workings of her heart. Dear Maria had been almost recovered from this disposition when he had seen to reintroduce himself into her life.

'Upon my word, you look very handsome to-night, Maria. Although I wish you had taken your father's advice for styling your hair. It does not become you, draping down your back so. But it is no matter. Mr Jackson shall not mind it when held against your pretty face and fine figure. Though you would be better to put your shoulders back just a little, for you do have quite the habit of slouching, my dear!'

Maria smiled at Pearl's near-exact repetition of her father's earlier words of advice. The two young ladies waited in the drawing-room while the gentlemen did whatever it is that gentlemen do when ladies retire from a dining-room. It was for the best that Maria was not cognisant of her father's present conversation; he was rather crudely and indelicately suggesting to Mr Jackson what prosperity Maria's future husband would have, with her being her father's only child and the bridge to a grotesque fortune. Very favourable agreements could be drawn up for a gentleman of suitable birth and standing.

'Upon my faith, I have seen her make no smile at any gentleman such as she makes at you. Indeed, I was once very glad of her fancy for writing plays and attending her little church above the amusements which many young women involve themselves in. But she cannot sit in her apartment writing these trifling scenes forever, and she is of an age now to make a gentleman of a good family a handsome wife in both her countenance and her character. Do you not agree, sir?'

Mr Jackson answered his agreement on both counts, declaring Maria a very charming and pretty sort of girl.

'To be sure, her complexion is not as fair as I had hoped it would become with age – despite her being so often indoors – it is on account of her taking very strongly after the image of her maternal grandfather. What thick blood that family has! Ah, but he was a fine gentleman, to be sure he was. And it shall be plenty thinned out by the time she has children of her own.'

Mr Jackson said not a word in response to this comment.

When the gentlemen joined the ladies in the drawing-room, Maria was sitting in one corner reading the first volume of *Clarissa*; Pearl was in the other playing the pianoforte. Mr Harrington made haste in fabricating a reason to quit the room and left Pearl to perform her role as his eyes on the pair.

'Indeed, my love, they shall be more disposed to developing affections if her old father is not in a way to listen to their conversation. And you must play something inspiriting. There is nothing so potent as music to lend a well-matched pair to love making,' he had said to his lady before Mr Jackson's arrival that evening. Of course, she agreed with him absolutely.

Maria did not look up from her book nor acknowledge the young gentleman taking a seat next to her.

'Your stepmother plays very well,' began Mr Jackson. 'Do you play, madam?'

'She is not my stepmother. Pearl is not married to my father.'

'I beg your pardon,' replied he with a sincere air of apology.

Maria had first thought to leave him in his silent confusion and return to her reading but could not keep herself from saying quietly, 'Your misunderstanding is hardly your own doing. Pray, do not think too ill of my father. They are not married because they cannot be married, and not by a cause of their own design. My father has every intention of honouring his commitment to Pearl, and without the persuasion of a judge, which I believe makes him a far better man than many.'

'I agree, madam.'

What had been her scheme in telling him such? Maria hardly knew herself; perhaps she had hoped to improve the gentleman's judgement of her father. There was surely some hope this divulging of information would deter Mr Jackson from any ideas involving herself – what an imprudent marriage it would be for him. If there was any success to that end, she could not determine for his countenance changed not at all.

'Your father informs me that you enjoy writing plays. I am a great lover of the theatres, especially those here in London.'

'Oh,' smiled Dear Maria, somewhat facetiously, 'I am sure *that* you are, Mr Jackson.'

His composure could not disguise his amusement at her accusation. Quickly she returned him a look that gave no doubt at her finding no humour in their present situation. After a moment, he tried again to engage her conversation. Maria would not tolerate it, but the wretched fiend would not desist.

'I understand you are quite fond of the music of your own voice. I do not much enjoy reading aloud, but I am always glad to listen to a book read even if the reader is entirely intolerable.' Here she forced, with some might, her book into his hands. 'Do you know the novel, sir?'

'Ashamedly, by title alone, madam,' answered he, subduing a laugh. 'I do not read many novels.'

'I see,' Maria replied, feeling rather offended on behalf of novels, 'well, the tale follows the life of a young woman from a family of significant fortune, who is viewed by her kin as little more than a means to social advancement, as she is pursued by a duplicitous and immoral man.'

'It sounds rather grim.'

'Oh, yes, it is very grim. Page after page of an innocent young woman's wretched despair – it is my favourite book in the entire world. You may start from the top of this page, sir.'

The gentleman released another smile that she would not return.

'And, so what of it, madam? What news have you for me?' asked Mr Harrington to his lady as they made their way to bed later that evening.

Pearl related her observations with no detail spared.

'A book you say? And do you suppose this is a good sign, madam? Aye! To be sure, it is! Is there not some intimate affection in a gentleman reading a book to a young woman?'

'Oh, to be sure, sir, it is a *most* intimate activity. When she passed him the book, I was already quite certain she was in love with him. And the affection in her eyes while he was in the course of his reading – and I must say, sir, he has a *very* handsome voice – well, they could not disguise her feelings for him.'

'Ah, very good, very good indeed, madam! I believe we shall see the two married before spring.'

'Without doubt, sir, nothing could seem more certain!'

CHAPTER FOUR

AN INTRODUCTION TO, AND
CONVERSATION WITH, RALPH.

Invariably, the greatest love of Maria's life had been Ralph, her cousin who was five years older than her. Though, it was not a romantic love. Oh, how furiously horrified were both Maria and Ralph whenever they encountered even a hint at their marrying. For a thousand thousand worlds, there could not be found a single man as wise or as good as Ralph Paterson – to Maria's mind, anyway. Ralph was the only surviving child of Maria's maternal uncle, Mr Paterson; God rest his soul.

Mr Paterson might appear an unlikely name for a gentleman whose father's family descended from a small village in Maharashtra, and perhaps it was. The Paterson name was no lineage of the male line. When Miss Paterson, the glovemaker's daughter – Maria and Ralph's future grandmother – found herself in love and on the cusp of marriage to an officer with the *East India Company*, it elicited delighted cries from all her family, till that time when they discovered her beau to be a native of East India. The family blessing was dependent upon many conditions, one being that her husband must give up his name. Earlier that week, the following intercourse of letters had occurred between the two cousins:

'Oh, my Ralph! I have so very much to tell you; I do not know what you shall make of it! Allow me to elaborate: you must remember last summer when we attended a series of talks by Mr Garcia, we became well acquainted with a gentleman by the name of King, who entirely disappeared after Violet's party – of course, you shall remember him, you told me upon a multitude of occasions how little you liked him – well – who should appear at my father's party before Christmas but this very gentleman himself; only, he was not introduced to me as Mr King, but the Honourable Mr Jackson. He is a politician, Ralph, can you believe it! It seems you had good reason not to trust his word!'

'I beg you do not chastise me for mentioning nothing of this till now. I hardly knew what to think of this circumstance, let alone how to articulate it to another. I hope you are not too cross with me! Oh, please do not be cross with me, Ralph; you know I cannot bear it when you are displeased with me. You know I would care nothing for this duplicity in any ordinary circumstance. In fact, I should laugh heartily to discover such a gentleman parading about as a commoner. Oh, but you must surely understand how it pained me to be reintroduced to him – and worse, now he is the latest object of my father's scheming. Every day I must hear the praises of this gentleman sung in my own home, and with each new morrow, I feel myself closer to blatting the truth of this gentleman's duplicitousness to my father. La! What little difference such a declaration should make! What is honour and decency in comparison to pedigree in the eyes of my father?'

'I write really to ask you to walk out with me on my return to our church on Sunday morning – do you remember Joanna is to give her first sermon? Pearl conveniently requires the carriage herself. You know that my papa shall not let me walk out or even take a hack without some escort – and he will never spare a servant for me. If I notify him of my plans without already having secured you as my watchman, I am certain he shall have another in mind. Then I am sure that I shall scream and run away from this place forever. Or perhaps I shall throw myself from my window into the street – what a pretty scene that would be. If I wore one of my white morning dresses, I would look like a little dove flown into a window, all broken-necked and beautiful. I beg you reply quickly with your answer. I am very dependant upon your indulgence for my happiness, cousin! Yours always affectionately, and now most desperately,

Maria.'

'I am very happy to oblige.

Yours, &c., Ralph Paterson M.D.'

It must be noted here, for the sake of not diminishing the character of this young doctor, that he was neither haughty nor unfeeling; he simply had not the time to be an attentive correspondent. Particularly to his cousin. Maria sent him page after page of her thoughts several times a week. The meeting was not till nine o'clock, nor more than a quarter of an hour from

Bedford Square; regardless, Maria had instructed her cousin to collect her at eight. Consequently, their walk to the meeting house took several scenic tours in the locale.

'I must say, you are very handsomely dressed this morning. Oh, will you be such a kind cousin and hold my reticule for me, Ralph?' The young Dr Paterson returned this compliment to his cousin and need not ask Maria why she could not hold the bag herself. Maria had a maxim that all men liked to be made helpful to young women. How obliging she was in always finding some way for any gentleman in her familiar acquaintance to be of service to her. 'Ah, do not attempt to disarm me by commenting upon *my* fine clothes, Ralph Paterson. You do not commonly dress so fashionably as this; I would call you a dandy if I did not think it would risk you returning me to Bedford Square!'

A disapproving look was returned, confirming to Maria this particular comparison would not be warmly received. Unable to question her cousin any further on his suspiciously well-put-together attire, Maria related every detail of her present misery minutely:

'…since sending my letter to you, Mr Jackson has *twice* more been a guest at our home. And now I am beginning to fear that he is not at all being put off by my father's imprudence; rather, he appears to be encouraged by it. What can *he*, a man of such an honourable and ancient family, mean by entertaining these ridiculous advances from a brewer? Certainly, my father has been encouraged by the gentleman's compliance; he has instructed me to *write* to Mr Jackson. Write to him! Can you believe it? What possibly might I have to say that I could not have said in the three visits he has made to our home in this one week? Indeed, it is my father who ought to write, for it is *he* towards whom Mr Jackson directs his courtship. You must know, any man who considers my father with any seriousness is almost certain to be motivated by the plumage of my inheritance. And I have not a single doubt that Mr Jackson's ideas are all mercenary.'

When her cousin appeared to be distracted by his own thoughts, Maria demanded that he must join in her misery. 'Ralph? He does not even listen to me! La! What are you men but handsome dolls to hand bags to and hang arms upon?' This declaration did not, to her disappointment, provoke him at all. His disposition was now disconcerting in its pensiveness. 'Are

17

you quite well, Ralph? Really, I thought you would revel in learning such, as you had been so certain of Mr King's poor character.'

Indeed, Ralph was perfectly well, corporeally speaking. But since receiving his cousin's letter, there had been a weight upon his mind that he was forced now to relieve. Before a word of this thought was imparted, he asked Maria to not despise him too strongly when she was to hear what he had been keeping from her. Maria reacted to his confession with predictable spectacle:

'Oh, Ralph! No, no, it cannot be! You knew all the while, and you said nothing to me? Oh, how could you, dearest of all men to me, knowing how I cared for him so, not have said a word of it? You treat me as ill as my father!' The lady appeared on the cusp of sobs. 'There is now not a single man in the whole world who I can say treats me well! And you *are* dressed like a dandy to-day!'

Dr Paterson and Mr Jackson had been acquainted for some great time when the latter presented himself as Mr King at Mr Garcia's first talk. The two young chaps had met nine years earlier as new students of Gonville and Caius. If they were to give their word, these gentlemen would surely own to having been close confidants for the first twelvemonth of their studies; both young men of even tempers and attentive to their learning; one an antiquary, the other, a man of science. Howbeit, this warm friendship came to a cold conclusion after their introduction to a young woman whose name is of little relevance.

What *is* pertinent, though, is that Dr Paterson held this young woman in high regard, as did she him, and after many long weeks of letter writing, she was enough enamoured to accept his addresses. The young man told nobody of his engagement but his closest friend, which relates what suffering was incurred when the young woman ended her engagement by reason of her affections for this very man. Though the lady protested these affections had grown through no little inducement, once she was free of her former beau, the new one wanted nothing of her. It seems superfluous to confirm that the two gentlemen did not remain friends; what Dr Paterson knew of Mr Jackson after this point was only by virtue of the talk that followed wherever he went.

'*Everything* he does is for his own amusement, Maria. The instant he believes himself in possession of your true admiration and regard, I assure you, he will care nothing for it.'

That she already knew.

'Oh, Ralph! This is not fair at all. How am I to be angry with you now, knowing what a broken heart you had suffered? You were of such a miserable humour all that summer when we stayed with Grandpapa – Oh, and I did tease you for it so mercilessly, and to think of how you tolerated it all so well! And how sorry I am for every word of it. Any lesser man would never have condescended to be prated to in such a way, any vehement reflection I would have been most deserving of, and yet you suffered me with such dignity. Oh, but I was such a child then, surely you can forgive me for it?'

Ralph replied that he could forgive his cousin for having been the most insufferable tormentor in the world if she would absolve him of his omission.

'Oh, need you even ask? Of course, I forgive you! But you must allow me to chide you for it a little. I may not have owned it to the others, but I had told Penny of my regard for him the moment the thought first passed into my mind, and she tells you *everything*. I know that you knew of my affections even before I had confessed them to you myself. You might have saved me from a most wretched heartbreak of my own had you imparted the knowledge of your previous acquaintance with him.'

Penny *had* told Ralph of his cousin's growing regard for Mr King. At first, he had been set upon deterring Maria's affections by owning the truth but soon considered this action unnecessary; Mr King or Mr Jackson (whatever he was to be called) continued to be committed to the same inducements as he had ever been. The young woman who might have been the object of his affections impeded her elevation to that vacancy by wearing her sentiments too visibly. This twice named gentleman had already redirected his flirtations to another young woman of the group; Maria had begun to notice, and Ralph, knowing how this rejection would injure her, saw little benefit in adding to her grief by revealing how she had been duped in more ways than one. Once Mr Jackson had imprinted himself upon Maria, there was nothing Ralph could have done to spare her misery.

A letter from Miss Penelope Stuart to Miss Maria Harrington. Thursday evening, ten o'clock:

'I write, my love, from the depths of the most wretched concern. You have not visited your cousin's home a single day this week, and now you have missed two evening services. Are you ill? My mind has conjured every most awful conclusion for your absence. If I have not a reply from you by to-morrow, I have it on his solemn oath that your cousin shall be to Bedford Square to discover the cause of your disappearance. If you have not a good reason for your absence, prepare yourself for an earnest chiding.'

'Thomas was reading from Revelation this evening; your favourite book, my dear. I am afraid to say he plans to read from Genesis on Sunday morning, but if you are certain to come, I can attempt to persuade him to include some gnashing of teeth and hellfire to satisfy you. What did you make of Joanna's sermon? She is far cleverer than I am. My argument against this Curse of Cham − as they call it - as you know it already, my dear, is that, as it was men, and not God, who have interpreted that particular history, I shall take no notice of their claim that a man seeing his father's nakedness hundreds of years ago should necessitate my being beneath anybody, simply because I am black and they are white. Have you anything cleverer to add than I have, my love? Pray, let it be nothing too profound − you know I am the weakest link in a chain of sharp-witted Stuarts − how fragile my ego is because of it.'

'I am much enamoured with the peach pelisse your father had made up for you − really, I do not know why you did not like it − I have embroidered a pretty floral scene on the collar. Your cousin complimented it twice on the first morning I wore it. Now, dear madam, in reply to your coy whisperations to me on Sunday morning, I cannot understand why you should suppose your cousin saying to you he "does one day plan to marry" equates with his wishing to marry me. Declare me his *Pamela*, and he my *Mister-B*, would you? Involve me not, sweet lady, in the romantic dreams you conjure from your beloved novels. Besides, I am not so certain I have such iron-clad virtue as young Pamela. Pray he does not *Mister-B* me; then again, pray he does! Oh, will you scold me for saying such about your cousin? If you will, I bid you remember the year you found yourself indefatigably in love with my brother − I certainly have not forgotten it. Burn this after reading, will you? Or hide it very well, that nobody but you will know the inner workings of the heart of, your,

Penny Stuart.'

A letter from Miss Maria Harrington to her friend Miss Penelope Stuart. Friday morning, six o'clock:

'Lord! (forgive me, I know you do not like when I exclaim such, but when you read what I have to tell, you shall understand why I begin in such a manner) I had hardly thought that my present circumstances when last we spoke at the meeting house could descend into greater absurdity, and yet they have! I am not ill, my love; how much I would rather be struck down by the most wretched of fevers than be plagued by my present torment! But I shall answer your letter before I begin recalling my misery: La! Penny! How may you suppose I should have anything clever to add about that peculiar passage – whatever Joanna and Thomas say, I agree with wholeheartedly, though I understand none of it at all – unless they disagree, in which case, I shall side with Joanna; it is better to be a traitor to my minister than my sex. The practical application of faith is all that is within my power – my mind begins to spin me into a nauseous turn just contemplating such conversation, so I shall say no more of it.'

'By the bye, have you noticed my cousin is dressing with a suspicious flair for fashion of late? You see him oftener than I do. I could not press him on the matter. I wonder he does not do so to impress you, my dear friend! Truly, I am very sorry if my whisperations bring you grief. I shall say not another word on it after this: if my cousin wants not for you, then may he forever remain single, for there is no woman but you I consider fine enough to marry him. I have affixed a note within this letter. It is for the good man himself, do pass it on to him for me. If my father thought I was writing to Ralph asking him to come to my rescue, then he would never allow it to leave the house, so I am forced to conceal it within my correspondence to you.'

'Now I shall relate to you my present misery. Oh, and how greatly I suffer, my dear! When my cousin returned me home to Bedford Square, who should be there in the sitting-room, but of course, Mr Jackson! He was to remain the whole afternoon, and within moments of my arrival, my father and Pearl abandoned the room themselves (each with an equally weak excuse) and left me alone in his company. Having nothing more to say to him than on any other occasion, he soon tired of his attempts at conversation with me and offered to read aloud again. Anything to avoid talking to the man, so naturally, I agreed to it. In his favour, I will say only this – he has a very even and pleasant reading voice. If he were not so cunning, then I would believe it rather charming. Little passed between us during that afternoon, except his questioning whether the entire story was related through the medium of letters and then later declaring what a morbid and unromantic tale he thought it to be. I have yet to tell him how many volumes there are!'

'I had thought to myself when he had left, "Really, that was not too great of a trial!" Only, that evening after dinner, my father informed me that Mr Jackson very much intended to make his addresses to me on his next visit. "Well," said I, "you ought to tell him he need not expend the effort, for I shall only reject them!" Oh, Penny, I have never seen such a countenance of fury upon my father. Once he understood I was very serious in wishing to decline Mr Jackson, his rage was most earnest; he upbraided me for my selfishness and banished me to my apartment. Later, Pearl came to me with some supper and divulged (although I am certain she was instructed to do so by my father) that if I would not have Mr Jackson, there is another gentleman, who is expected to soon receive a peerage (La! What is that to me?), who is ready to marry me after we have met only once. You shall never believe who it is!'

'Pearl said to me, "Mr Adams, that is to be the man your father will make you marry if you will not have Mr Jackson. And you shall be sent to live with him in Kent." Mr Adams (you must remember) is older than even my father and is an ugly and odious man, and I really think nothing of Kent! "No," said I, "no, I will not marry him!" No doubt recalling my father's exact words, Pearl said that I would be then best to accept Mr Jackson, for if I married him, my father would rent us a house in town, and I may spend my hours writing plays in my apartment of that home and still attend my meeting house. "It will be little different than your life is now," she remarked. Yes, little different, excepting my being married to a man I care nothing for!'

'I have been now, for five days, confined to my apartment. At first, I had thought a night of rest would quell my father's vehemence, but it did not. An unexpected benefit of my imprisonment is that I have had no cause to wear shoes and have changed myself each morning only into a new nightgown; what luxury is idleness! I would be quite happy with the solitude if only I were able to write, but my thoughts have met with some obstacle, and I cannot remember what it means to have an imagining. Always, you know, I must walk when I happen upon such a blockage in my mind, but as I am permitted to take a turn of nowhere but the floor of my apartment, the ideas will not come. I might accuse my father of purposely taking from me the method of my artistic conjurings, but I do not believe he is clever enough to be credited with that. Upon my word, I shall never forgive him for making me endure such boredom. Do tell my cousin to read my note immediately. You know he will forget otherwise, and what a desperate need for his service has your most affectionate and admiring friend,

Maria H.'

'My dearest, dear Ralph, My father has me confined to my apartment and will not release me till I agree to marry Mr Jackson (if you can believe it!). Penny shall fill you in on the other details. Please come quickly and make him see reason!

Your, most obedient and eternally lovingly obliged,

Maria.'

CHAPTER FIVE

IN WHICH WE VENTURE THROUGH TIME TO THE PREVIOUS SUMMER.

That most recent summer, Mr Garcia, a minister of a small and little-known church, had distributed pamphlets among the streets of London, entitled, *Do Not Ye Become Haughty with Paradoxical Morality.* Much was expatiated in these three-penny pamphlets, though very little was read of it, and only then by a few. One of those few was Mr Thomas Stuart (the older brother of Maria's dear Penny). Mr Stuart was himself a minister of a small meeting house. Though let it be made clear, the meeting house was small only in its construction; few ministers in London, nay, in England, could claim the crowds of Mr Stuart. Mr Stuart's father had come to London from Brazil in the penultimate decade of that century last, having stumbled upon a fortuitous friendship with a wealthy and Portuguese speaking Englishman who secured his manumission.

The elder Mr Stuart did not live to see what claims would be held against his son's name. If he had, oh, how he should have smiled and laughed. Young Mr Stuart was renowned for giving sermons of such a conquering and rousing nature that many women were said to faint from the high flutterations of the spirit he moved within them. What a great number of young ladies were moved to hear the calling of Wesleyan Methodism by this beguiling young minister! Penny and her younger sister Joanna were perhaps the only women in his sphere who were not infatuated with every word that sprung from Thomas' mouth. Maria had spent one whole winter and half of the following spring when she was eighteen, sighing helplessly on the front pews, certain that she would marry nobody if it were not Thomas Stuart. Of course, her father would never allow it, and Thomas was resolved never to marry; so, with dozens of other young women, Maria had found her heart quite broken from the unrequited love stirred by this gentleman's ferocious sermons.

Endeavouring not to stray too far from the important facts of this tale, it is now prudent to return to Mr Garcia and his pamphlets. After perusing this text for some time, Thomas Stuart found himself most interested by the back page, which advertised a series of talks on the Roman Empire. The gentleman later shared that which had gained his attention with his sister, who next related it to Maria.

'Oh, most certainly, I should like to join you. So long as my cousin accompanies me, I see no reason why my papa might object to it. As they are to be on a Monday and Friday evening – Lord, is it not a little ambitious to hold two talks a week, really, how much can there be to say on the subject? – I shall come hither directly, and then we may all travel thither together. I can only hope that Ralph shall deign to bestow his time upon me for yet another outing.'

It might be of some illuminating effect to state here that the two young women were presently sitting in the by-room of Dr Paterson's office; Maria being bored to distraction as always, and Miss Stuart being the clerk of the aforementioned doctor. It is surely known that the educated role of a physician's clerk could never be taken up by a woman. 'What absurdity!' some may cry – a thought my esteemed readers might find themselves expostulating rather often during the course of this tale. Cry they may, but it would be the truth of the matter all the same. Miss Stuart had been Dr Paterson's clerk for three years.

'And when, *Miss Humility*, has your cousin ever shewed reluctance in assisting you or given license to any thought that to do so would be a condescension and not a pleasure?'

'Quite right you are, Penny! Which happy memories do I possess of recent outings that are not mine only by virtue of his generous nature? If it were not for my cousin, then I should be the most miserable girl in all of London, all of England, in fact! For my father is so unjustly paranoid that *I*, or should I say, *his fortune*, will be wooed away from him by a poor suitor. When have I been allowed to walk out alone since being without a governess? Never! And yet, my papa is far too fond of his own repose to escort me anywhere. What a dull life I should have if it were not for my dear Ralph. What faults are his – that he works too hard? That he is too generous or too tolerant of even the illest of humours? There is not a better cousin in the world, I say, and doubtless, he shall be the same breed of husband.' With a wicked smile she imparted that last utterance.

'Away with you, cunning madam!' replied Penny. 'I shall not be tricked into this conversation to-day.'

Ah, but could Miss Stuart hide the smile from her face? Never. Not from the only person acquainted with the truth of her heart. Penny silenced her friend as the doctor was heard re-entering his office. Maria quickly offered a whispered defence, 'Oh, you need not instruct me so. Have I not held this secret of yours for years? Besides, for a clever man, my dear cousin can be an utter blockhead. Combine that with his modesty, and he should never believe me even if I told him straight to his face!'

Dr Paterson opened the door of the by-room to find the two young ladies still engaged in this intimate conversation. What intimidation is brought by two young women engaged in such giggles and whispers! Even if he did know them both so very well.

'I beg your pardon. I did not mean to disturb you.'

'Lord! It is *I* who should beg pardon, Ralph, for I have been disturbing your good lady here from her work. She has not done a single thing for at least forty minutes!' Oh, that wicked Maria smile appeared again before taking a more earnest countenance. 'Do you know that you have blood on your shirt?' said she, poking at a crimson patch as large as a saucer on his stomach.

He replied in the affirmative.

Penny set to fetching a clean shirt for her doctor – if only she could truly call him *her* doctor – and Maria took her leave, though before parting, remarked to her cousin, 'Really, Ralph, you did ought to furnish yourself with better clothes! You dress like my father, and there is no compliment in my saying *that*. There is nothing young ladies admire in a gentleman more than a keen eye for fashion, is that not right, Penny?'

Penny allowed only her smile to be her reply. This young woman herself was the most fashionable lady in Maria's acquaintance. No insignificant portion of the good wages Dr Paterson paid her was spent on beautiful things. And which physician could claim an office with such cheer as he? But it was not just her happy fashions that had brought colour to this otherwise gloomy room that day:

'Who are the flowers from?' the doctor asked with some curiosity.

27

'Oh, they are from me. I wandered down to the flower seller when I went out for a walk. I thought that they would cheer the room a little. You do not mind, do you, Dr Paterson?'

'No, I do not mind. They are very–' He paused to find his thought. '…pleasant.' *This* was the word he settled upon.

'And they distract very well from the jar of Mr Bert's urinary stones,' said she, looking upon him in the way she always did, watching as he decanted the bloodied tools from his bag. Dr Paterson agreed, lifting his head briefly from his employment. Always he looked at her to respond. 'Your ring, Dr Paterson,' said she, coming very close to grasping his hand. His answer was but a noise of confusion. 'It is now rather more red than gold. Would you like me to clean it for you?'

What a pause ensued!

Any one of his servants could have, and probably should have, been tasked with such a thing, but Dr Paterson so often found himself helplessly agreeing to any suggestion from this happy young woman. While Penny set about cleaning his instruments and ring, the doctor sat at his desk, still in his bloodstained shirt, at last having his first meal of that day, and began tackling the pile of unread letters before him. Penny distracted him all the while, relaying the information about Mr Garcia's talks. Dr Paterson did not find it very easy to concentrate when surrounded by conversation but did not mind at all. Penny might talk of nothing and all day long, and he would mind it not for even a moment. Nothing gave him greater pleasure than returning from his work to her. After half an hour or so, they were disturbed by a note brought for the lady. 'Oh, you shall never guess who the letter is from!' Penny declared, leaning herself against the other side of his desk.

'I do not believe I shall. But I suppose you shall make me attempt it.'

She smiled as if to say, '*Oh, absolutely, I shall.*'

'Maria?'

'What a waste of a guess that was, Dr Paterson.'

'You never said my guesses were limited in number!'

'You have only one guess remaining. Pray, sir, use it wisely.'

'Only *two* guesses? What an unfair game this is! – I can always tell when you have spent too long in Maria's company because you are infinitely more contrary.' Penny offered him only a smile, and so he answered further, 'Your cousin near Dartmouth, that is my best guess, madam.'

'No,' she answered, looking unimpressed. 'Here – I shall begin. *Dear Cousin–*'

'I said it was your cousin!'

'Yes, but the wrong one. It is from Violet,' she riposted. '*Dear cousin* – something about housekeeping – something about the duties of a wife – ah, here is the purpose of her letter, I did think it odd that she should write to me, but I suppose she thinks it necessary to commit it to paper: *I write only to remind you of the party my husband has organised for my birthday. It is to be three weeks on Saturday. Do not forget, as you were so close to doing my birthday last.* I do not know why you are smiling so, she has invited you also. Oh, Thomas has told her about the lectures, and she and Mr Featherstone will be coming – well, now you really must come, for she is always much nicer when you are with me. *There is no need to concern yourself with choosing me a gift, I have my eye on a new velvet bonnet, so you might be pleased to gift me the money for that or get me no gift at all.*'

How vexed dear Penny was. Being so enrapt in his clerk's passionate haranguing, Dr Paterson answered only two letters from a pile of thirty that afternoon, each response with fewer than four lines. Never could he bear to contemplate the days his office would be without her voice, even if he did pass most of every evening doing that which he had been so happily distracted from during the day.

29

CHAPTER SIX

CONCERNING STILL THAT SUMMER LAST.

Violet's party was handsomely planned, and why should it not be? Rather, how could it not be? If Mr Featherstone did not ensure it was so, he would surely never hear the end of his having ruined his wife's twenty-first birthday. Oh, yes, Violet was just to turn one-and-twenty, three years younger than her cousin Penny and had married a man so grateful for her attentions that there was not a thing he would not do to provide for her constant felicity. In capturing the eye of this retired tailor, Violet had pulled herself above the means and prospects of every other woman in her family. She loved him as well as she would have loved a man half his age. And twice as much as a man of half his wealth. Both were supremely content in their marriage, so what more is there to say of it?

Though, one disadvantage of this marriage was the haughty airs it gave to Mrs Featherstone, who, now a wife, sought to impart her expert knowledge upon her cousin at every opportunity. 'I see that you are wearing a lavender petticoat, although you know very well that is *my* favourite colour,' Mrs Featherstone said to welcome her cousin into her party.

'I thought that violet was your favourite colour, Violet?' The two blinked incredulously at one another for some time before Penny's attentions were distracted by the sight of Dr Paterson talking with Maria in a corner of this hired hall. The musicians had started, but no dancing had yet begun, much to the doctor's relief, she knew.

Viewing the hall from the very opposite prospect, Maria waved happily at her friend before catching sight of Mr King, who had now entered the hall himself. Having caught his gaze, she dropped both her smile and her wave and turned her back to him. What determination she had begun the evening with to ignore him entirely; now he might feel what it was to be spurned. This was perhaps the only time she had willingly allowed Pearl such a hand in designing her attire and style. She did not, for a moment, doubt how handsome she looked. That was till the gentleman seemed to notice nothing of her, not even when she stood up twice with Thomas Stuart and once with his equally handsome – though rather more serious – younger brother James. It did not matter how many gentlemen she danced with, for she danced with them all excepting Ralph, and still, Mr King was entirely ignorant of everything she did, and Maria checked often enough to know. Seeing his cousin's sulky disposition, Ralph paused his conversation with Penny to say, 'Are you quite well, Maria? We can go home if you would like.'

That was a welcome prospect but seeing the two who she wished to find their happiness together in such contented conversation, she would not break them apart for her sour mood. 'Thank you, Ralph, you are always most thoughtful. Really, I just feel a little faint. I think I shall go outside for some fresh air.' The hall was situated at an inn some few miles from London. It was rare Maria had an opportunity to breathe such pleasant air, and for some moments, she took in every aspect of the beauty of a summer's evening away from town. It was just as she began to settle into this meditative pursuit that Mr King made his appearance.

'Forgive me, I thought that I had seen you come out here. Are you quite well, Miss Harrington?' She answered only to turn her face from his, causing him to smile, though she did not see it. 'Your hair looks very different. I think I prefer it as you usually wear it, when it is down and resting upon your back.'

'My! What penetrating observations you make, sir! And what consequence are your preferences to me? It is clear you know me not very well, for I often wear my hair in this way.'

She did not.

'I must confess, I have been quite resolved upon ignoring you all evening, madam.'

Maria could only but release a laugh at the gentleman's honesty. 'And what would you have me say to *that*, sir?'

'Trying and failing, I might add,' he smiled with an affectation of admiration. 'It is not in my power to return to Mr Garcia's final lectures. I am called away from town. How determined I have been to banish you from my thoughts before I came to leave. Yet I find myself here to-night because I have so comprehensively failed in that determination.'

'What artful words you possess, sir! How can you bring yourself to speak so freely to a woman you know so little?'

'Decry them artful if you will. I shall call them truthful. Pray, forgive the liberties I take, dear Miss Harrington, but I must ask before I leave, would you permit me to write to you?'

'Write to me! What bold libertine behaviour is this! Why should you wish to write to me if not for some reason very improprietous?'

'Oh, madam, can you be so cruel as to desire the exposing of my heart in such a way? Surely you must know why I wish to write to you, why I have attempted in vain to avoid your gaze. I would fall to my knees to beg your pardon for presuming to importune you in such a way. Oh, but Miss Harrington, I can no longer stem the frenzy you have driven into my heart. Let it be so contrary to conventions of propriety, I own that I adore you, and I must die if you refuse me one letter!'

At last, she returned his smile. 'My father would not take kindly to the arrival of any letters from a gentleman professing adoration for his daughter. Though I should be very uneasy to have the death of a young man fall upon me. If you would like to talk to me, sir, then you shall find me at the meeting house on Dean Street every Sunday morning and Tuesday and Thursday evenings.' At this, she gave a little curtsey and made off to leave, but before she could, he reached for her hand.

'*Dean Street?* I shall remember the name, madam. Oh, but will not you stay a moment longer? I must be gone from town this evening!'

Damn his handsome devil voice!

'And what reason could I have to stay out here, sir? There is merriment inside I should like to return to. You might engage me for a dance or two if you would like to see more of me.'

With what proficient eloquence did he beseech her, clasp her hand and press it to his lips. For those better acquainted with the world, his would have been recognised as such typical words from the mouth of any cunning gentleman seeking to charm a young woman whose naivety was as apparent as her innocence. Maria was not acquainted with the world and certainly not with a man of the world such as this. Perhaps it was the impassioned tone in his very charming voice, or maybe because she was entirely unwilling to let go of his attention now that she had it within her possession once more, but whatever the cause, Maria did stay with Mr King. She would not return to the party for a very long time.

Dr Paterson could never be obliged to dance, neither by Penny nor Maria; the only two women in the world who could talk him into anything. Though usually, she would tease her cousin for his pretension, Maria was glad to arrive back in the hall, her long absence quite unnoticed, to see her Ralph sitting alone.

'May we go home now, Ralph?'

'Whatever is wrong, Maria?' he said, beholding the traces of some recent lamentation upon her cheeks.

'Nothing is wrong, Ralph. Only, I would like to go home now.'

Violet's party was the last Maria was to see of Mr King. With great quivering anticipation did she arrive at her meeting house, thrice a week, every week for two months, before she, at last, accepted that the man she had thought herself to be in love with was never to be seen by her again. As abruptly as he had entered her heart, he had vacated it.

CHAPTER SEVEN

A RETURN TO MARIA'S PRESENT PREDICAMENT.

Being disallowed from sending any letter from her apartment and no means of defying her father, Maria instead wrote the following letter to her grandfather, who had passed some two years previous:

'Oh, with what a heavy heart I write to you. I am to marry Mr Jackson, and the date shall be whenever is soonest to be fixed. Ralph has attempted four times (all in vain) to bring my father to reason. I have not been permitted to see even my dear cousin. I only know of his efforts because I have heard such great shouting between him and my father, and Pearl has been kind enough to tell me the rest of what has been said. If it were for my own sake, you know that I would not marry Mr Jackson for all the world. I would happily forfeit all that my father holds over me. Did he really believe me so attached to a pocket-allowance and a fine home that I would submit to such a violation of my own will? Indeed, it appears that he did.'

'Oh, but he did not rely upon it, for once I shewed him my resolve, or my "obstinate saucy airs" as he has accused me of, and seeing that I would not yield, he has taken up the most perverse and cruel means of bending me to his will. He says (though you must already have seen and heard all that has gone on) he will cease supporting the care of my mamma unless I submit to accepting Mr Jackson. What wickedness is this, Grandpapa? If only you could answer to tell me, for you have seen every face that belongs to man, encountered every illness of soul and spirit – you would know exactly what should bring him to reason. I beg you find some method to impart this knowledge to me; Mr Jackson is to return this evening to make his addresses, and for the fear that my father would enact his wicked threat, I have submitted to accept him.'

'Before he left my apartment, I said, "From this day, sir, you shall never again be known to me as my papa. You will not be deserving even of the title of my father. Mr Harrington is all that you shall be to me; you shall be nothing more to me than a man who has done business with my husband." He laughed and remarked upon with what warm passions young women always speak. Can it be, Grandpapa, that I had so poorly judged this man all my life? How could he covet the elevated esteem of strangers induced by Mr Jackson's birth at the price of the eternal loss of the love of his only child? What damnation he brings upon himself, making a plaything of the life of not just one person but three! For, though I care little to consider Mr Jackson's plight in all this, I gather, from the insistence of my performing the role of a woman most affected by love, he knows not that he is soon to be married to the most miserable woman in the world.'

'My final hope, I believe, is Pearl. Though she has yet to contradict my father, she no longer speaks in his support and offers me the most sympathetic eye whenever she is in my company. Though, she has as much reason to reconsider defying my father as I and none of the predisposition to do so. Still, I hope to persuade her to reflect to my father the abhorrence of his actions. If you hold any influence in the minds of we mortals, I pray you will–'

At this moment, Maria's writing was stopped as Pearl entered her apartment to inform her of Mr Jackson's arrival. Not a moment was wasted by Maria in the pursuit of her last hope of avoiding the fate that ever narrowed upon her. The instant Pearl was seated, Maria threw off all her pride and swelled herself with deference for the woman who sat before her, at last throwing herself to the lady's feet.

'Oh, please, Pearl, please, there must be something you can say to prevent this, at the very least to delay the matter? You may tell my father that I shall attend all the balls with him, every ball in England if I must. I will make myself the most amiable and affable catch for every young man of consequence if only he will not force me to accept *him* downstairs!'

Pearl appeared for a moment as if she may yet yield, but it was not to be. She resumed her usual feather-headed facade. 'For all the balls in England, you shall not find a better match than Mr Jackson. He is everything a young man ought to be and thinks not his noble birth too good for your origins. Defiance for defiance's sake shall only bring you suffering; the sooner you submit to the plans, the sooner you shall be happy, Maria.'

'But you must know that I can *never* be happy with him; I know far more of this man than my father does, and I cannot conceive I shall ever know happiness again if I should marry him!'

'Your cousin has informed your father of all the charges you would lay against Mr Jackson. He is certain that there is nothing of his character that cannot be altered by the affection of an attentive wife.'

'Lord, I beg you tell me these are not really my father's words! But he does not know it all. Even Ralph does not know the entirety of it. Pearl, you must believe me when I tell you he is a most immoral sort of man.'

This conversation continued in much the same way till the two were disturbed by a servant who wished to know how long it should be before Mr Harrington and Mr Jackson would be joined by female company. Maria had, by this time, worked herself into such a frenzy of wretched sorrow that one glance at her countenance from Mr Jackson would surely reveal the inducements employed to bring about the acceptance he was soon to receive.

'Maria, you must stop your crying now.'

Through great sobs, Maria replied that such a power was not in her possession.

'You must. You must think of your mother and stop your crying.' Maria saw that Pearl said this with none of the menace or threatening present when her father took to reissuing his threat. No, Pearl spoke with the spirit of a woman who had long since submitted to quiet acquiescence as her *mode de vie*. Owing to the stubborn redness now etched upon Maria's cheeks from her distress, it took some time for Pearl to ready the young lady for her presentation downstairs.

'Maria, you must try to smile at least a little.'

'Smile! Madam, how can you ask me to smile when I am forced to accept a man I cannot abide?'

'Very well – if you cannot smile, then you must slacken your jaw, Maria – like this, see. Loosen your lips just a little. Yes, keep your face like that, and your father and Mr Jackson shall both think you overcome with the quiver of anticipation. There – you no longer look forlorn nor defiant, only scared. And really, I think few men are not gratified by the sparkle of a little terror on the face of their young bride!'

So long were the two women occupied that Mr Harrington became quite concerned his daughter had retracted her submission. Having grown impatient, he came to fetch Maria from her apartment and took her directly to the drawing-room in which Mr Jackson waited. She entered the room alone. The head of this broken young lady felt as heavy as her heart; both throbbing from an hour of begging mercy from a lady who could offer none. One lingering reserve of resistance subsisted, and as Mr Jackson stood to greet her, Maria handed him a note she had written earlier that day:

'Perhaps you will be amazed to receive this note from me – I hope I shall not be obliged to hand it to you myself, but if needs must, hand it to you I shall. I have been much amazed of late. Amazed that you, with all your name and connections, should so happily lower yourself to such a steady acquaintance with the Harringtons. My father has informed me of what a favourable eye you have cast over me, and I come to learn that our brief period of courtship is to end this evening with your proposal of marriage. What a courtship indeed, sir! Like any other of my father's business dealings, you have inspected the goods and agreed terms over dinner and cards. And what agreeable terms they are, for you, sir.'

'Knowing your behaviour towards me during our last acquaintance, I know it cannot be affection for me that induces you to degrade yourself in such a match. Money must be your only motive. Having perused the terms of our marriage, it appears there is almost no circumstance in which you would not have everything that would be mine if I had been a son and not a daughter. But are you truly so mercenary, so resolved to have an ugly fortune that you would throw away the chance of a match of love that may await you in the future? Would you make us both unhappy simply for greed?'

'I am absolutely convinced that you could never make me happy, and I have no intention of making you happy a single day of our marriage. What if you should fall in love with a woman after we are married? How miserable you should be to be attached forever to me. Will you not consider deferring this proposal so that you may think on the permanence and severity of what it is you are to propose? For both our sakes, sir!

I am not, your obedient servant, M. Harrington.'

'May I answer you now, or do you insist I write my reply, madam?' he said with a smile once he had finished reading her note. When she permitted him to speak his answer, he continued, 'I have considered already this proposal a hundred times before to-day. I am absolutely certain of my wish to marry you. But if you are convinced you could never be satisfied by me, then you need not accept my offer.'

How wrong he was. But he seemed to care little for their being not in love, nor could she detect any shame in his openly mercenary behaviour. Only for the thought of her mother, Maria replied as such:

'Oh, I shall accept you, sir. Let your pride worry not. I beg you spare me whatever romantic speech you have devised; I wish to hear no more of your false affections. And you ought to expect no pretty exclamations from me; I shall accept you, but I shall say nothing more of it. Now, if you would excuse me, I have quite the headache and should like to retire to my apartment. I am sure you and my father have much to plan for the day. I trust that you shall pick only the most handsome patterns of silks for us, *honourable* Mr Jackson.'

This abusive quip brought a smile of some great amusement to the gentleman's face, but Maria would not be won and left him with nothing but the most earnest of miens.

CHAPTER EIGHT

A VERY SOMBRE WEDDING DAY

Three weeks came to pass before the unhappy day arrived, and in all that time, poor Maria had not been allowed to leave her apartment nor write to anybody except Mr Jackson, who she was forced to tell of her excitement for their upcoming nuptials. These lines were convincing enough for Mr Harrington, who superintended their construction, but not so for Mr Jackson, who believed himself to be very much engaged in a game of winning the affections of a woman who had good reason to dislike him. It was evident to him that despite her abusive quips and forcing upon him the task of reading perhaps the bleakest and most tedious novel in the world (or so he thought), she was very much expectant and hopeful of his efforts to win her good favour. '*And why should not she play so coolly with me*?' he considered. After all, he had used her very ill.

In the days leading to her union with Mr Jackson, the young lady was acquainted with great despair. With no one to speak to, it was very hard to revel in her misery. And misery that cannot be revelled in is simply grief, and she could find no comfort in being reacquainted with that state of sorrow. Who would be at the wedding, Maria knew not; the answer would be revealed to her upon entering the church. On her side, there was only Mr Harrington and Pearl, and on the bridegroom's, his eldest brother. Mr Jackson was quite surprised when his brother had not only accepted his invitation to the wedding but actually kept his word and had come.

If I could be once again permitted to address my beloved and most respected reader, I should say that the rapid succession of the many strange and tumultuous events to take place within this tale may alarm those of a rational disposition. Were I to be in the habit of dispensing unsolicited advice, I should also venture to add, as a cook will describe how best their recipe might be served, this story is to be best enjoyed alongside a minor suspension of any firm attachments to our good friends reason and logic.

And now we shall return to that miserable little scene in a cold and gloomy church:

This brother, Mr Richard Jackson, was the severest man Maria thought she had ever seen. He seemed as though he could have passed his entire life without smiling once. How glad she was to not be marrying *him*, misery would not be the word for a life attached to such a man, although she did consider there was a peculiar allure to his angry eyes. His wife Jane stood at his side, young, supremely pretty, and as haughty as her husband, though not nearly quite so cross-looking. It was no disappointment to Maria when they excused themselves shortly after the service; her new family appeared as unlikable as her old one. Unfortunately, Mr Harrington and his lover were not so obliging as to disappear immediately after the deal had been done, insisting that the couple join them for a celebratory meal at Bedford Square. The scene was mostly built from sorry glances passing between Pearl and Maria as Mr Harrington imparted his wisdom for the new husband:

'May you learn this lesson sooner than I did, good sir – beware the crocodile tears. Just like her mother, this young madam has taps affixed behind those dark eyes. To be sure, there is not a single inconvenience for which she will not spill her pretty tears. Do not get enwrapped in appeasing her hysterics. For years, I employed that tactic, and I warn you, it will only encourage more of these little fits. I learnt it is always best not to admit her in your presence till she has composed herself. After a few days of lamenting to her maid, she will return to you quite cheerily, to be sure, sir! – Say, how do you like your ring, dear Maria? I picked very well, did I not!'

Maria cared nothing for the ring. It was like everything her father bought her, expensive and garish. 'Yes, you picked well. It is a very pretty thing, thank you, Papa.'

Before the new couple departed to their home in Russell Square, Pearl required a moment of Maria's time to speak in the adjoining parlour. Oh, how grim! Though she was glad it was not Mr Harrington who had decided to undertake this particular task, Maria was little less horrified at having such a conversation with the woman who spent every night in her father's bed!

'Really, Pearl, not a word of this is necessary. Everything I need to know I have read in the books at my cousin's home a hundred times over – I dare say, I know far more of it than any other bride. And besides, I have absolutely no idea of being a-bed with Mr Jackson a single night of my life. We may be married, but we need not be bedfellows. I tell you, I will not have him!'

'It is not your choice, Maria,' her companion said with a great deal of compassion in her fluttering, pretty eyes. 'Your father has dropped some hints to Mr Jackson that you may be a little reluctant in that respect. And he has very indulgently engaged the good man's patience for a few nights. But if you care for my advice, I think you would be better to have it done with sooner. Even if he is patient with you – which your father believes he will be – you will only grow more anxious for the inevitable. And with anxiety, you will grow frigid, and frigidity, my dear, will make the ordeal quite unpleasant, no matter how kindly he is. If you can adjust your thoughts and soften your heart to the man's many good qualities – and to be sure, he is very handsome, which is not something every bride may say of her husband – you will find it very little of an ordeal. Even less so the second time.'

Like many girls do, Maria had spent a great number of hours of her childhood drawing sketches of wedding gowns and flowers and imagining the spectacular and felicitous day. How sorry that little girl would be to see herself now. And as some young women do, Maria had passed a great number of quiet evenings in her bed meditating on the thought of her wedding night and what scenes should take place then; that too was to be so very different than she had ever imagined. Having familiarised themselves with their enormous and stark new home, the couple shared a silent supper before Maria excused herself to her foreign apartment. Shortly thereafter, Mr Jackson disturbed the scene of her undressing, sending away the maid and offering his own services for that employment.

'Thank you, but truly, I would be much happier for Sarah to do it.'

'Then I shall return to you when it is done.'

She could not help but to release a sigh, seeing that he mistook her resistance for shyness. 'I am not being bashful, sir. Surely you can understand, given the history of our acquaintance, there can be no happiness on my part at the thought of spending the night with you.'

Now he released a sigh. 'I am sorry if how we left things before upset you, Maria. But we are married now, and our situation is quite different.'

A disbelieving look was soon etched across the face of his new wife. '*We* did not leave things, sir. The leaving was all yours. And I was not *upset*. I was terrified, beyond terrified; I was beside myself with fear for months, not knowing if there would yet be any consequences to that night and without the slightest idea how I could have found you if there were. And what a mercy there were no such repercussions because you clearly had no intention to shew yourself again. There is nothing you could ever hope to do or say that could induce me to be with you, in that manner, ever again! Unless, of course, you seek to oblige me through my promise of obedience; be pleased to know that in doing so, you would ensure the permanent loss of what little hope there is that I might ever love you. Certainly, some women find a pretty fantasy in the thought of reforming a man's character through marriage, but your wife is not one of them. Seek not redemption from me, *honourable* sir, for you shall surely never find it; you may keep all your "*sorries*" for another lady.'

'So that is to be it then, you shall make a nun of yourself and our home your convent?'

'Why dance around it, sir? Ask what you mean to ask!' She paused for a moment, but when he said nothing, for truly Mr Jackson knew not around what he was accused of dancing, Maria continued thus, 'Then I shall save you the trouble. You have been my first and shall be my last encounter of that kind. Is that not what every husband should like to hear? How pleased you must be! Do with yourself and with whom, Mr Jackson, as you like, I shall not pine with jealousy for a man for whom I have no respect.' He made no reply. Maria could not determine if his countenance was one of anger or upset. When his silence would not relent, she could little resist the urge to fill the heavy air between them. 'I would feel pity for you if your enticement for marrying me had not been so mercenary. Simply, the property of one man has been passed into the possession of another. What possible romantic sentiments could be affected by such a dealing?'

'By Christ, Maria, you speak as if you had no choice in the matter!'

Now was her turn for a silent and impenetrable gaze. Whether it was by way of reason, or the passion of her hurt that gave cause for her to speak the truth, Maria did not know. She spoke before she had truly considered the weight of her words. 'I speak as if I had no choice, *Husband*, because that is entirely the fact of the matter. By what inducements I was made to accept you, I shall not express, but know that our marriage was against my every will and protestation till the very hour we were wed.' What look he held now was entirely undeterminable. 'There – now you know it all, and you are free to hate my father as much as I do. At least we may have *that* to unite us if nothing else.'

'You must believe that if I had known–'

'What use are ifs to us now, sir? It is done. At least *you* have substantial compensation for your troubles.' Maria considered that he did look most affected by this knowledge.

'I shall take my leave of you now,' said he, 'goodnight.'

CHAPTER NINE

CONTAINING MANY OF MR JACKSON'S THOUGHTS AND SOME NEW CHARACTERS.

Maria remained the first two days of her marriage in her apartment. Had her husband not coaxed her from her confinement, she would have stayed for quite some time. To begin, he had no thought of inducing her to hasten the end of her solitude; he had no right to do so. Never had this young man considered that Mr Harrington – who had appeared significantly more enthused by the match than his daughter – had, in fact, forced that daughter's acceptance. What was to be thought on the matter? In the first instance, only mortification that he, though unknowingly, had been party to such an abominable violation of the will of a young woman. In the second, the disquietude that Maria should truly have been so opposed to marrying him.

Yes, he had used her very ill. But what in his previous conduct could not be remedied by the respectability of their marriage? Knowing what tenets of her Christianity she had been moved to disregard for him, and not certain till their wedding night that there had been no other men since, and not forgetting the lowliness of her birth and connections, really, it was *he* who had every reason to be against their marriage. In the third, he thought his lady correct. What had been done was done, and once she had overcome her present dissatisfaction, the best could be made of the situation. His plan of leaving Maria to her own space and ideas was disrupted on this third day of their marriage after Sarah, his wife's maid, had come to him in a state of some worry. The lady, he was told, would eat nothing of the food sent to her, returning every meal in the same state in which it had been presented.

'Not a thing, sir,' Sarah repeated when pressed. 'Not a single thing in two days, and she surely cannot survive for long on tea alone!'

And what was *he* to do about this? Indeed, anything that could be said would be better done so by his wife's maid; delicacy was required for delicacy. Sarah had said all that could be said, encouraged in every delicate way, when she had told Maria she would make herself quite ill, her only answer was, 'I know', and when the maid protested that no person could live for long on only tea, Maria's reply was simply a repetition of her first. When Mr Jackson entered his wife's apartment, he found her writing a letter at the desk that had a perfect prospect of the street below.

'Who are you writing to?' he asked when she did not acknowledge his entrance.

'Does it matter?'

'No, not at all.'

She would say nothing more and looked at him not once. The conversation would have to be carried by him alone. At length, he decided on the tactic of bluntness and directly asked Maria why she would eat no food sent to her, half-expecting that she would deny such a thing; she did not.

'Because the pain in my stomach serves as such a good distraction from that in my heart, husband.'

What was he to say to *that*? But he knew something must be said. Maria appeared the type of woman who would starve herself to death, for what; spite, anger, revenge? I can inform the reader that simply, the lady was broken-hearted, and she was rarely able to resist the embrace of her own misery. Each wound must be further mutilated till it festered and spread into every opening of her mind. Fortunately for Mr Jackson, it would only take a little hope of felicity to bring his wife away from the edge of all-consuming despair.

'Tell me – how can I make you happy, Maria? I have perhaps a se'nnight in which I may take my leave from town. Allow me to take you somewhere, anywhere you could want. Surely there must be someplace that should make you happier than here?'

At last, she turned to behold him. Despite her melancholic countenance, he considered that she was far more beautiful than he had ever before allowed. 'I would like to visit my mamma. She lives near Dulwich.'

'*Near Dulwich*,' he said, offering a smile she did not return, 'then that is where we shall go, as soon as we have our things packed.'

Gingerbread; that is what Maria decided would be the meal to break her fast. Howbeit, Mr Jackson firmly insisted to his wife that they would not leave for Dulwich till she had eaten at least something that resembled a proper meal.

'Then we shall not go to Dulwich, husband.'

Mr Jackson stood in disbelief. He would have admired his wife's resolve to have it her way if there had been any logic to her position. He believed she was being awkward simply for the sake of being awkward; a conjecture further compounded when came his eventual acquiescence: 'Fine, Maria, if that is what you want to eat, then you shall have some gingerbread. I will send a servant out to a bakery.'

'Oh, no, sir, I shall not have just *any* gingerbread. My particular desire is for the gingerbread from a charming little place we shall pass on our journey. I always stop on my way to visit my mamma.' She smiled in defiance of her husband's rapidly increasing infuriation.

It took a moment before Mr Jackson was assured the next words from his mouth would not be shouted. 'Maria, you must eat before we leave, or you will surely collapse on the journey. You have not eaten a thing for two days!'

'I feel quite fine, sir. I see no reason why you should disbelieve me. What greater exertion is there to be had from sitting in a carriage compared to sitting here in my apartment? And by the time someone has been sent and come back again, we should be nearly arrived at the bakery. Besides, my mind is already so firmly set on that particular substance, I have no hunger for anything else.'

It seemed to Mr Jackson that his new wife could subsist on stubbornness alone.

The carriage was readied, their trunks attached, the lady helped to her seat by her husband, with, of course, the second volume of *Clarissa* in hand. Despite despising this book more and more with each never-ending, tragic correspondence, Mr Jackson was worried that giving his wife any opportunity for conversation would lead to another nonsensical demand; thus, happily, did he offer to read to her.

'Good God!' he declared moments into their journey, browsing a line he had spotted further along the page. 'What do you have me reading, Maria? This man's letters get ever more horrendous – *Her grandmother besought me, at first, to spare her Rosebud: and when a girl is put, or puts herself into a man's power, what can he wish for further? While I always considered opposition and resistance as a challenge to do my worst!*'

'Do you know,' she answered, not taking her eyes from the window, 'I had never imagined the voice of Clarissa's villain before – but I think you have exactly the voice Lovelace would have.' A little smiling glance was cast in his direction at these final words.

The bakery was not very far from town, and after much harrowing lamentation from Clarissa Harlowe and villainous plotting from Robert Lovelace, read in an unenthused, though still charming voice, they arrived. Need it be said, the purchasing of the gingerbread could not pass without some small protestation; the driver would not be sent into the bakery, Maria would herself go, it was most important she saw the offerings before making her selection.

'For God's sake, Maria – will you please allow John to go into the shop, for I am not convinced you will make it so far as the door!'

'Then why do you not escort me for support? Should I be at any risk of crumbling to the ground, I am sure you are quite strong enough to hold me upright.' A teasing smile was produced by the lady. 'Ah! I have it. You believe yourself above such a place. Mr King did not think himself too good for the haunts of we common people, but then what a very different man he was!'

This was not the first that Maria had reminded her husband of his former duplicity, but it was the first she had spoken the name he had assumed for his holiday in the lower circles of London. It shamed him a little. Wanting to avoid her penetrating, dark eyes and determined he would not be drawn into another tedious negotiation, Mr Jackson answered, 'You will not argue with me on this point. *I* shall go into the shop, and *you*, Miss Contrary, you shall wait here.' This was said with enough humour that Maria was satisfied not to argue further. Mr Jackson returned with all the gingerbread that had been for sale, unwilling to risk any opening for further objections from Maria. She chid him for his wastefulness with a smile and remarked what a shame it should be for so many other customers to be met with disappointment. But she could not keep herself from feeling a little pleased with his efforts.

Maria's mother was just as the young lady had hoped to find her: cheerful, well, and safe. There was every good reason to disallow Mr Jackson to join her visit to this cottage near Dulwich. But when he had declared himself very much wanting to meet her mother, Maria believed him and was pleased to believe him. Unaccustomed to explaining how her mother was and how it had come to be, Maria prepared her new husband for the meeting with only this caution, 'Owing to a dreadful accident some years ago, my dear mamma has not the memory she once had. You will find her very charming, I am sure of it, but do not mortify yourself if your charm fails you, sir, for you will be forgotten by her before we have returned to the inn.'

Mrs Harrington was found by her son-in-law to be an amiable lady, of the most open and warm disposition, asking always so many questions and so enthused by all his answers. It did strike him as odd when first it appeared the lady was as unfamiliar with her own daughter as she was with him; Maria had not detailed quite how affected the lady's memory was. The gentleman had forever heard his wife refer to her mother as her *dear mamma*, but here she addressed her as Mrs Harrington.

The society of this unfamiliar young couple brought such evident pleasure to the lady, who looked perhaps much older than she was. 'When had they been married – and where – which flowers were chosen – how many bridesmaids had there been – how unusual it was to have had no bridesmaids – where had they first met?' This last question was answered by Maria before Mr Jackson had the chance to think, let alone speak, 'A little meeting house, if you can believe it, at a lecture about the Roman Empire. I cannot remember a thing of the talk now, but I very distinctly remember seeing Mr Jackson for the first time.' All this was said with a smile.

Mrs Froggett, the lady who cared for Maria's mother, seemed very glad to hear of such beginnings and said to the gentleman in a whispered tone, 'Oh, how happy I am that our dear Maria should have met her husband of her own accord, and was not paired off by her father to some high and mighty fellow who wants only for her fortune.' Mr Jackson smiled but did not answer. The woman continued her whispered conversation, 'And I dare say you cannot forget the moment you first set eyes upon Maria. Oh, is not she the most beautiful creature you ever have seen, Mr Jackson?'

'Indeed she is, madam.'

The conversation continued with no greater awkwardness, and the newlyweds were implored to remain longer. 'They would stay for tea, would they not? And cake, they must absolutely stay for cake! But not coffee nor supper if they were too fatigued from their travelling.' Of course they would stay. Maria would never leave this place again if she could help it. Tiring a little from such exciting society, Mrs Harrington was encouraged to rest before the tea things were brought into the sitting-room. Maria took this opportunity to shew her husband her very favourite haunts of this small village.

'Tell me, Mr Jackson, can you swim?' asked she. The two stood beside a small fishing lake adjacent to the house.

'Indeed, I can.'

'I cannot. Not at all. If I were to fall into any deep water, I should surely drown.' What a morbid conversation this was beginning to be, though Mr Jackson was noticing that any conversation with Maria ran the risk of taking a sudden macabre turn. 'If I were to jump into this lake right now, what would you say to me?' asked the lady with a smile.

'What an odd question, Maria.'

'Oh, you are no fun, Mr Jackson!'

Lord, what beautiful, mournful eyes she is in possession of! 'Very well,' said he, at last. 'I would say – why, when you cannot swim, Maria, have you jumped into a lake?' This was said with very little seriousness.

'That is a good answer, I believe,' she smiled. 'Would you be cross with me?'

He laughed. 'Yes, I suppose I would be cross with you. For I have no spare clothes with me, and it is very cold out to-day. In fact, I would be *very* cross with you!'

'That is a good answer,' she said, smiling again. 'And would you hate me for it?' she asked, with no smile at all and a disquieting earnestness.

'I do not think I like this game very much anymore, Maria.'

Taking his hand in hers and standing with her gaze fixed upon the water, Maria turned the conversation upon another question, 'Have you ever read Hamlet?'

'Yes, I have.'

'And what did you think of it?'

'I did not care for it.'

'Curious!' she replied, now turning her eyes to meet with his. 'Whyever not?'

'I do not much like tragedies, Maria.'

'Hmm,' she pondered for a moment, 'how very different we are, Mr Jackson.'

Maria soon returned to the cottage, expecting her husband to follow closely behind; he did not. He remained a little longer by the water. There was rarely any quiet when Maria was about, and if there was, it was a purposeful, vengeful quiet – her silence carried a point as well as any words might. His repose was not long-lasting. Mrs Harrington had volunteered to fetch the gentleman in for tea, watched by Mrs Froggett and Maria, who were busy talking at the kitchen door. Maria's mother performed the duty perfectly, the best china was out she was pleased to inform him, and a cake too. '…ginger cake, do you like it, Mr Jackson? It is my daughter's favourite.'

'Your daughter? Do you mean to say Maria?'

'Yes, that is right, Maria. How did you know? Oh – I must have mentioned her to you earlier. You must forgive me, Mr Jackson. I am so often forgetting the things I say.'

'Oh, worry yourself not, madam. You did not say – how old is Maria?' he asked with an uneasy curiosity.

'She will be five in September,' the lady answered with a contemplative face. Before the gentleman had the chance to ask any further questions, Mrs Harrington had turned her gaze and asked, in the revenant of her daughter's voice, 'Tell me, Mr Jackson, can you swim?' Mr Jackson was so bemused he could not answer. The lady cared not and instead began

53

another thought, '*Here lies the water. Here stands the man. If the man goes to this water and drowns himself, it is, will he, nill he, he goes — mark you that. But if the water comes to him and drowns him, he drowns not himself.*'

'What!' Mr Jackson replied with a rudeness that shocked himself. Though it did not phase his partner in this bizarre conversation.

'Hamlet,' she said, turning to him with a serious sort of smile.

A letter from Mrs Maria Jackson to her friend Miss Penelope Stuart, written the following morning:

'Oh, I have done what I said I would never do for the world, thrice! It would have been four times had he not said himself to be so very exhausted just now, la! So, I am sitting down to write to you instead. Be free to chide me for it, my love! How weak I am! Lord, help me when that man opens his mouth to talk. I am resistless! There can be no annulling the marriage now, though I shall not have him again, be assured of that. How I wish I was as obstinate as my father accuses me of being, I should have liked to have held out a little longer than this, for I am sure he thinks himself absolved of his former crimes. I beg you say not a word to Ralph, I should not like him to know such things in any case, but he has such a low opinion of Mr Jackson, he will surely think less of me for acquiescing so easily to his charms (and what potent charms they are, my dear!). If he asks, you may be pleased to tell my cousin that it has been a very sedate trip, with nothing of any interest coming to pass.'

'I am so absolutely conflicted; I rather believe I could already be in love with him again, and yet I still loathe him so bitterly. Visiting my mamma has reminded me of the wicked threat held against her to unite me with this man. She is ignorant of what cruelty would have befallen her, but I am not, and I greatly fear that by submitting to become Mrs Jackson, I have given my father a tool by which he may bend my will whenever he feels it justified. A tool that shall likely be inherited by my husband, leaving my sweet mamma forever at the mercy of the benevolence of these tyrant men. La! I talk myself out of being in love with him already, and yet I anticipate my resolve shall break the moment at which he wills it. What a charming devil I have married!'

'Enough of my misery, I shall no doubt have a lifetime of it, and if I am to fill page after page with my self-pity every time I write to you, then I believe you shall quickly be in search of a new companion. When I return to London, the first thing I shall do is visit you, my dear, and I promise to say not a word of the honourable Mr Jackson nor the dishonourable Mr Harrington. If I cannot have felicity in those branches of my life, then I am determined to know it in every other, and nothing shall make me happier than to be in your company and talk of what a happy life you shall have, my love. To his credit, Mr Jackson has given no objection to my continued attendance of services at the meeting house and has given me his word that he shall join me on the first Sunday after our return. Perhaps it is best if you explain to your family why my husband bears a striking resemblance to Mr King (if you have not told them of it already).'

'One must always find the positives even amongst the most objectively miserable circumstances, and I rather believe that this horrid affair will give me much inspiration for writing my next lovetragedy. Though perhaps you will agree that the tale of a woman forced to marry a man she despises is a little unoriginal. The man himself calls me now from my letter and wishes to go for a walk whilst the weather is fine. Is he not supposed to be so very exhausted! Oh, but damn his handsome devil voice! I agreed to it without even the semblance of a potential refusal. I really believe he could talk me into walking off a cliff, and I should think of nothing but his voice as I fell. This is not a very good start to my renewed vows to refuse him. I shall have to begin again to-morrow! Pray, will you, my dear, for the Lord to see fit to swell the resolve of ever your,

Maria Jackson (What strangeness it is to write that).'

As she had very much expected to, Maria did falter on her renewed vow of refusing her husband that day, and the next, and the day following that too. In fact, she faltered every day till they returned to their new home in London. What a tumultuous scene lay within her mind. When first she had given herself to this man, the disdain he inspired was unadulterated, having abandoned her mere moments later and never to say another word. Howbeit, as her husband, he had shewed himself to be not entirely coldhearted, giving Maria on this trip as much of his attention beyond their bed as he had bestowed when inviting her to it. Yet she was resolved to be miserable with this man, for anything less than feeling utterly despondent every day of her marriage would risk validating the means her father took to bring about this pairing. *Whate're the course, the end's renown*; not if Maria would have her way, all would not end well in this tale, nor would it *be* well, as a matter of principled revolution against the tyrant Mr Harrington, she would never allow herself to be happy with her husband.

This resolution was a little less difficult to keep in the days following their arrival home. Having passed almost the entirety of the morrow in his study and the whole of the evening playing cards at his brother's home, Mr Jackson first gave thought to his lady as he came to return to his bed. He stirred her with a knock at her door. Though she had not been sleeping, Maria had been quite anticipating his return home.

'It is three o'clock in the morning, sir,' said she, disguising her avidity behind feigned perturbation. 'Is something wrong?'

'No, nothing is wrong,' said he. 'I have only now returned home. I would have been here earlier, but I won the last six games.' After offering her sincere congratulations, the lady assured him that she would have been just as glad to receive this news over breakfast. This elicited a smile from her husband. 'When I was sufficiently satisfied with that occupation, my thoughts naturally turned to you.'

'Naturally, indeed, Mr Jackson.' The two remained in silence for some moments at her door before he said,

'Would you like me to stay with you in your apartment to-night, Maria?'

'You are welcome to stay, Husband, though I cannot yet say whether I shall like it.' She could not quash her wicked smile. *Damn his handsome devil voice!* She did damn his voice again when the morning came, and Mr Jackson was gone not just from her apartment, but from their home, without a single word to her.

CHAPTER TEN

DETAILING AN UNHAPPY AFTERNOON.

Maria forgave her husband with rapidity. Maria forgave everybody with great rapidity; excepting, of course, her father, what he had done could never be forgiven, even by her. She passed near an entire day being convinced, over and over by her own ruminations, that there must be something *she* had said or done wrongly. Wrongly enough that Mr Jackson should not want to wake her before his leaving that morning; when at last he arrived home that afternoon, Maria was determined to repair the fracture she had caused.

'Hello,' said she, finding her husband sitting on a couch by the fire in his study.

'Hello, Maria,' he answered, with not half the spirit with which she had greeted him. He had not, at first, looked up from his book, but sensing the lady lingering still at the door, he lifted his head and asked, 'Is all well? Why are you standing at the door in that way?'

'Yes, all is very well.' Maria took this as an invitation into the room and joined him on the couch. 'What are you reading?' she asked when he said nothing more. 'Ah, you need not answer – I see the title now - *The Iliad of Homer*. I have started it a hundred times but never finished it once.'

Mr Jackson did not answer but for a short diversion of his gaze in the direction of his wife.

'It is fish for dinner to-night.' Having paused to allow for a response, she continued, 'Do not ask me what sort of fish, for I really have no idea. It'll be white fish, I suppose, but then aren't most fish white? Oh, really, I don't know!' Again, without any response, she asked, 'Did you have a very busy day?'

'Yes, quite busy.'

'Well, that is good, I suppose. I always find it diverting to be busy, though not *too* busy, mind.'

As she began her next attempt at conversation, the lady was stopped by Mr Jackson, who said himself to be finding her constant talking a great distraction from his reading. *Oh dear, Maria. You are only making things worse.* 'Oh! Of course, I am sorry,' said she, drumming her fingers gently on a little table standing next to the couch. 'Here – what an idea I have – lift your book up for a moment.' She took the cushion from behind her and placed it upon his lap. 'There! Now I may rest my head upon you and gaze at the fire, and you can read your book in peace. A good compromise, I dare say!'

'No,' answered he, brushing the cushion aside. 'Maria, you are not a dog. Why do you wish to rest your head upon my lap? There are still many hours before dinner; cannot you find some entertainment for yourself that does not necessitate disrupting my reading? Oh, Lord! Maria, do not look at me as if you shall cry. Why must you always be crying!' Mr Jackson finished with a sigh.

She answered to say that she could surely not help such an expression on her face and quit the room before there was a chance for anything more to be said on the matter.

Having already visited Penny and Ralph earlier that day and hitherto neglected a call to her new sister-in-law, Maria decided the remainder of her afternoon would be spent belatedly making this courtesy. Jane was a pleasant enough companion, full of condescensions and advice for a new wife; there was a decided kindness to her air that gave Maria no reason to resent such instruction. It was only once she was admitted to the house that Maria was to learn her sister-in-law was not at home. She would leave and happily did attempt to but was persuaded by Mr Richard Jackson to stay a little while. He appeared unexpectedly open and affable, *smiling* even as he greeted her. Maria's suspicion that there was some liquid influence upon his current disposition was confirmed when he led her to the drawing-room, where was sitting his friend and the evidence of their refreshments. The lady was introduced, followed by the gentleman, 'Mr Ashby – a friend – a colleague – a good man indeed.' Shortly the lady would find her thoughts at odds with that last charge.

'And here – what anticipation I had to be proven wrong, Jackson,' Mr Ashby began no sooner than she was seated. Evidently, the man was in want of notice for his mysterious exclamation. Such notice was not given by Maria or her brother-in-law, which shortly found the gentleman continuing his thought without provocation, 'There is much talk about – is not there, Jackson? – of your youngest brother's new wife. What a curiosity it is that he should enter into such clandestine dealings with a gentleman brewer – can there be such a thing as a gentleman brewer? – the money, that was always my answer for his motives, but some who have met you, madam, have insisted that when I see this lady for myself, I will judge fortune could have only been his secondary motive. What nonsense I have declared it to be. Her beauty would have to be very striking for such a thing to be true. Now here I have you before me, and I must say, I regard nothing remarkable in your appearance and even less in your airs and manners. And your complexion, I have heard it described as a little exotic – I see nothing of it myself. It is more reminiscent of a sickly fieldworker to my eye.'

Mr Richard Jackson simply laughed in response. Maria thought for a moment that she would cry for the second time that afternoon, but after composing herself, replied to insincerely beg pardon at having been such a disappointment to Mr Ashby. An onslaught of malicious questioning began, 'Was she musical – artistic – a linguist – could she really not read or write in French – was she a talent with a needle and thread – a good housekeeper and economist – how could a woman of such means be so unaccomplished – had she any purpose at all?' At length, he remarked, 'I continually find it is the same with these ill-bred merchant families. Their daughters are always without talent or grace and have every expectation that their position in society can be bought – a wife can never be made from materials fit only for a mistress!'

Mr Richard Jackson laughed again, though with less enthusiasm this time; Maria did not reply at all. Mr Ashby seemed little in need of an answer to continue his performance. 'Tell me – Mrs Jackson,' he said after a moment of pause, 'do you always wear your hair flopping down your back like a common street whore?'

'You are very rude, sir,' she answered with an earnest mien. 'I suppose to think of such a thing, you must be well acquainted with many women of the town. I cannot see that you might convince any woman to have you without payment, and your preoccupation with my fortune rather makes me believe that you must have very little of your own. I hope for the sake of these street ladies that you are just as generous in dispensing the contents of your small purse as you are the contents of your small mind.'

What amusement this brought her brother-in-law, who remarked, 'Ah, she has you there, Ashby! And how I do enjoy a woman who can respond to taunting with some sauce.'

'I would very happily give you no enjoyment, Mr Jackson, but if that is the price I must pay for slighting Mr Ashby, then I shall accept it with grace.'

How disquieting! Her brother-in-law said not another word and smiled at her in a manner she had seen before on the face of her own Mr Jackson most frequently. Attention to the man supposed to care for her resulted in being thought a nuisance, and a rebuke to a man who she cared nothing for, gave her all the notice. *There is no winning with these men!* Maria had preferred the eldest Jackson brother when she thought him to be always cold and angry, and now she was tasked with the trial of adequately displaying her perfect indifference to him. If he had not such handsomely furious eyes, she believed his unwelcome smiles should have been quite mortifying indeed.

'My – she is an upstart little thing. I say, for all the money in the world, I could never be induced to set my sights so low for marriage as did Sidney Jackson.'

'Enough now, Ashby,' his friend insisted, still smiling at the lady. And henceforth, the conversation turned to that which Maria understood not at all and had no wish to understand. She remained only a little longer, in spite of encouragement from her brother-in-law to stay. With still much time before dinner and nothing else to do, Maria asked the driver to take her on a turn of the town.

Mr Ashby was very rude, but he was also not wrong, not by Maria's estimations. Really, what talents had she beyond the most basic skills afforded to women of education? In her possession was nothing that might have her called accomplished, and she had only the lightest hand in the running of her home – almost everything she entrusted to the judgement of her housekeeper. As to her looks, she had gazed for long enough into her mirror and had met with enough young women to know that nothing in her appearance was extraordinary.

No matter how long she slept, she always had those horrific dark circles under her eyes. Pretty, she had been decided many times, though she did not see it herself, nor did she think it any great compliment. Most young women were declared pretty simply because time had not yet diminished their full cheeks. Maria had only to be so very lightly pushed in the direction of despair or joy, and she would leap to it with all the force she could muster. By the end of her carriage tour of town, Maria could not conceive of a woman with less beauty, less grace, or less knowledge than herself. *That rude gentleman was entirely correct; you serve absolutely no purpose at all, Maria.*

She wanted nothing for her dinner, so did not stir from her room once she returned home. This caught the notice of her husband – though that had not been her direct intention – he came to her apartment and was sorry, so very sorry. Obsequious declarations of regret soon formed into those of spirited passion. *Damn his handsome devil voice!* When all had come to pass, he would not stay, owing to an engagement to play cards with his eldest brother and a friend.

'Oh, do not cry, dear Maria! To-morrow, I shall set my whole afternoon aside only for you, I promise.'

His wife did not entirely believe him, but she would not attempt to carry her point further. As quickly as he could be redressed, Mr Jackson was gone. The following afternoon came and went, with no appearance from the gentleman at his home. When he did, at last, make his arrival, he found not Maria in his study but a half-burnt *Iliad of Homer* discarded on the floor by the fireplace. Some men, Mr Jackson considered, perhaps even most men, would not tolerate such an igneous temper in a wife. But there was something both amusing and alluring to him about the combustion of her flaming humours.

Maria found nothing amusing in inhabiting such a state of mind, she would be far happier feeling sad than angry, but there were times when she simply could not help it. In her rage, she had burnt not just his book but every play she had ever written; years of imagination, toil, and catharsis reduced to ash in the fireplace. How, at that moment, she wished she might end her time so beautifully and easily. Still, Maria could not turn Mr Jackson away when he knocked on her door.

CHAPTER ELEVEN

CONTAINING MANY THINGS, BUT MOST IMPORTANTLY, GILLY'S ARRIVAL INTO THE STORY.

A letter from Mrs Maria Jackson to her grandfather, written at her home in Russell Square:

'What shame becomes me that you should be required to remind me that it has been now seven weeks since last I wrote to you. It is my greatest pleasure when you appear to me in my dreams, but I am sorry that such a rencontre has come to pass owing to my negligence. It was a pretty thought to meet with me at the shrubbery behind your old cottage. Oh, how I felt as if I were ten years old again, to walk about the place, my hand in yours, and hear you say to me, "Come, child, tell me what weighs upon your mind." And how forlorn I was to find you disappeared before I could answer, which finds me writing this letter to you now.'

'It was a very pretty garden in the spring, was it not, sir? I wonder if you knew the sprouting of those new blooms would be your last. Did you know it? I am certain this spring shall be my last. My heart could barely endure the bleak wretchedness of winter before, but if I am already so listless at the approach of spring, then what hope is there that my heart shall not shrivel and cease to beat when faced with a winter as the most unloved daughter and wife in the world? But enough of my plight, if I am destined to endure it till the age of one hundred, then I suppose I must, though I hope relief will come rather sooner than that.'

'Mamma, you will be pleased to know (though, of course, you must already know it) is very well and was in a good humour for my visit. For all his ignorance towards me, Mr Jackson was most attentive to her and asked many simple questions about her poultry and how she cares for them. He indulged her with his interest, although she explained to him things he must already know and in the most rudimentary of language. But I shall not allow this fact to bolster his character too much; he was a very different man the first week we were married, most attentive and obliging in every way a husband ought to be. Now – well, you know it, but I shall say it anyway – he cares for nothing but his books, his friends, and his card games and placates me with promises of what he shall do when he is not so busy and what he shall do to-morrow; and yet, when to-morrow comes, he remembers not his promise, and instead seeks to make new ones! "How many to-morrows are there to be, Husband, before it shall be to-day?" I ask him. He is *sorry*, and he is *busy*; always this is to be his answer.'

'And this, Grandpapa, is my husband upon our honey-moon, well then how am I to suppose he shall act when my novelty and beauty has faded? But I do not think I am for this life long enough that either should have the time to diminish. Let us hope his second wife may benefit from the lessons taught to him by my suffering. Enough of me! It is your birthday very soon. I have not forgotten; you must know that I would never forget such a day. As last year, and the year before that, Ralph and I shall get ourselves each a wretched pie and sit by that filthy and awful river, as you did when first you came to London. I miss you very much, rather more now than ever.

Forever your most loving and admiring, and wanting always for your presence, Maria.'

It might be remembered that on their excursion the week after their wedding, Mr Jackson had promised his wife that he would join her at her meeting house for a service the Sunday after they were returned. Second only to the home of her late grandfather, this meeting house on Dean Street held the greatest value in her heart.

Many years ago, upon overhearing his young daughter acting out the most despairing and self-deprecatory conversation with companions whose existence was limited to the confines of her mind, Mr Harrington had demanded young Maria's governess determine what was the cause of such madcapped behaviour. A want for companions was the lady's answer. '*Was not she,*' riposted Mr Harrington, meaning by this the governess to whom he spoke, '*intended as much as a companion as an educator?*' Indeed, but this wise woman replied that even the most obliging of adult company could be no replacement for playmates of a child's own age. After very little discussion, it was decided that Miss Jones would take young Maria to her Methodist meetings, where there were always a great many children.

Miss Jones had been gone from London four years, but Dean Street had become as much Maria's home as she might hope to name any place in the world. Being of a very different situation in life than most amongst the congregation, much of Maria's pocket-allowance had been given to the church's relief fund no sooner than it had been given to her. So dear was this place that it caused the greatest pain to her when the first Sunday after their return, her husband faltered on his promise, owing to his being too busy to attend. The following Sunday, it was then the greatest injury to her, as he had promised twice as passionately as the first time that he would join her, but of course, he did not. It was now Thursday, the day of another meeting, and after weeks of being ignored by her husband till the hours before dawn, Maria could take no more of his false promises.

'How can you mean to tell me that you cannot join me *again* this evening!'

The lady was standing over her husband, who was fixed to his writing desk, mid-way through the composition of a short letter. Though at the time, Maria had been quite pleased to hear her husband knock at her apartment door when he came home that afternoon, now she very much resented him for it. For, what could be less welcome to a lady who had happily passed no insignificant length of time in a vehement, and we might venture to say, rather furious, rendezvous with her husband than the prospect of sitting on a hard church pew only hours later! And now, that husband would not even be sitting beside her.

After some sighing, Mr Jackson gave his answer, 'I have told you, I had every reason to believe I should be able to join you, but just now I have received a note from my brother stating some business upon which he needs to speak with me urgently.' At last, looking up from his writing, he exclaimed, 'Oh – no, do not be brought to tears, dear Maria!' This was said with some frustration. 'What might I do to remedy your distress?'

'The meeting will be done by seven o'clock. You might delay your visit to your brother by a few hours and, at last, observe a promise you have now made to me three times and broken twice already.' That would not be done, although Maria suspected that it could be should he wish it, despite his protestations contrariwise.

'Say – by the time you are returned home from church, I will be finished with my brother, and you shall have my attention for the rest of the evening. You may decide anything you like for us to do. In fact, why don't you put on a nice gown, and I shall bring the carriage to collect you after your meeting, and we can go out somewhere. I give you my word, we'll have a prime evening together!'

'You may give me your word, *honourable* sir, but what value has it to me? I rather believe you shall promise me this, only for me to find you have unearthed some other very important business that requires your immediate attention, lest the world should collapse around us!'

'Forever as witty as you are pretty, my dear. Perhaps if you allow me to write without such distractions, I could leave sooner for my brother's home, and I might yet fulfil this promise even if you have decided already that I shall not.' Oh, what a satirical smile he offered with this riposte. It was too much. Maria had met with her limit for promise-breaking husbands for that day and impulsively knocked all his papers onto the floor, spilling ink on both her husband and his letter.

'There – now I can smile in amusement also,' said she before quitting the room in a rage.

Maria arrived at her church having already forgiven her husband for faltering on his promise a third time and was expectant and content with the knowledge that she would soon have an entire evening to command his attention. When anybody mentioned the fineness of her attire – and many did – Maria, with the fullest of hearts, professed it was because, 'My husband is taking me out somewhere after the meeting!' More than a little disappointment, it can be imagined, was felt when the young lady was returned home by her cousin, who had insisted she would catch a cold if she waited outside any longer. Upon arriving at Russell Square, Maria was informed that Mr Jackson had not yet returned from his visit to his brother's home. An hour passed, and she thought, *'Perhaps he has stayed for supper.'* After a while longer, she reasoned, *'Perhaps he has stayed for a drink.'* And when another hour passed by, *'Perhaps they were talking about something very important!'* When came ten o'clock, she could make no more excuses for her husband and accepted his breaking of yet another promise.

The sounds of an arrival in the foyer elicited a confusing combination of excitement and anger. Feelings soon to be replaced by absolute confusion itself, owing to a gentleman she had never before seen being presented to her in the drawing-room as Mr Jackson. It was Guilielmus Jackson, the middle of the three brothers and known always as Gilly. Maria quickly determined Gilly a coxcomb: fashionable and vain. The sort of man she should have liked to marry had she been given the choice. He looked just the type to make her only miserable enough that she might be happy.

After the introductions had been made, Gilly explained that he too had been at his older brother's home. On the return to his own and not realising how late it was, he had decided he must at last visit his new sister. The handsome fellow begged pardon twice for his attentions being so belated – he had only just returned from a trip to Italy. Twice he declared neither of his brothers to have done justice to her beauty, how glad he said himself to be, to encounter it with his own eyes. 'His brother had married the prettiest girl in London – Had not they met before? He felt sure they had. He knew her face from somewhere. He would not forget such a pretty face–'

'Upon my word,' Maria said, allowing herself a pleased little blush, 'I do not remember ever meeting you, sir.'

'Very well!' he answered jovially. 'But now I must insist you tell me everything about yourself, even the dull things. In fact, *especially* the dull things. I shall return home a miserable wretch unless you tell me every dull thing about yourself, Maria!' What an intense character, indeed. '*Such devilish charm!*' thought Maria. And how naturally the two slipped into a most pleasant conversation.

'So, dear Maria,' began he again after a moment of quiet, 'if my brother makes himself too busy for your company, what is it you occupy your time with here?'

'Oh – very little, truly. I am most unaccomplished, though I do enjoy writing sometimes.'

He appeared delighted by this revelation. 'And what is it that you write?'

'Plays mostly.'

'Romances?'

'Oh, no. Never romances,' said she with an earnest mien and the doe-like gaze she had inadvertently adopted from watching Pearl perform it so often.

He smiled. 'Comedies then.'

'No, I only write tragedies, sir.'

'How macabre! Ought not pretty young women spend their time thinking of happy things?'

'Oh, absolutely! But I am most fond of feeling miserable.'

'Then how satisfied you must be married to my brother, dear Maria.'

She returned his smile.

'I expect you go to the theatre often,' said he.

'No. Not at all. I cannot remember the last time I went.'

'Does not my brother offer to take you?'

'He has promised that he shall when he is not so very busy. I had thought we might go this evening, but he seems always to decide himself too busy to take me.'

'Well,' Gilly said, beholding her fluttering gaze most earnestly, 'he is not busy to-night, and yet he does not take you. Instead, he has spent his evening having bawdy conversations and playing cards, leaving you, his angel of a bride, here alone. I am sure it is the most scandalous mistreatment of a wife I have ever known! Indeed, I always consider it a crime worse than murder for men to remove the prettiest girls from the match table only to ignore them once the deal is done. If my brother married you without the singular intention of laying the world before you every day, he ought to have given way to a man who would prostrate a thousand worlds at your feet before breakfast!'

Maria laughed and replied, to this rather forward and amusing gentleman, that there was some truth in his observation. It felt gratifying to be sympathised with, and it took almost no persuasion for Maria to be convinced into an outing to a theatre with her brother-in-law that very

68

evening. At first, she was a little suspect of his motives, as he did converse so flirtatiously, but the evening passed with true pleasure. Gilly, though clearly a fashionable free-liver of the town, was in every way a gentleman. Maria was very glad to have at least one person in her new family whom she could rely upon to bring her good company. A friend, at last, in this new and lonely world.

After many hours in the green room of a very respectable theatre, meeting many fascinating characters, the lady returned home having entirely forgotten her displeasure with her husband. She was soon to be reacquainted with it. Mr Jackson came to meet his brother and his wife in the foyer before enough time had elapsed for them to remove their outerwear.

'What in God's name are you doing here?' he demanded from his brother.

Maria sought to answer this question, despite it not being directed at her, 'Gilly took me to the theatre this evening; he was only seeing me inside.' She smiled with not so much sauce as she might have given.

'*Gilly?* Oh yes, I am sure that he did wish to see you inside!' her husband replied bitterly. He was drunk. Maria did not suspect so herself, but Gilly declared it, and Mr Jackson did not deny the charge.

'Oh no, I will not have it, sir!' cried out Maria. 'You are not permitted to be angry with me, *honourable* Mr Jackson, when it is you who is deserving of all *my* scorn!'

'Oh, enlighten me, please, what have I done to upset you now, dear Maria?' her husband said with that infuriating, facetious smile. Any other person might have seen this as a suitable time to take their leave, but Gilly Jackson was most curious to remain and witness how this scene should end.

'You treat me like a doll, sir. You simply pick me up to play with and put me back down when it pleases you. I shall not allow you to make a game of our marriage, in which you inspire me into hating you only so that you might win my affections again. What reason can you have to greet me with such contempt if it is not simply for the sake of upsetting me?'

He replied only to instruct her to be gone to her room.

'I am not your child, sir. You cannot send me away to my bedroom.'

'To your room, Maria!' he now said very sternly, gazing only at his brother.

'No!' replied she, making her way by him.

Though he did not make himself very deserving of the title at that moment, the gentleman would not let her pass and turned his lady towards the stairs. 'For once, Maria, might you behave like a wife deserving of the many freedoms afforded to you and do as you are told?'

Oh, what rage this inspired! 'Do not touch me, *Husband*, do not touch me ever again!' She made her way now up the stairs but stopped to provoke him once more. 'And do not come creeping to my door to-night. If there were not another man in the whole world, I would sooner spend every night of my life alone than with you. And what a sorry picture that must paint of you and your feeble talents, for I so very much hate to be alone in my bed!'

All this gifted much amusement to Gilly, who had brought far more destruction to his brother's marriage than he had hoped to achieve in just one evening. And with such little effort on his part! Maria's coat, gloves, bonnet, and shoes were strewn across the stairs, and as she reached the first landing, she called down jovially, 'Do be careful not to trip on your way to bed, *Husband*!'

Perhaps we might feel most sympathy for the poor butler who had never been dismissed from the foyer.

In spite of her taunting, Mr Jackson was not angry with his wife. His anger was only by reason of his brother's meddling. Yet it had been she who felt the greatest force of his wrath. A trifling amount of foolish shoving and jostling occurred between the brothers, insults were exchanged, and warnings expostulated, but it all resulted in nothing more than Gilly's increased amusement and Mr Jackson's further inflamed rage. Gilly had, earlier that evening, promised his brother he would stay away from Maria.

After some hours, as the new day began to break, Mr Jackson's temper calmed, and having reflected on by what reasons Maria had been so upset that evening, he felt very sorry for behaving so coarsely with her. What contrition he felt when thinking upon his wife, in her lovely gown, waiting for him outside her meeting house. Remembering the last occasion when Maria had told him not to come to her room and how, after he did heed her warning, his *not* contravening her direct instruction had caused his

70

wife the greatest injury and upset, Mr Jackson went to the door of her apartment. The door was open, and his wife was gone.

CHAPTER TWELVE

TAKING PLACE CHIEFLY AT DR PATERSON'S HOME.

Maria did not stir before lunchtime, remaining in her room at Dr Paterson's home for a long while after she had woken. This left the morning for Penny Stuart and her doctor – sorry, *the* doctor – to work unobstructed. As pained as she was for her dear Maria, Penny was not unpleased to have the sanctuary of their morning routine preserved. *Le Bonheur*! That is all the lady knew on her stroll to her work each day. And how many clerks might say that? The first hour of the day always passed with cups of tea and conversation, primarily to tell the doctor the design of his day, but so often did their talk stray.

'*Lily of the Incas,*' said the lady as the doctor searched for one of many misplaced letters. He responded with that regular sound of his confusion. '*Lily of the Incas*,' she repeated, 'or *Alstroemeria,* that is the name of the flowers you have here on the side table. Did you buy them, Dr Paterson?'

He appeared a little abashed at the question. 'Yes – yes, I did.' He gazed at her most intently for a moment before returning his attention to the mass of papers on his desk. 'I was going to give them to Maria, but she has not yet woken.'

'That is very thoughtful of you. I believe she will like them very much. They are one of my particular favourites.' Penny paused for a moment before saying, 'How is Maria? Did she say what has caused her to seek refuge here with you?'

'She did say, but I could not claim to understand much of what passed in our conversation last night. You know how she can become when she is distressed. Something about a theatre and Mr Jackson's brother – I do not know, truly. Perhaps you could speak with her about it?'

Once Dr Paterson was gone on his first call, Penny did speak with Maria. A night of rest had done little to improve Maria's steadiness in communicating the circumstances that had caused her to flee her home. Still, her friend understood the cause of her flight without trial. It was not one event but a multitude. When Miss Stuart explained this knot of heartbreaking happenings to the lady's cousin upon his arrival home, it was accompanied by a declaration from Maria that she would never return to Mr Jackson or their home in Russell Square.

For several days Maria did not leave her bedroom. In part, because she wanted for nothing but to sleep and stare solemnly at the ceiling, but also because she knew by now her cousin would be acquainted with the entire truth of her history with Mr Jackson; she was too much ashamed to look him in the eye. Ralph's eyes were quite the same as their grandfather's had been, in their shape and their near-black hue; usually, they gave her great comfort, but at present, they should only make her feel more wretched.

Aware that so much of her pain at her husband's recent actions came from the foundation of those of his past, it seemed implausible to Maria that she could competently communicate the narrative of her misery and omit that particular detail any longer. Earlier that day, she had confessed the truth to Penny in a letter, for she could not bring the bitter words to her lips. Here lies below her letter:

'Will you think me strange for writing to you when we presently exist under the same roof? I have teased at it, hemmed again and again as I tried to confess the whole truth of my former acquaintance with Mr Jackson. You must see by my unsteady hand how my pen trembles even at writing the words. Forgive me, then, for not saying them aloud.'

'Oh my dear, I must confess to you, I lost far more than just my pride to Mr Jackson when I knew him as Mr King. I was so ashamed of it, Penny. I could not bear for anyone to know such an awful thing about me, not even you. Before your mind rushes to those unpleasant questions that are so often whispered between ladies at such times as these: A *brutish seduction*, a *violent coercion*, an *unwelcome union*. Oh! How words will be made to dance around such a thing! I must give him credit for there being no charge of that sort, none at all. All the worse I must be in your estimations to own the truth, but I must answer truthfully.'

'What a poor friend am I to you with my immoral weakness! My yielding required no coercion but that which came from his nimble words. I can only say it is because I thought myself to be very in love with him. And for those moments, he appeared to have a real regard for me – oh, but when he had had his fill, he walked away from me as if I were a three-penny-upright! – and I fare little better as his wife. He is all charm and attention till the game wears thin. You know, I would not be surprised if he took up patting me on the head afterwards.'

'No sin shall go unpunished. I surely should have known. There could be no greater punishment for me than to be forced to marry the man with whom I engaged so wickedly. Does God not make his point so poetically, my dear? Is our sex not the original source of suffering to all mankind? Is not that why we are to be punished with the pains and dangers of delivery and are so weak in our design? Why should God require a vow of obedience from a wife to her husband, but never a husband to his wife, if it is not by reason of our natural predilection for sinfulness? And here, I defy the Lord once again by running from that which was designed for me. Oh, but I cannot go back, Penny! You must know I cannot! Will you confess this to Ralph for me? You have my express permission to do so. I beseech you think not too ill of your,

Maria.'

An hour later, the following reply was delivered to Maria's bedroom:

'You were quite right, my love; that was the first thought to enter my mind. For shame, what sort of friend do you think me, that I would prefer you to have done so *unwillingly*? And I could hardly agree that it is to his credit. Surely it is a rudimentary civility of all who wish to claim their being a good man. Might I reassure you, sweet lady, that I think no less of you. More, in fact, owing to the dignity with which you have borne this secret alone for half a year.'

'As to your present disagreement with Mr Jackson, I believe a little time to calm your thoughts shall be of great benefit. And as to your disagreement with God, I shall say only this – God did not write the Bible, and He does not write the sermons preached in our churches, Maria, men did; fallible, human men. There is wisdom and foolishness and every contradiction in between. Read and listen with a critical disposition, my love, and make up your own mind. Do not allow yourself to be resigned to a status of innate wickedness and a marriage of misery simply because a man tells you it is the natural order of things. You are sounding positively medieval in your theology – you must never let Joanna hear you talk in such a way!'

'I shall speak with your cousin on the matter. Though would you have me implore him not to lay the charge on Mr Jackson? For, if I know him as well as I believe I do, I think this shall be his first wish. I leave you with the knowledge that you are very much wished for in my company, and there shall never be the winds of judgement in the eyes of your,

Penny Stuart.'

Penny did share with Dr Paterson this confession. *'Oh dear, Maria!'* was his first thought at this news. His second was of great anger towards her husband – and this remained with him for much of the day, distracting him greatly from his work. It is perhaps for this reason that before returning home after his final call of that day, Dr Paterson directed his carriage to Russell Square. Penny had besought him, on Maria's behalf, not to lay any accusations at Mr Jackson's feet – the folly was, in Maria's eyes, as much hers as his.

'Why are you here?' Mr Jackson said with all the contempt of a man who had spent his afternoon alone, drinking something he did not much care for till the third glass.

'Are you aware Maria is staying at my home? I know she has not written to tell you such – I thought you might be worried about her.'

'I had assumed she would be hiding with you. I have no plans to come for her. She will come home when she is ready, I am sure.'

'I do not think she will be ready any time soon, Jackson. Maria is quite certain she will not return at all.'

'Well, then, I shall have to wait a little longer. If I come for her now, she will expect always to be chased around each time we have a minor disagreement. No, she will learn her lesson the first time. I shall not come looking for her when she runs off!'

'Really, it is no wonder Maria believes you have no regard for her. You speak about her as if she were a child.'

'I speak about her as if she were a child because she is a child, Paterson. The moment I return here each day, I am followed around my own home from room to room by a whining little girl hanging off my neck — *I am a bore. Why will I never play with her?* — can you tell me that these are the words of a wife? I have no more patience with her! In the afternoons, Maria is declaring what abject misery I bring by my ignorance towards her and imploring me to take a mistress so she might be spared her marital duty. By the evening, she expels continual languid sighs, which she attributes to being so very hopelessly in love with me, and then demands to know what time I shall be to her bed — every day it is the same thing!'

'Come now, Jackson—'

'No! Indeed, she bemoans so much at every meal brought to her that I have been obliged on more than one occasion to slice up the food on her plate and negotiate her eating each mouthful! Oh, and the slightest inconvenience is likely to bring forth tears. By God — she burst into sobs one afternoon because the tip of her pen broke off! And I think I have yet to mention she insists I choose her outfit whatsoever place we visit. She wants only to wear whatever *I* like best. But, hang me, I could not care less! Even when she does nothing but sit at home all day, *I* must choose what she sits in! Everywhere I go, she must go too. Every book I read, she must read also. I tell you, I have married a spoilt little girl!'

Dr Paterson smiled at this. 'In for a penny, in for a pound, Jackson! That is the only way to be closely acquainted with Maria. You cannot suppose to isolate and exploit those parts of her character that please you and ignore her when she presents those parts that do not.'

'That is very easy for you to say, Paterson. I do not believe I have managed to pass a single hour in her company without some exaltation of her, *dear, dear Ralph.*'

Dr Paterson now laughed, rather in disbelief. 'And what do I do to be deserving of such praises—'

'It needs not explaining. You indulge her every whim, dare never to correct her childish temper and feed ever into her dramatic conjurings. If that is what I must do to win her praise, then I shall accept always to hear my name said with contempt from her lips.'

'You only further exemplify how very little you know your wife. The only whim she has ever asked me to indulge is the giving of my time

77

and my ear. And if – as on many occasions is the case – I am unable to offer her either, she is satisfied with my answer. As to her childish temper and dramatic conjurings, I cannot deny their existence. But once you know better the music of her manners, you will see the slamming of doors and throwing of her head upon you in wretched despair or in utter contentedness are simply the flourishes of her emotions. I do nothing more for my cousin than any man ought to do – less perhaps – and my reward for this basic kindness is to be forever regarded as the best of cousins, the best of men, and the best of all God's creatures!'

The estranged friends exchanged a silent gaze before Dr Paterson continued thus, 'I doubt not that despite the mercenary and cold circumstances of your address, and the wicked threats pressed upon her to accept you, that should you be slightly less determined to dislike her nature, and only a little more giving of your time and attention, she would soon declare to everyone who would listen that there could not be a better husband in all the world as her dear Mr Jackson.'

Mr Jackson regarded his old friend pensively. 'And why should you care to tell me this? Is not this the outcome you must have always desired?'

'I will own, I would happily see her never return to you again.'

A moment elapsed before Mr Jackson replied, 'Is there some further amendment to this declaration, or have you come here simply to gloat?'

'I shall not endeavour to implore you any further. Cling to your pride if you will, but I would warn you not to underestimate Maria's willingness to carry her point when sufficiently provoked, nor her willingness to forgive when sufficiently attended.'

CHAPTER THIRTEEN

A SHORT TALE OF FRUSTRATION AND IGNORANCE.

The following morning a parcel arrived at Dr Paterson's home addressed to Mrs Maria Jackson, the note attached was as follows:

'Dear Miss Contrary, I hope the contents of this box shall be agreeable to you. Be pleased to eat whichever you like best, all, or none of them at all.

I am, your most obedient servant, and obliging husband,

Mr Sidney Jackson Jnr Esq., M.P.'

'Postscript – It might gratify you to know that I awoke an hour early to fetch these for you myself.'

A note from Mrs Maria Jackson directed to Russell Square. Addressed to her husband:

'I write only to inform you that I have to-day committed myself to abstain from sugar. You need not waste any further mornings in search of gingerbread.

I am, your unhappy wife, Mrs Maria Jackson.'

Once each week, Dr Paterson would have the Stuart family come for dinner. He was rather similar to his cousin in the respect that he made little effort to make new acquaintances and even fewer efforts to make new friends; Thomas Stuart was easily the best contender for his closest friend. James Stuart did not dislike Ralph, but neither would he commit himself to full approbation, owing to a long-standing suspicion that the doctor was in love with his eldest sister. Joanna, the youngest Stuart sibling at nineteen years, found Dr Paterson to be tolerably intelligent and a better influence upon Penny than Maria, who she considered unpardonably ignorant and rather unhinged.

Much of the dinner passed Maria by, as she fluctuated between feeling rather pleased by her husband's parcel and then chiding herself for falling for what was so clearly another of his games. She should not have responded – she should have responded with something more severe – oh, but if it was not a game, and he truly was sorry, then she ought to have responded with something softer. But it was done; the note had been sent, and she would not make a fool of herself by sending another. Such extremities of emotion were experienced by Maria at the table that she gave little notice to her food, prompting both Ralph and Penny to ask if she was not hungry. The second time this was asked, she replied with, 'Oh, no, I am not really hungry at all.' After pausing as if she had finished but deciding she had not, Maria continued, 'I am still quite full from gorging on an entire box of gingerbread to-day. Ah, but it was my last hurrah, for I am resolved never to touch sugar again from this day forth.'

'Did not you already resolve to abstain from the product? I am sure you have said before you would do so,' replied Joanna, knowing very well the answer to her question and receiving for it a forbidding look from her sister.

'Perhaps I did, Joanna, though I cannot swear that I remember saying so. But here – you may all be witness to my solemn vow to-day!'

A little further conversation revealed that, somehow unbeknownst to Maria, every other person at the table had been abstaining from sugar for quite some time. Penny, two years, the same as Ralph (what a coincidence that should be), Thomas and James, both approximately five years, and Joanna had been in this state of self-denial since making her pledge at the tender age of six. It was not entirely Maria's fault; often, it appeared to her that she was incapable of fixing her mind to anything for more than a few moments; a thought, a conversation, a feeling. The slightest distraction could cause her mind to jam – the irritating scrape of a knife upon a plate might render her ears all but useless to any noise but that which disrupted her thoughts. To everybody else in the world, Maria believed she must surely appear forgetful, rude and simple – an affable and open demeanour was her attempt at a cure. This often only seemed to make things worse. As a consequence, Maria could find no enjoyment in any circumstance in which she might be required to be in the society of those who she could not be certain would forgive her nature.

This conversation did not occur without leaving Maria feeling a little foolish, a state of being in which she so often found herself. If the lady felt foolish now, she was soon to doubt herself capable of a single intelligent thought. Another conversation was shortly underway between Joanna and Thomas. Less of a conversation and more a fierce debate; Penny and James sank into silence as they habitually did when these two locked horns. Dr Paterson did not shy from the conversation and was of the same mind as his friend; reforms and regulations for the protection of those enslaved should be made till abolition could be achieved.

'No, I will not have it, Dr Paterson,' answered Joanna. 'I understand, for most, these measures are thought of with the best of intentions, but it will have entirely the opposite effect: rather than reducing the suffering of those enslaved, it will prolong it.'

'Tell me, how could offering these people more protection result in their increased suffering, Sister? – In what world could outlawing the flogging of women make their lives worse and not better?' replied Thomas with a distinct air of frustration.

'On two counts, Brother,' replied Joanna, matching his tone. 'Firstly, any perceived infringements upon slavers will give them cause to increase the suffering of their slaves. Was it not just a few years since Mr Wilberforce simply *gave notice* of a bill, causing widespread panic among the slavers and resulting in the massacre of a thousand innocent people falsely accused of insurrection? On the second, *Brother*, is that any perceived relief in the conditions of slavery will give cause for the public to avert their eyes from the cause. How many years passed after the Zong massacre before they put an end to the middle passage?' When Thomas gave no response, she continued, 'Over twenty-five years! And that was *with* a public outraged at the inhumanity of the trade. It must be immediate and total emancipation or no emancipation at all.'

'Yes – it is all very good playing at politics, but if you saw what it is they suffered, Sister, as I have, and did not only read about it in books, then I do not believe you would be so quick to martyr them. Any relief that can be offered must be.'

The conversation continued in much the same way, both becoming further entrenched in their original position and Dr Paterson trying his best to suggest some middle ground. Realising how long she had been silent and knowing no more than the peripherals of the conversation, Maria added her thoughts, 'Oh, but what a great shame it is that we can so little influence these foreign governments to follow our lead.'

Nobody understood truly what Maria had said or why she had said it. A little further dialogue between herself and Thomas revealed that Maria was perplexingly under the illusion that the British abolition of the slave *trade* some ten years earlier was one and the same as emancipation; of course, it was not.

'And does this not perfectly illustrate my point,' Joanna said, 'if Maria, who is supposed to have benefited from a lady's education and had also the education of being so well acquainted with our father – who passed the first twenty years of his life in bondage – can be so unforgivably ignorant about the cause, then what hope can there be once the wool descends over the eyes of the public in the form of regulations? I wonder half the population of Britain is not stupid enough to confuse the trading of slaves with owning them!'

The weight of her own idiocy felt to be crushing Maria's body into her seat. Thomas offered her a kindly smile, rendering her only more distraught; the disappointment in his eyes could only be superseded by that of God himself. It was too much to bear; Maria could prevent her fit of tears only long enough to quit the room in a most awkward and clattering manner. The door to her bedroom was locked, and she could not be compelled to stir by the attempts of either Ralph or Penny. At length, Joanna came to her door, and though she could not bring herself to apologise for pointing out the inexcusable nature of Maria's ignorance, she was sorry for having upset her friend. '…if you are wishing to learn more about the cause, I might suggest that you begin by asking your new brother-in-law, Mr Richard Jackson. He is very much in support of abolition. I heard him speak at a meeting recently.'

CHAPTER FOURTEEN

IN WHICH MARIA AND RALPH CELEBRATE
THEIR GRANDPAPA'S BIRTHDAY.

A note attached to a parcel delivered to Dr Paterson's home, addressed to Mrs Maria Jackson:

'Dear Miss Contrary, How glad I am to hear it – I have denied myself the product for near six months. How much easier it shall be to abstain without the temptations brought by fetching sweet things for my dear wife! I took the liberty of having some baked apples (sans sugar) made for you; I hope it aids with the transition into your life of self-denial. Enjoy!

I am, your most obedient servant, and obliging husband,

Mr Sidney Jackson Jnr Esq., M.P.'

'Happy birthday, Grandpapa,' Maria said in a hushed voice as she sat herself precariously close to the river.

At no great length, Maria and her cousin garnered strange looks from bypassers; a well-dressed young pair sat on the floor like children or beggars – how very strange! But Maria did not notice, and Ralph did not care, although he apprehended the glances. 'Come, Maria, you must eat your pie. You shall be in better spirits for eating something.'

'No, you must have mine, Ralph. I do not feel like eating. I am full enough on my own stupidity.'

'Maria, nobody thinks you are stupid.'

'No, they do not. Worse – they know beyond all doubt that I am and that I am ignorant and selfishly minded.'

Such thoughts had consumed her every waking moment since the dinner with the Stuarts. Receiving the parcel from her husband had only added to her despair when she discovered that she had been also entirely without knowledge of his abstaining from sugar.

'I do not believe you are any such thing, Maria. You are a dreamy creature and easily distracted, but if you were to direct your passion towards something, I am sure remarkable things might happen!'

Maria did not reply. Her mind was not open to compliments and would hear only affirmations of her most wretched qualities. Eventually, Ralph did have Maria's pie after she had threatened to throw it into the river if he pressed her to eat it once more. After a lengthy silence and with no warning at all, Maria's manners took on a livelier appearance. Looking her cousin in the eyes with a wicked smile, she said:

'Ralph, tell me – tell me the first answer that comes to your head – what should you say if I were to throw myself into that vile river right now?'

'Well, I do not suppose that I should say anything. I would likely be entirely preoccupied with getting you out.'

'Yes, that is a good answer, I believe. But what would you say to me afterwards, would you be so very cross with me? Tell me – would you hate me forever, Ralph?' She smiled all the while.

'Oh, certainly, I would be most cross with you, if only because I should not like to ruin another new shirt. And you know nothing could make me hate you, Maria.'

As quickly as her face had broken into happy smiles, it suddenly took on a countenance of mournful curiosity. 'What do you suppose Grandpapa said to my mamma when he fetched her from the river?' Ralph did not answer. He hated the besotted infatuation with which Maria forever spoke of that scene. 'Do you think he was very cross with her?' said she to prompt his reply.

'I do not believe so, Maria. I think he was just very sad,' he, at length, replied. Ralph watched his cousin, whose focus was consumed entirely by staring at the dark water below. He said her name several times, but she did not stir. Temporarily she had been quite immobilised. 'Come, Maria, you must eat something,' he said, shaking her by the arm.

With sorrowful eyes and a serious sort of smile, she turned to him and answered, 'I have told you, I really am not hungry, Ralph. If you keep pestering me, then I shall – well, I shall cut off all my hair – and then what will you have to say for yourself!'

'Well, now I know that you must wish me to pester you further, for not – as you would say – in a thousand thousand lifetimes – could you be convinced to cut more than an inch from your hair, no matter how much I were to annoy you. Tell me what takes your fancy, Maria. I have still some time before I must needs return.'

'Oh, how I wish you did not know me half so well, Ralph! Upon my word, I swear nothing takes my fancy. I am far too unhappy to think of eating. You must tell me what *you* fancy I should eat.'

'Ah! I shall not be drawn into that game again – everything I suggest will be met with declarations of it being the most intolerable and repugnant food in the world – and before I know it, you will have drained half an hour forcing me to list every food I can think of, and then I shall have to return without seeing a thing pass between your lips. A clever scheme the first time you did so, perhaps, but I am wise to every one of your tricks now!'

Maria took in a very good prospect of her cousin before squeezing his face between her hands. 'Do not dare die before me, Ralph Paterson! I know very well that you shall survive without me. Nowhere except in the house of God himself could I bear to live without you. And if you do, I shall throw myself into the ground on top of you and how very pleased I shall be to drown amongst the scattered earth!'

'I see even in death I shall not escape you! Look, Maria–' he began, ready to chide her for her morbid fancy.

'No, *you* look. You must swear to me now that you will not die before I do!'

'Maria, I have sworn this at your request more times than any man ought to be asked to swear anything. Do not think I am insensible to this being yet another distraction – I shall be buying you boiled eels at this rate, and you will eat whatever I choose for you!'

Not a secret could be kept from Dr Paterson by Miss Stuart – well, excepting one – and the fear of owning that truth might explain part of why the young lady shared everything but this single truth with him. What a very perfect listener this gentleman doctor was, and what more could so many young women wish for in a beau than a man so highly talented in such a skill. Dr Paterson did not simply listen to Penny without interruption; he invited her to share her thoughts, with questions not quite severe enough to be considered prying, but neither trivial enough to be the work of only polite conversation making. Penny could undertake all her work with no difficulty at all, dancing about his office – doing this and that – never a step wrong – all while giving a near-constant account of her musings. Dr Paterson could neither talk nor listen and perform his work well. He would happily read a letter six times over if it meant having the music and dance of this lady's soliloquies before him. Maria, now being gone to her brother-in-law's home, the two had time to recommence their usual way of being.

'Yes, you are quite right, Dr Paterson. It is a good sign that Maria has declared herself to be most unhappy; it is always when she insists upon her being very well that one ought to be most concerned. Joanna was mortified by what she had said to Maria– well, perhaps not *what* she had said – but *when* and *how* she had said it; it was a little cruel. Though I think she was not entirely wrong to be irked at Maria's absent knowledge – do you believe she was wrong?'

Dr Paterson looked up from his desk and replied, 'No, I do not believe she was wholly wrong.'

'Sometimes,' the lady said with a smile, 'I think the second coming could happen and entirely bypass Maria. It is a blessing– and a curse – an enviable talent, I think. I dare say, if I could command myself to hear nothing of these fierce battles between Thomas and Joanna, then how soon I would live among my own thoughts.'

'But not, I know, for lack of a depth of your own opinions and conjectures on the subject.'

'No, indeed. To my mind, the evil situation appears to be such a great, tightly wound knot of a thing, with so many contradictory conjectures as to what shall loosen it and what shall tighten it. A wicked conundrum, and one that it pains me greatly to think on – though the cause is in my prayers every night, of course, and in my thoughts oftener than that. But I do not wish to be faced with such heartache at every meal, every cup of tea, and every game of backgammon! Sometimes, I should just like to be able to enjoy my own comfort, without meditating upon someone else's misery. Oh, what a selfish creature I sound. Tell me, I permit you to be entirely unreserved in your reproach – does that make me sound so very selfish?'

'No, not at all. If you were selfish, the thought of such suffering belonging to another would cause you no such grief that you might wish to avoid thinking of it from time to time.'

In this interval, Penny stood herself upon a stool for her next order of administration in a manner that quite distracted Dr Paterson with concern that she might fall. Penny felt all the kindness of his response and allowed the greatest intensity of her flutter to pass before continuing her thought. 'Thomas has been indefatigable in his interest in the cause since his trip to Spanish Town. What a lionheart he has to agree to such a scheme – and what a lamb's heart have I? I do not think I slept a single night till he returned home.'

'You should not reproach yourself so. It is natural for a sister to worry for her brother in such a way.'

'Yes, perhaps. But Joanna did not fear for him. She would have gone with him had he allowed it. How very different we are. She has, I believe, more of our mother's spirit. I do not know what my father would make of it – such a peacemaker to us all – oh, really, I had only organised this cupboard two days ago! How can it be so jumbled already?' No sooner than this thought had been communicated, Penny released a shriek that started Dr Paterson in such a way that he quite leapt from his seat in anticipation of her falling. 'It is almost three o'clock, Dr Paterson, you must be gone, or you shall be late to Mrs Jenkins!'

CHAPTER FIFTEEN

IN WHICH WE RETURN TO BEDFORD SQUARE.

A note from Mr Sidney Jackson to his wife, delivered the following morning:

'My dear Miss Contrary, I have it that you were gone to my brother's home yesterday to make use of his books on the subject of slavery and abolition. I can happily inform you there are many books on such topics in my own library, any of which you are welcome to read whenever you should want. If it should please you better, come when I am gone from the house – it is your home too, after all, and I should not like to think you believe yourself unwelcome. Or, if you should prefer, I shall have a selection sent to you at your cousin's home. A letter came for you this morning. By the hand, I guess it is from your father – I have enclosed it.

I am, your most obedient servant, and obliging husband,

Mr Sidney Jackson Jnr Esq., M.P.'

A letter from Mr Harrington to his daughter:

'You need not work yourself into another frenzy, child – this letter is only of a practical pretension. Though, if your revengeful and proud heart might make any allowances, may I suggest you invite your stepmother to pay you a wedding visit. My poor Pearl is most distressed to be disallowed from offering such a basic civility. Your sulking has been tolerated for long enough now, madam, and your perverse moods shall sour the air of my home no longer!'

'A married woman you may now be, and you might refuse me the designation of your father as long as it pleases you, but you have not yet been excused of your filial duties. I am to hold a dinner party this Friday. I shall expect to see you there with your husband – and in a cheerful humour. You need not reply if there is no acceptance amongst your answer – if that be the case, I shall next pick up my pen to write to Mrs Froggett about the suitability of her situation for your mother.

I am still, in my heart, if not in your own, Your father.'

'Postscript – do not arrive looking like a slum child with your hair draping all over you. How you wore it on your wedding day would be sufficiently suitable.'

A note from Mrs Maria Jackson to her husband, delivered the same morning:

'Dear Honourable Husband, it seems I am to have no secrets from you. I thank you for your kind offers, though I must inform you, they are entirely unnecessary. Your brother has offered me the use of his study as often as I should need it. I find the room is most superiorly furnished and benefits from very well-placed windows, and your brother is most obliging in answering any questions I have. We have been summoned to attend a party at Bedford Square this Friday. You may collect me at five o'clock from my cousin's home. You might ask Sarah to send over my black silk gown and any mournful accessories she believes might best communicate my displeasure with my father.

I am, your very unhappy wife, Maria'

For many days Maria could not quite decide if she was more furious or horrified at the readiness with which her father took up again his threat, for nothing more than securing her attendance at a dinner party. He could not be certain that had he simply asked her, without any such menace, she would have refused his invitation. Maria had often observed, through her study of human nature in plays and books, that fortune and fear so often corrupted the soul. The former had long since been the most treasured thing in her father's heart. She had always known him to be a man of greed, though, till most recently, Maria had never considered her father to be cruel.

As she readied herself for the party, and with a soft sigh, she thought, '*Some men, I believe, once they discover the efficacy of rule by fear, choose to use it to command their will in even the most unexceptional of circumstances. And soon, they cannot ask for a cup of tea without employing wicked threats. A party, indeed! Oh, my poor mamma, her comfort threatened to secure such an ordinary and inconsequential occurrence. And this from the man who coaxed me to his parties when I was a child with – "Oh, tell me, little queen of my heart, what shall sweeten it for you?" – how very far we have come from that!'*

Mr Jackson could hardly contain his amusement at the sight of Maria, resembling rather more a young widow than a new bride. Not willing to directly disobey her father, her hair was fashioned as it had been on their wedding day – her husband noticed such and spoke of it with an affected sentimentality that she could not return. For the duration of the carriage journey, his determined felicity quickly threatened to dissolve her unhappiness, but not so once they arrived at Bedford Square.

Here – for the first time since leaving Russell Square – Maria was quite glad to be at odds with her husband. The thought that her father might in any way satisfy himself that she was happy in the marriage he had so violently forced upon her could not be borne. The resolution to be miserable before the gaze of her father, coincided very well with her resolution to be miserable before the gaze of her husband. Dinner passed with all the expected questions for a newly married couple. Maria left her husband to burden the most part of the answering. She considered that Mr Jackson was most talented at conversing with people he cared nothing for with a truly convincing enthusiasm. An obvious skill for a politician to have, the more she thought on it.

'Hello, Maria. I like your hair this evening,' said Pearl with her usual smile as the ladies made way to the drawing-room. She held on to Maria's arm, keeping her back, and once the others had passed by, she continued, 'Oh, Maria, I must warn you, your father is not best pleased with you.'

Maria returned a look of frustrated disbelief. 'Heavens! What should I care if he is pleased or not!'

'Cheerful, Maria, you must look cheerful!' Pearl replied with a solemn urgency. 'And when the men join, you must stand with your father and talk with his friends. Do you understand, Maria? Really you must.'

Pearl's demeanour was disquieting, to say the least. But Maria would not be bullied by her father. When the men arrived, she did stand by him and smile at his jokes, talk of her happiness as a wife, and laugh at being so poorly skilled in the talents of housekeeping. And then, when a suitably large crowd had gathered, Mr Jackson, who had been encouraged to join this circle, witnessed an odd happening overcome his wife in the corner of his field of vision. He had seen it before once. He was sure that he had, on his wedding day, in fact. For many moments Maria went very still, and her eyes began to strain and water.

'Oh, Mrs Jackson, your lips have gone quite blue!' remarked a lady standing across from Maria.

In a moment more, Maria was entirely gone. It was only owing to his watching his wife so intensely that Mr Jackson was able to catch her before she was brought some injury by being met with the hard floor. It was a habit unintentionally formed in her early childhood to hold her breath when she was overcome with any emotion. With time, this habit became a skill. Maria had, as Mr Jackson now suspected, attempted such a thing on their wedding day. Wanting the moment to be perfectly dramatic in its timing, she had waited till the exchanging of vows to enact her plan. Before her lightheadedness could progress into a ringing in her ears and a distinct dizziness, she was compelled by the reverend to open her mouth and speak.

In a scene that pleased everyone with its theatrics, Mr Jackson had carried his wife from the drawing-room and taken her to rest upon the bed of her former apartment. *Bother!* Unwittingly, Maria had given her father cause for much pleasure – with the keen ear of all his guests able to profess what a delicate creature his daughter was and what a gallant and gentlemanly husband she had – and perhaps worse, she had opened herself to the powers and charms of Mr Jackson's private society – in a bedroom no less! It had not taken long for her to stir and find him, in such an unfair handsomeness, sitting at her side.

To Maria's great fortune, there was a particular natural barrier that would fortify her resolve to resist Mr Jackson's charms. Her will alone seemed of little use. She was, at this time, in the later stages of that regularly occurring inconvenience. Not now plagued enough that attending a party was any great strife, but not quite cleared of the valley of danger that she would risk provoking a final hurrah of that female suffering.

'I must say,' began he, 'I am in awe! Of all the talents in the world, I believe this is by far the most useful I have yet to encounter!'

'Perhaps I am not so very unaccomplished after all,' Maria replied with a tinge of humour.

'I have never thought you to be unaccomplished, Maria.' After a moment of severe pause, he asked, 'Will not you come home with me tonight?'

'No.' How difficult that one word had been to say.

'Why not?'

She did not answer his question and instead posed one of her own, 'Though I did not know your true name, you knew I was Miss Harrington when first we met. Tell me – did you know I was my father's daughter when you agreed to attend his party in December?'

Little expecting such a question, he took a moment to respond. 'I did not know, not for certain. I suspected, and I hoped; that is the only reason I agreed to it. When Providence thrust me into your path once again, I could hardly ignore the opportunity to redeem myself.'

'Redeem yourself? Is *that* what you believe you have been doing, Mr Jackson – in whose eyes, God's or mine?'

'I care far less for God's opinion of me than yours, dear Maria. It is *you* who is my redeemer.'

'Do not believe you can charm me with blasphemy, Husband. You are beginning to sound rather unnervingly like the villain of my favourite book,' she answered only half-seriously.

What a smile this brought to his face. In an instant, he was dropped to his knees at her bedside and took Maria's hand in his. '*But dost think I will lose such an angel, such a forgiving angel as this? By my soul, I will not! How she wounds me, how she cuts me to the soul, by her exalted generosity! But she must have mercy upon me first!*'

'I see that you have been reading it without me, sir,' Maria replied, unable to repress her own smile. *Damn his handsome devil voice!*

'Oh, indeed, I have finished it. And what a harrowing and miserable tale it is – I understand now why you like it so very much.'

'Do you? Is that for knowing the book better – or me?'

'Both, *my forgiving angel*,' he replied with that wretched, beautiful, will-breaking voice, retaking his seat on the bed. After a moment of pause, he asked again, 'Will you truly not come home with me, Maria?'

'No, truly, I will not.' She paused for a moment to enjoy her own resolve, having not, till she had spoken, been certain that she would refuse him. 'But if you would like to see me, then you shall find me every Sunday morning and Tuesday and Thursday evenings at Dean Street.'

Mr Jackson beheld her earnestly. Maria could not quite understand his expression. At length, he replied, 'Then you shall see me every Sunday morning and Tuesday and Thursday evenings at Dean Street, dear Maria.'

CHAPTER SIXTEEN

CONTAINING A SCENE VERY TYPICAL OF MARIA AND JAMES STUART.

James Stuart offered his arm for Maria to take; through politeness and courtesy and because Maria would surely chide him if he did not, and not because he was one of those men who might feel in anyway unfulfilled when the crook of his arm was not home to that of a pretty young woman. The Sunday service at Dean Street had now come to its end. The two were walking to visit Mr Carrey, a member of their congregation afflicted with old age and decrepitude. The walk was no greater than a quarter of an hour, but a walk of even just that length alone with Maria was enough to make the younger Mr Stuart uneasy.

Not for any unrequited affectionate sentiments, although there had been a period of several weeks when he was seventeen and Maria was sixteen when he had panicked himself at the thought that he might be in love with her. This had passed with no struggle greater than relieving himself of a common cold, and soon Maria was, by him, thought of with equal irritation and familial fondness as she had ever been. No, he was uneasy simply because Maria was Maria, and he was himself.

James Stuart was a quiet man, a goldsmith who, for much of his day, worked by himself and liked it that way. He was sometimes mistaken for being reserved or shy. He was neither; he was quiet through no effects of anxiousness or secrecy. He was very simply just quiet. When not entranced in one of her many dazes, Maria was the very opposite of quiet and would talk incessantly, leaping from subject to subject and so loudly that she might be heard by the inhabitants of every home they passed. A girl like Maria, perpetually spilling over the neckline of a very expensive looking gown, hanging adoringly on the arm of a young Black fellow of far more modest attire, brought enough attention as it was. Long since had

James discovered that the best hope of moderating Maria's talking was to answer her.

'Tell me,' Maria began as they set off, 'how is Violet? I have not seen her at church for such a long time. Is she going to another man's sermons again because she has fallen out with Thomas? Lord, they do fight terribly those two – but he is right to keep her manners in check, I believe. She can be sometimes a little rude. When did I last see her? It must have been when she and Penny came to visit me at Russell Square after I was first married. Or have I seen her since then – tell me, do you remember, James?'

Pausing only for a gasp of breath and not long enough for a reply, she continued, 'No, I am sure that was the last I saw her – oh, I was furious with one of our footmen who kept gawping at dear Penny and Violet, you know what sort of way I am talking about! I might have excused him if he were fresh from the country, but he has lived in London his entire life – odd creature, staring and glancing at them in such a way! When Mr Jackson came home, I told him all about it, and so he said to me, "If you believe him to be ignorant and prejudiced, then dismiss him, you have my permission, or would you like me to do it?" – Well, what was I to say to that? I could not be entirely certain that prejudice was the cause of his odd staring, so I decided that I would leave the matter unless he did any such thing again. Do you think I was right to leave the matter, James? – Oh, do watch out! There is something awful vile on the path coming up on your side.'

'Violet has long begun her confinement, several weeks now, I believe.'

'Oh – has she really? I did not think she was so far along as all that! She is one of those fortunate women whose personage looks so well in such a state. I know I shall not have a single edge in sight when my time comes – I dare say, I shall resemble a stout little ball with a head on top!' Maria stopped to laugh, giving a window of opportunity for her conversation partner to change the subject.

'I see your Mr Jackson finally made his long-awaited appearance this morning.'

'Yes, he did. I was quite as surprised as everyone else. Do you think very poorly of him for his deception last summer?'

'I think,' began James, formulating a politic response, 'that he would not be the first gentleman of consequence to amuse himself pretending to be a man of none.'

'What mischief must lie within a man's character that he can find amusement in dishonesty and deception?' Before James had the chance to answer, Maria continued, 'Speaking of marriage–'

'Were we?'

'Yes.' She jabbed him playfully in his side. 'Mr Carrey's daughter, she is very beautiful, is she not? And the same age as myself, she has many more years of beauty ahead of her.' James replied with nothing and gave a not too serious warning look. 'Oh, no, please, do not be cross with me, James!' said she with a smile. 'Well, perhaps a little. You know it pleases me when you are a little cross because it puts such a pretty look on your face.' James answered with only that cross and pretty look. 'Lord! You men are always so boring to talk with about these things. If you insist on being so very coy, then I shall make myself quite brazen. I know you are in love with her!'

The smallest, slightest smile crept upon his face.

'You must tell her!'

'It is too soon, Maria. Her husband has not been dead a year.'

'True, but he was a horrid man, and everybody knew how very unkindly he treated her and that poor little girl. I doubt her heart is at all broken by his passing. Dear Mr Carrey, he is surely not long for this world, and when he has passed, she will have nobody but her child and nothing at all to support herself. And she will be so reliant on finding a husband that before we know it, she will be married to some other unworthy, jealous creature. You must tell her before it is too late. You simply must!'

'What good shall I be to her? I cannot marry yet. You know I cannot.'

'Why are you and Thomas always professing that you *cannot* marry? La! Yes, because of Penny and Joanna, and – Oh! – whatever shall become of them if their brothers do marry?'

'Say it with all the sarcasm you like, Maria, but neither of us could afford to keep a wife, children and two sisters. Does not everyone say that a man is not wise to choose a wife before he is five-and-twenty? When I am older, wiser and a little richer, then I shall marry.'

'Do they? Why would everyone say that? I always thought, for the good of a man's soul, he was best to marry as early as possible. It is very easy for bachelors to fall into mischief; they only need engage in a trifling flirtation, and it can quite break a girl's heart. But married men can flirt monstrously to no consequence at all. In fact, I'm sure people quite encourage it. I have encountered many a married man known as foul-tempered and dull simply because he will not flirt with his friends' wives or his wife's friends! But very well, you need not marry her immediately. Many young couples are engaged till such a time as their circumstances allow for marriage.'

'I may be at liberty to wait, but – as you have already expertly said – her circumstances cannot permit the luxury of dallying.'

They were now at the door of Mr Carrey's lodgings, and so their conversation was forced to end. This did not prevent Maria from continuing to think on the subject at great length. It would not do. She could not bear to think of poor Mrs Stephens, who had once been Miss Carrey, submitting to another miserable marriage. No, she would see no marriages of convenience amongst her friends – *everyone must marry for love*. Mrs Stephens was a quiet woman with good manners, a mind well-educated by her father, and possession of a very handsome smile. A smile that was very often engaged in the presence of James Stuart. Caroline, her daughter, of somewhere between two and three years, shewed no restraint in her delight in Mr Stuart's company. His gift of dried figs was very happily received by the child and her grandfather, who was situated in a chair by the fire of the small sitting-room. The lodgings were humble; a sitting-room and one bedroom to provide accommodation for all three. By no means the worst situation Mr Carrey had happened upon, but far from the best.

Mr Carrey had been among the elder Mr Stuart's first friends when he arrived in London and was his first Black friend in that city. Mr Stuart was the new protégé of the fashionable elite. Mr Carrey had long been under the patronage of this set, having, at the age of six, come into the possession of a young Earl who, being rather bored and moderately benevolent, sought to amuse himself by making an educated gentleman of the child, gifting him his freedom as an eighteenth birthday present. As Mr

Stuart's fortune and prospects were on the rise, Mr Carrey's were soon to be ripped from beneath him.

When first Mr Stuart came to London, abolition was not the moral bread and butter of good people as it is to-day; it was the talk of radicals and religious zealots. In the infancy of the London movement, meetings were fortunate to see a dozen men. How fortuitous for human decency that this handful of men, and their counterparts brewing fervency across the nation, were so indefatigable. With revolution carried to the London airs in the winds from America, France, and Toussaint Louverture's Black republic, radicals rattled the repose of many men. Mr Carrey, having endured the middle-passage at the tender age of four, soon found himself an inspired radical, sharing this wild idea of emancipation at inns, theatres, and parties alike. Soon after this, he found himself violently disrupted on his evening walk home, and shortly after that, situated on a slave ship, and given a choice: be an overseer or be bound in chains once more.

Having known the funny little creature for much of her life, Mr Carrey was always happy to see Maria, though he was equally happy to see her leave within fifteen minutes of her arrival. She did rather have a habit of rattling off news at the speed and volume of an auctioneer at a cattle market. '...Ralph told me the most awful thing to-day – oh, but really, I should not tell you, Mr Carrey – it will upset you, I think. No, I shall not tell you.' Mr Carrey gave Maria a look as if to say, '*Now that you have begun, you must finish.*' She answered this glance by exclaiming, 'No, no really, it is a very sad, horrible affair! James, you know of what I speak. Do you think I am right to not tell Mr Carrey? – James!' But young Mr Stuart was distracted in conversation with Caroline at the table and did not hear her or pretended not to.

'Really, girl,' Mr Carrey sighed, 'you will drive me into a nervous paroxysm with all this wittering. Tell me, or do not, but you must stop this prattle, dear.'

'Oh, well then I shall tell you, Mr Carrey, as someone is bound to at some juncture, and I really see no reason why it should not be me. I never get to tell anybody anything! This morning, when we were all gathered and talking after Thomas' sermon – which was, by the bye, very rousing, how sad I am for you that you are forced to miss his sermons now – Penny said to Ralph, "Will you tell the others what you told me yesterday?" He replied, "Of what do you speak?" For you see, at first, he did not recall what she was meaning…' Maria continued in much this way, frequenting many needless details of the particulars before Mr Carrey understood the facts of the conversation. Ralph had come to hear of an exhibition at The Egyptian Hall, the preserved body of a young boy who had died while living as the slavechild of a baron and his wife in England.

'Is it not the most horrifying thing you have ever known in all your life, Mr Carrey?'

It was far from the most horrifying thing Mr Carrey had known in his life. But considering all he had known and seen, this story pained him more than he could understand.

CHAPTER SEVENTEEN

IN WHICH WE LEARN MARIA'S THOUGHTS ON LOVE.

M r Richard Jackson's study *was* very well furnished and *did* have superbly situated windows. It was larger and brighter than that of Maria's husband and, most importantly, had little risk of Sidney Jackson being there. Little risk, but not no risk at all. When Maria arrived there later that afternoon, she was pleasantly surprised and monstrously infuriated to find the eldest and the youngest Jackson brothers together. Accompanied by a butler and a footman, Maria stood at the door with a countenance so furious, neither gentleman could help smiling. *That wretched, handsome, Jackson devil smile!*

'What are *you* doing here?' she said to her husband, with arms folded and a surly, open-mouthed pout.

'Well, I can leave if my being here is a problem, Maria.'

He was not quite certain if she was entirely serious. It was difficult to make out such things with Maria. She was at least half-serious. Attending the morning service at Dean Street had put another good mark against his previous misconduct. What a distraction he would be. Thomas' voice that morning had been particularly thundering, yet for much of the sermon, Maria had been at risk of barely finding her heart to swell or her mind to throb with the fervour of her faith. This was owing to her being very distracted by her husband, who juvenilely insisted on whispering to her throughout in his handsome voice.

Maria was concerned not only about the distraction he would serve here but for the increased risk that she might reconcile with him prematurely. With every communication and rencontre, her will to stay away from Russell Square dissolved a little more. She would have been much happier to have found the eldest Jackson brother alone; having benefited from their recent shared company, Richard Jackson had very much improved in Maria's estimations. He was quite serious still, but very knowledgeable about the cause she cared for, spoke at length to answer any confusion on her part; and, to her surprise and contentment, asked for her thoughts on the issues, and not only so he might exercise his own superior knowledge in correcting her.

'Before you begin, Maria,' Richard said after several moments of silence, hoping to bypass any domestic disharmony occurring in his study, 'I have a gift to give you.'

'You do?' said both Mr and Mrs Jackson in a curious union. Maria, with a smile, and Mr Jackson, with a frown. Richard Jackson held out a book-shaped parcel in his hand.

'Oh! What a torment you are, Richard!' she laughed as she opened the parcel to reveal a copy of *Frankenstein*.

'Richard?' Mr Jackson echoed quietly, frowning now rather more. '*Richard?*' he repeated with greater force. 'Why are my brothers to you Gilly and Richard, and yet I am invariably called *Mister Jackson*, or worse, *Husband?*' This was said with an air of jest but had a foundation of seriousness.

Maria glanced at him for a moment with thought behind her eyes. 'I have called you by your Christian name on two previous occasions, and neither brought me much joy. Besides, I like calling you Mr Jackson! It makes me happy. If you insist that I call you Sidney, then I shall, but you must know that each time I utter a syllable of that name, it would be as if prodding a needle into my heart. Is that what you want, Mr Jackson?' Mr Jackson did not reply to his wife but for that look of amusement he so often wore when on the receiving end of Maria's serious-smiled abuse. 'Really,' she said, turning to the other Jackson brother, 'you are very bad, Richard, very bad buying me such a teasing gift. For shame, what unbrotherly behaviour this is!'

'For shame that you can so heartfully declare yourself a lover of all tales tragic and not have read this book!'

It is always an awkward circumstance to be party to a conversation founded in prior amusements to which you were not privy. Mr Jackson did not escape any such feelings as he sat as the audience to this interaction.

'Ah, I have told you, sir, I do not care for modern literature. And here you are, forcing it into my hand as a gift. I doubt not that from now till the end of my life I shall be greeted by you with – *Maria, have you read the book yet?* – you intend to wear me down by your demands. Very well, I shall read it. But I am determined not to like it!'

'Very good, Maria. I cannot argue with that,' Richard Jackson answered with a steady humour.

Shortly the lady's intended purpose was resumed, books were discussed, and at length, one was chosen. The Jackson men were in perpetual discussion, and for a long while, Maria did well to ignore them. That was till she heard her husband relate to his brother the information shared by Dr Paterson after that morning's service. 'Oh, it is horrid, is it not?' Maria said, turning in her seat to face her brother-in-law. 'Do you not think it is a horrid affair, Richard?' she prompted again when he did not answer.

'Yes, it is,' he said, drumming his temple and deep in thought. In the next moment, he was lifted from his seat and scanning the shelves of his library. Maria and her husband exchanged a look of intrigue and confusion. 'Here – *The Diary of Horatio Beilby.*' He lifted five thick books from the shelf. 'In one of these volumes, I am sure there is some mention of a dead boy being preserved on the insistence of his mistress. I remember clearly reading it and thinking what an absurd and unchristian thing it was.'

'Have you any idea in which volume I might find such a passage?'

'Not at all, Maria, but you are welcome to take the books with you.'

When Maria arrived at Dr Paterson's home, she was shortly informed the doctor was at the Stuart residence. When she arrived thither, Ralph was not there, neither was Thomas. The two had left to indulge in some manly activity that Maria cared not to enquire after further. With her stack of books in hand, Maria was led to the sitting-room, where sat Penny on a chair, with Joanna on the floor between her sister's knees. James was nearby, in another chair, reading aloud a book in one hand and holding in his other a comb offered with an outstretched arm for his elder sister to retake it as she pleased.

'No,' interjected Penny, when her sister offered to help scour through the books, 'you are wobbling your head about enough as it is without a book to distract you. James can help you, Maria.'

'Offer my services, would you, Sister? Perhaps I am too busy to help dear Maria,' replied James, who added, upon looking up from his book, 'Oh, Heavens! Do not cry, Maria. Yes, I shall help you!'

Quickly wiping the two little tears from her chin, and with a mischievous smile, Maria took the book from his hand and replaced it with the first volume of the diary of Horatio Beilby. 'Unless you plan to visit Mrs Stephens, in which case, I would very gladly forgo your assistance.'

A look of riposte was the only answer her toying would receive, and soon Maria and James made gains in discovering the boy at The Egyptian Hall. Being very distractible, Maria spent far more of her time daydreaming and chatting to Penny and Joanna than reading and was periodically jibed by James for her slowness. 'Really, Maria, I have now skimmed the pages of the entire first volume, and here you are not even a quarter of the way through the second – Oh no, no tears, please, Maria, you shall not read the book any quicker for blurring your vision!'

'Yes, you are of a peculiarly sensitive disposition to-day, dear Maria, is all quite well?' asked Penny.

Maria thought for a moment before replying, 'Penny, my dear, I have decided to love Mr Jackson. Tell me – what do you make of that?'

With this revelation, James decided he wanted no more for the company in the sitting-room and took the remaining three volumes of the diary under his arm to an adjoining parlour.

'La! Are not these men strange creatures?' said Maria. 'As I was saying, I think I shall love Mr Jackson, I have considered it at great length, and I believe it is the most reasonable course of action.'

'Most reasonable course of action, Maria, how strange you are,' said Joanna. 'I am most curious to understand your train of thought.'

'Well, as I have said, I have thought on it at great length. Mr Jackson is my husband, and there is nothing I might do to change that. Is that not true?'

'Yes, that is true,' answered Penny.

'And it is an unavoidable duty of all married women to place the judgement and instruction of their husband above all others, second only to God, is that not true?' – 'It is true, is it not?' asked she again when neither Joanna nor Penny appeared willing to answer.

'Yes, it is true,' at last Joanna replied, reluctantly.

'And what an impossible thing it would be to so exalt a man I did not love. You know, I have always been very gratified to give over my submission to the wisdom of the men I love. What instruction has my cousin ever given that I have not willingly undertaken? And my dear grandpapa, and your dearest papa, did I not always most happily have them decide such a great many things for me?'

Again, with hesitation, Joanna replied in the affirmative.

'It takes, therefore, no struggle of computation to understand that if I am to do my duty by God and enter into the willing submission required in the married state, I must love my husband. So, I have simply decided that I shall love Mr Jackson.'

Before Joanna or Penny could answer this conclusion, in walked James with the third volume of Horatio Beilby's diary in hand. 'Here, I have it!' he exclaimed. "*At Foston Abbey, the mistress of the house shewed me a Black boy they had kept, who she particularly had loved very well. At eight, he had died of consumption and, unable to part with the child, his body was dried in an oven and lies now in a velvet-lined box in the library. In the gallery, I looked upon a portrait of the boy with his mistress.*"

'Oh, how wretched!' remarked Penny, clasping one hand to her heart.

How wretched, indeed. Foston Abbey, James informed the young women, was only so far as Surrey, giving Joanna the idea to visit the house to learn more about the boy. 'To what end?' was the question from James, and his younger sister answered to say that if people knew more of the boy or even saw a little sketch of him – for she was very good with a pencil – then they should be all the more horrified in his being presented for amusement at The Egyptian Hall.

'I shall ask Mr Jackson!' declared Maria. 'He seems to know every land-owner in the country; I am sure he will be able to get us a visit to Foston Abbey.'

Returning to her home at Russell Square was an odd thing. A house chosen by her father and husband and that she had first seen on the same wretched day when she exchanged one poisonous name for another. There was, though, a distinct sentiment of homecoming hovering in her chest. She did not entirely understand it. Mr Jackson, she had come to understand, she had missed very much.

'Maria!' her husband said with surprise. The lady's loud conversation with the butler *en route* to the drawing-room had announced her arrival before that good servant had the chance. Mr Jackson stood at the door to greet her.

'You are busy, I see,' replied she coolly, peering beyond his shoulder in curiosity at the sound of other gentlemen in the room. 'I can return another time.'

'No, you need not leave. I am only playing cards. I would hardly call myself busy. They can leave, and you can stay, Maria.'

'You need not turn your friends out onto the street, Mr Jackson. I am only here to talk with you briefly.' Shortly, the estranged pair left for his study, Maria's favourite room in the house. 'In future, would you please use the ugly drawing-room for your card games? I really cannot bear the thought of the nice drawing-room smelling constantly of smoke and alcohol.' Really, Maria hated the ugly drawing-room. She talked about it every time she walked by the door. Everything was an awful peach colour that did not suit her complexion at all. Though, she would never be convinced to engage the expense of redecorating the room – *what a waste of money that would be!*

'Is this what you have come to talk to me about?' he smiled.

'No,' she answered seriously. 'I have only two things to say to you; one is a question, and the other is a statement.'

'How you intrigue me, dear Maria.'

'You need not become over-excited. Neither is very interesting.'

First came the question, although, really, it was less of a question and more of a demand. If he did not already know the family who owned

Foston Abbey, he would make himself known to them and find an invitation for his wife to visit the gallery there.

'Very well,' he replied, amused by her serious little face, 'and what is your statement?'

'Oh, that?' Her face remained unchanged. 'I have thought about it, and I have decided to love you, and I see no reason why I should not tell you. Oh, actually, there is a third thing – you shall need to buy me a new wedding ring as I threw my other into the Thames.'

'You have decided to love me? Does one not *fall* in love with another?'

'No. I have fallen in love with you twice before, and how very quickly I found myself falling out of love with you. A falling love is very fickle. This time, I have *decided* to love you. I have thought about it, and as you are my husband, there is no sanction divine nor legal for me to love another in that way. And while you have given me much cause to be your greatest critic, I do not believe it is a wife's place to dislike her husband for any significant length of time unless he is habitually unkind to her. And there is surely not another man in England with a reading voice as pleasant as yours – so I have decided that I shall love you.'

'I see.'

'That is all I have to say on the matter. You need not get anything very expensive. My last ring was wretchedly gaudy. Just a gold band would do.'

'She could not come to him and make such a declaration and simply walk away again! He really could not burden to see her leave the house to-night – he would not sleep for thought of her. How could he work when her face stole from him all his sensible thoughts? She needn't even look at him nor admit him to her apartment. Just to inhabit the same air as she breathed would be sufficient. He would sleep on the floor at the foot of her bed if that was what she required. Whatever it was she wanted–'

'Really, Mr Jackson, enough of these obsequious declarations!' *Damn his handsome devil voice!* 'You may tell your friends to leave, and I shall wait in your apartment, *not* mine.'

And here, our scene shall, as it is so often called, *fade to black*.

What humour that the two plaits of Maria's waist-length hair should, as they so often did, have become loosely wound about her neck as she slept. Her tossing and turning as she awoke pulled this knot each time a little tighter, causing her to break from her dreaming and pull the lengths from about her neck. '*A very pretty scene should that have been,*' thought she, '*if my body were to perish where my will that night had done.*' And seeing now Mr Jackson was not at her side, she considered, with an absurdity induced by her anger, how apt it should have been for him to find her in his bed, drained of her happiness and of her life. Yes, how charming she would look, strangled by a rope of her own hair in her husband's bed! After musing that handsome scene for a few moments in her mind, she took to the dressing table, loosened her plaits and amused herself by wrapping the black curls taut about her neck – like a deadly silk scarf.

Mr Jackson had left a note on the table nearest her side of his bed. She had found it soon after waking and read his words with her hair still playing out the scene of one of her many pretty deaths:

'My dear Miss Contrary, before you commit to despising me again, please read this: I am already late, but I shall take a moment to explain my absence to you. It is nine o'clock, and I have attempted many times to wake you (as you had so forcefully instructed I must do), but you will not wake, dear Maria. If it were not for the regular despondent sighing you so adorably expel, I would frighten myself that you were quite dead. What an angel you are when you sleep, Maria. I could sit like this with you forever – ah, but I must go. How you have not been disturbed by the damned pigeon flapping constantly at the window, I do not know. I swear, if it is still here when I return home, I shall shoot the thing! I hope to be home not long after noon. Will you wait here for me till I am home?

I am, your most obedient servant and obliging husband,

Sidney (Is it not such a fine name, my dear?).'

'Postscript: I have decided that I shall love you too, dear Maria.'

A note left for Mr Sidney Jackson in his study:

'Do I understand you mean to say that I am not like an angel when I am awake? How I am sorry that my own husband should prefer my company when I am asleep. I am to be gone shortly. I am too busy to-day to wait here for you. I am sure I shall see you again soon, by and by. Good God! Please do not shoot the pigeon! What an awful joke that was (I hope it was a joke). Do you keep a gun in the house? Pray, you do not, and if you do, pray, get rid of it! Oh, and be pleased to make the arrangements for my visit to Foston Abbey as soon as you are able. I shall be most unhappy if you do not.

Your indifferent wife, Maria.'

'Postscript: I have just found a horrid little gold box in the nice drawing-room. Pray, tell me it is not yours, for if you have taken to chewing tobacco, you will remind me only of my father, and there shall be no hope for us. If you have taken to snuff, then you shall remind me of Pearl, and I shall mock you whenever I see you holding your thumb and finger together. I hope you have taken to none of it, but if you must, let it be cigars. A pipe would age you terribly, and I trust my Ralph when he says that cigarettes are made from the most inferior tobacco. As you will not abstain from drinking alcohol or gambling; for the sake of your own soul and that of your wife, I am hopeful you will not engage with yet another vice. I shall ask Thomas to talk particularly on the matter on Tuesday evening.'

CHAPTER EIGHTEEN

CONTAINING A RENCONTRE WITH GILLY.

Obedience and duty, both filial and marital – and by the nature of the subject, aimed more at one sex than the other – had been the subject of Thomas' Tuesday evening sermon. This was much to the amusement of Mr Jackson, who entertained himself by whispering to his wife at first ridiculous and subsequently lewd suggestions for employment in which a wife's obedience might be commanded. Though she could not absolutely deny all displays of encouragement on her face, Maria was determined to find as little humour in it as possible. She did chide her husband for taking such liberties in a place of worship.

'You shall not bring me round with your depraved sense of humour, husband. You must stop with such perverse quips,' said she as the crowds around them began to depart from their seats after the service.

'Ah, dear Maria,' he answered, leaning into her ear, 'but then you would have nothing for which you could admonish me. And I believe there is nothing you enjoy quite so much as an opportunity to prove to me how much your soul is above mine.'

'How freely you speak to tease me, sir. It behoves me to remind you, Mr Jackson, that I have not yet said you are forgiven for your earlier imprudence!'

'You have told me that you love me. Therefore, is your forgiveness not implied?'

'Most certainly, it is not. Not by me!'

'Well – then tell me; do you forgive me, Maria?' he said rather seriously.

Damn his handsome devil voice!

A blank-faced pause here ensued as the lady wrestled with the overwhelm of the chattering crowds to know her own thoughts. Maria had forgiven Mr Jackson. Quite some time ago, and for far longer than she had the wish to acknowledge. If her piety could be thanked for such easily obtained clemency, then there would be no cause for shame. Howbeit, her readiness to pardon her husband, appeared not, to Maria, to be of the strength found in submitting oneself to powers divine, but the weakness of acquiescing to the powers of man.

'I shall think on the question, Husband, and give you my answer on Thursday.' Though some tenderness had broken into her countenance, Maria was satisfied that she had spoken sufficiently coolly.

Between a Tuesday and Thursday usually comes a Wednesday, and on this particular Wednesday, Maria and Joanna were to travel to Foston Abbey. This arrangement had been formed after some impressively expeditious enquiries made by her husband, enquiries that had, unfortunately, led him to his brother Gilly, who was presently laying his suit on the reasonably pretty Miss Cosway, the great-niece of the old bachelor who owned the place. The master was rarely home, but this lady would be most pleased to welcome the friends of her charmer for a visit.

Owing to her duties in Dr Paterson's office, Penny regretfully could not join the excursion. Mr Jackson, though also duty-bound elsewhere, made himself available for the trip when he could not overcome the fear of Maria spending a day in the close company of his mischievous brother. The journey was, as journeys from London to the country are, long and a little dull once the novelty of fields and cattle had worn. The three played Travelling Piquet, which was tired of after spotting the ninth flock of sheep. Then came the word games; a game of The Old Soldier, Substantives, and Relations. Maria had brought her copy of *Frankenstein* and asked Mr Jackson, at first sweetly and then sharply, to read it to her. He would not pander to her. No matter how watery her eyes might become. He was in a mood for games, as was Joanna. They both came out with such clever things that Maria spent half of each game sulking, much to the amusement of both her companions.

Neither Joanna nor Maria had travelled much beyond London, and neither had ever visited a grand country home, certainly not anywhere known as an *abbey*. Maria was very nervous. Joanna was not at all. Strange

112

perhaps, as, in truth, Joanna had better cause to expect a less than warm welcome from Miss Cosway or the servants of the Abbey, who so very often could be haughtier than their employers. The youngest Miss Stuart made no habit of concerning herself with predictions of how she might be received by others; it was a very poor use of her time. Conversely, Maria passed a great deal of her time concerned with how she might be received, now somewhat regretting that she had tidied her hair only into a single loose plait.

Miss Cosway, already joined by Gilly, greeted her guests with very agreeable manners, and the airs of a lady much in need of amusement. Maria's hair was commented upon, though with more curiosity than malice. The lady of the house made herself known to be perfectly amiable and made only one strange remark to Joanna: 'Two of our housemaids are African, Miss Stuart. They are paid the very same as the other girls and are worked no harder. I can quite assure you, there is no prejudice here. Oh – I do hope we come across them; you might tell me which one you think the more handsome!' A train of spoken thoughts Joanna felt really required no reply. Soon the little party were seated in some very fine-looking room and deep in the throes of conversation.

'Do not you agree, Mrs Jackson, that marriage was a far better prospect for women when men were in the habit of dying sooner?' said Miss Cosway, clearly amused at her own thought.

They had come to search for the painting, and Joanna had made her desire to visit the gallery amply known, but Miss Cosway had insisted before any tour of the house, they must all take tea together. Having become distracted with a thought she could no better recall than the conversation taking place around her, Maria was startled to be addressed by their hostess and with such an odd question.

'Heavens! No!' Maria said with her serious smile. 'I have no wish to be made independent by the death of my husband. I hope very much that Mr Jackson will not die before I do. That would not do at all! I shall not be gratified unless I am to die at least forty years before his passing.' All were entertained with this answer, except her husband, who offered a disconcerted half-smile. 'I suppose to be on the safe side, I am best to die before you are thirty, my love.' What a toying and sweet disposition this was said with! Mr Jackson was a little undone by an uneasy tone of seriousness he had detected in Maria's words. Her eyes had not quite committed to the joviality of her smile.

'What a divertingly absurd creature you are, madam,' replied Miss Cosway, much amused by her new companion. 'And, my – what a handsome young widower you will be, Mr Jackson, if your wife has her way. And I find wives always get their way one way or another.'

'A monstrously rich widower too!' Gilly added with a laugh that sounded a jot angry. 'I would encourage you to think again, dear sister. Surely your poor grieving husband will be disallowed from taking another wife so long as your father is alive – if he wishes to cling to your pretty inheritance. And after having such a fine example of the gentle sex for a wife, you cannot expect the man to live single. You will push your Mr King to a life of great sinfulness!'

'Mr King!' cried Miss Cosway. 'Do you pretend to forget your own brother's name? What a jester you are, Gilly!'

'No, madam,' he replied with a smile directed only at his brother. 'It is an old joke between Sidney and me.'

'Oh, no, I shall not have this, sir! It is not genteel to converse of private amusements in the presence of those not privy to the joke. If you do not explain it to me, then I shall be very cross with you and think you no gentleman at all.'

It was evident to Maria that her brother-in-law should encounter few difficulties in securing Miss Cosway's heart and hand – if that was his intention – though she was not convinced it was. To begin, Gilly resisted the lady's pleas, though this was borne not of any real reluctance but his teasing nature. At last, he said, 'Really, madam, I believe my brother is better suited to explain the history of Mr King, that profligate adventurer amongst The Great Unwashed. After all, he was a character of your creation, was not he, Sidney?'

Mr Jackson did not reply and diverted a contrite look towards Maria, who proffered an accomplished pretence of ease.

'Is your husband always so severe, Mrs Jackson?' Miss Cosway said in a purposely audible whisper, leaning across the table. 'I am half-terrified to look at him!'

'Perhaps, Maria,' began Joanna, having known 'Mr King' herself and understanding the look of cresting distress upon her friend's face, 'we might go to look at the portraits now. You know I do not like to be rushed when taking in paintings. Miss Cosway, would you give us your leave that we might take a walk of the gallery?'

'Oh, let us all go!' the lady cried. 'I am quite tired of sitting. And I am certain I can answer any questions you might have, and those who truly love art always have questions, do not they, Miss Stuart?'

'I believe they do, madam.'

Once Miss Cosway had such a scheme in her sights, there was nothing more to be done. This unhappy set was to go together to peruse the gallery. Miss Cosway walked ahead with Gilly, leading the way, and Mr Jackson had his wife on one arm, and Joanna on the other. At some juncture during their acquaintance, though *when* Maria did not know, Mr Jackson and Joanna must have previously discussed missionary work in the colonies. In possession of a sharp memory that could recall the particular interests of even the most fleeting of acquaintances, Mr Jackson quickly engaged the interest of the young Miss Stuart. Maria found herself quite pleased to be the wife of a man who would endeavour to make her friends feel distinguished in his memory, even if it were nothing more than a politician's parlour trick.

Miss Cosway and Gilly talked loudly enough that their conversation could easily be heard over Joanna's soft ruminations of her hopes to travel to the West Indies, carrying with her God, comfort, and a zeal for the powers of education. Maria was unskilled in hearing conflicting conversations and, against her better judgement, concentrated her attention upon the one at the head of the walking party. 'Mr King is a most churlish character. A gentleman in disguise,' declared Gilly, 'whose adventures have been designed and written of by my brother and me alike.'

'How diverting!' came Miss Cosway's pretty cry. 'He must share some tales. She demanded he must!' And so he did. 'Inns? – little theatres? – the daughters of illiterates and labourers? – a farmer's young wife? – those religious zealot girls? – how amusing this all was to her ears – were these stories all formed entirely from imagination – not a jot of truth in it at all?'

'Oh, I am afraid to answer such a question, madam, for fear that you will threaten to strip from me the title of a gentleman once again!' Gilly replied with that devilish Jackson smile, turning his head to cast a goading look at his brother.

What a churn those words had brought to Maria's mind. Though Mr Jackson had never said as much, it had been her belief – and now she was not entirely sure why – that Mr King was an invention of a single, spontaneous humour, not a prolific profligate of deliberate design and iterant interaction with the lowly of London. A jolly good game between brothers.

'Fiends and villains, the both of you!' Miss Cosway laughed. Quickly the lady hushed her voice, though she spoke still loud enough to be heard. 'That is why your brother will not engage with us – his wife is present – oh, but upon my word, I have never known any of my sex ungratified at the prospect of reforming a philanderer, especially a handsome one. Mrs Jackson must be very pleased with the fruits of her labour.'

The party at the rear pretended not to hear a word of this, though all did. Gladly, they were now arrived at the gallery, and after a knowing look to Gilly, Miss Cosway redirected her attention to talk of the paintings. Somewhat unexpectedly, and not absolutely to Joanna's comfort, their hostess insisted that Miss Stuart, being so interested in art, should take her arm. 'Will you join us, Mrs Jackson? I rarely find gentlemen have anything interesting to say about paintings – unless it is of a young woman whose clothes have gone missing, then they all have an artisan's eye!' Her laugh was joined only by Gilly's. 'Come, dear lady, take my left! There is something so heart-filling to be found in walking arm-in-arm with one's own sex. Do not you agree?'

'No, I will not,' answered Maria rather more bluntly than she had intended. She could not walk arm-in-arm with Miss Cosway after overhearing these new revelations about Mr Jackson. She could not, and she would not. Though Maria declared herself to be blighted with a headache and needing *good country air,* the hostess proceeded to extend her arm and press our poor Maria to join their perusing party. She could not stay here. She simply could not. If she did, then she would cry, or scream, or throw a priceless vase onto the floor. Pressed and pressed again, there was only one thing to be done.

Seeing his wife had commanded her breathing to halt before beginning her walk of submission to Miss Cosway's arm, Mr Jackson said quite angrily, 'Good God, woman! If my wife says she is ill and wants to

116

walk in the country air, then you will allow her to do so!' Miss Cosway could hardly argue with such a directive and, with an arched brow, sent Maria on her way. Declaring to Joanna in a whisper that she was not sorry, for she liked her company better anyway.

'Shall I come with you, Maria?' said Mr Jackson. His question went unanswered as the lady passed hurriedly by without a look in his direction.

Tapping his brother firmly on the shoulder, Gilly parted his lips to prod a little further at the wound of his creation. Before he could speak, Mr Jackson had shaken off his brother's hand and gone after his wife.

CHAPTER NINETEEN

CONTAINING A LETTER OF SIGNIFICANCE.

Maria did not arrive at the meeting house the following evening. As such, her husband could not talk to her as he had planned. In vain, he tried for a long while to ask of her absence, but her friends were too busy discussing Joanna's discoveries at Foston Abbey. Maria had wanted to take her walk alone and quite adamantly sent Mr Jackson back to the gallery, where he found Joanna asking many questions about a portrait of the once mistress of this great home:

There he was, clinging to the hem of his mistress, her hand resting on his head. He was a prop, an accessory of fashion. The humorousness of his name, his ostentatious clothing, and the indignity of his resting place; in it all was the evidence of a boy beheld as an amusement. In every sense, legal and figurative, he was a possession. And yet, he was not. Not by the natural and moral laws of our unending universe. This boy had entered the world as every other before him, to a mother who could not believe that the trials and tortures of delivery could be washed away by the piercing cry of new life, not till she experienced it for herself. It was a boy! She always knew it would be a boy! Although she had benefited from the best part of a year to prepare herself, still the lady was dumbfounded by a kind of true shock and awe – that is known so few times in life – to find herself holding a baby, her baby. In her arms, she held hope. Hope that she was allowed to hold for two years more before her soul was ripped from her clambering fingers and sent to England as a gift from a husband to his childless wife.

'The boy was a romantic gift?' asked Penny in a voice of disbelief.

'Yes, that is what Miss Cosway said, was it not, Mr Jackson?'

He replied in the affirmative, and Penny eyed him with a severity that was most unusual for her habitually happy manners. At length, and after much further conversation about the boy at Foston Abbey, Mr Jackson managed to catch the ear of his estranged friend and ask after Maria.

119

'She did not much feel like coming this evening.'

'That is unusual for Maria, surely. Did she say why – is she unwell?'

'I believe your brother upset her when he came by this afternoon.'

'Richard?' Mr Jackson asked, somewhat hopefully.

Dr Paterson answered with a shake of the head. The two exchanged a strange, entirely indescribable look. When first Ralph Paterson had been acquainted with Mr Jackson in their younger days, his companion despaired at his brother Gilly: a prolific womaniser, a man insincere and immoral in equal measures, everything he did was only for his own amusement. After the consequences of Mr Jackson's betrayal, Ralph heard often that his estranged pal had tumbled into the influence of Gilly and his circle of unsavoury friends.

'Do you know what he has said to her?'

'No idea, Jackson,' Dr Paterson said, feeling unexpectedly sorry for the man. 'He brought a letter with him to shew her, that much I heard, but what it said, I could not tell you. She spent the rest of the afternoon in her bedroom and would not come out.'

'May I come by to speak with her? Lord only knows what Gilly has said!'

'If you would give me leave to say so, Mr Jackson,' began Penny, feeling quite fierce and knowing more than Dr Paterson on the matter. 'I do not think Maria wants to see you.'

A note delivered to Mr Jackson on Thursday evening, from his brother Mr Richard Jackson:

'Your breweress made a visit to my home this evening to call on Jane and told her (in a fit of deranged distress) of all the reasons she has to be vexed with you and our brother. I do mean all, Sidney – our wives are perhaps better friends than I had hoped. For the love of Christ, I thought you were long moved beyond this. I expect it from Gilly, but I believed you had learnt your lesson long ago. Less than a month before the election, and you were still up to these tricks – for shame, man! Wake early to-morrow, and come to my office before you begin your day. I would like to speak with you in person. Your wife left the sheet of scribbles she had brought with her. But, as they are your degenerate words, I enclose it to be returned to you, sir, so that you might think on your actions.

&c., R. Jack'

The included pages: From a letter sent to Mr Gilly Jackson from his brother Sidney in the previous July:

'Ah, yes, dear sir, I had thought you would be eager to hear the adventures of young Mr King – What a dastardly fellow is he! Come August, I believe I shall be forced to resign my old friend from action, and what despondency shall this bring upon the canaille of London! He has fallen in with a very pious lot, entirely by happenstance; I had come to a lecture as Mr Jackson, but upon seeing a flock of delicate young creatures among the crowd, I found myself leaving as Mr King. And among the pretty things is Miss Harrington, the cousin of my very old pal Ralph Paterson. He was unnoticed by me till after introducing myself many times, but he has not the gall to charge me publicly.'

'Ordinarily, I would be little moved by such an unremarkable sort of girl, but upon further glances, it is clear she is a bushel little bubby; dugs so well developed, they are up to her ears! Her manners are too open for my usual tastes. I have encountered books for children that are harder to read than her heart – it is obvious she is little acquainted with the ways of the world. Poor naïve creature, how she smiles at me so freely! God forgive me, but I cannot resist such a dewy-eyed lamb, nor the sport of injuring Paterson in debauching her. Less than a month will see her introduced to new knowledge of mankind – name your price, and I shall happily put a wager upon it.'

'You may keep your theatre wenches, Brother. Nothing worth having is had easily. Low hanging fruit comes to mind! These falling angels require far more patience than that of which you are in possession. Pick the right one, and you will never find your forbearance wasted – for all their praying, I find those with the yielding hearts make such capable and ready kneelers. How pleased I shall be to look down upon Miss Harrington's pretty, black, marble eyes. As to your invitation for me to join you in Venice this September, you must know I cannot agree to it. Though, if God has mercy upon me and I do not win this seat–'

121

The forty-minute verbal keelhauling Mr Jackson had received on Friday morning was small change when compared to the anticipation of his first interview with Maria; if he could convince her to speak with him. That which his eldest brother said had been heard many times before – he was a disappointment, squandering his time and intelligence, and for what; frothy, empty praise from Gilly and the licentious fools he calls friends?

'That you would use such language came as no great surprise to me – though I was forced to feign great shock when Jane shewed me the letter. But that the both of you would commit such words to paper is unfathomable. I have convinced Gilly to give over your letters on the promise that you will give up his. Did you write to anyone else of your lewd meditations?'

Mr Jackson shook his head.

'And then we have the matter of Maria – what in God's name were you thinking?' Richard paused for his brother to answer, but when he did not, he happily continued his chiding. 'Did not Jane and I suggest to you at least half a dozen suitable women? This was supposed to be a new beginning for you, Sidney. By Christ, the pains I went through to procure you that seat.' Here he slammed his fist onto the desk. 'And months later, with no previous mention of her, you tell me that you are engaged to a girl who – for her abundance of riches – is still the granddaughter of an East Indian and a butcher from Berkshire. And now I learn that you married her, knowing well her virtue was long gone. Were you really so bent on securing your financial independence? Christ knows what her history is. Now I shall be forced to quiz her to ensure there are no ghosts that shall return to haunt you further along your career.'

'You shall do no such thing! Say what you like of me, Brother, but I shall not have you speculate about Maria in such a way. With me was the one and only time she entered into such a deed before we were married.'

Richard Jackson laughed, 'Yes, well, I am sure she would tell you that to secure her new name.'

How wrong Mr Jackson considered his brother was. When they were first married, on their trip to Dulwich, Mr Jackson had attempted, on one of their long lovers' walks, to engage his new bride to speak on what her father had done to secure her hand. Maria would say nothing of it but begged her husband to promise that he would never speak to anyone of her

122

agreement having been coerced. Of course, at the time, he professed that he would happily swear to never speak of it. Why would he ever want to admit such a wretched truth? For a moment, he considered breaking this promise to exonerate Maria's name. Mr Jackson had been the one in such shameful parleys with Mr Harrington to secure a generous allowance while his father-in-law was alive and the entirety of Maria's inheritance upon his death, yet it was Maria who was viewed as the opportunist by his family and friends. Mr Jackson had broken his word to Maria many times, but having recently committed to ceasing that habit, he answered, 'It does not really matter if you believe her. I do.'

'Her prudence is your prudence, and – unfortunately – your prudence is mine. Speaking of which, I have told you, you must leave off this constant wittering about prison reforms, and do not you dare engage with the farcical fascination your little *breweress*–'

'Stop referring to her as such!'

'Very well,' Richard began again with a conceited smile, 'the farcical fascination *your wife* has with this boy at The Egyptian Hall. Did I not instruct you to keep your head down this year? Less time trying to impress your *ready kneeler* and more spent making friends in the House!'

Knowing of no better place to seek her – for Dr Paterson, cognisant now to the contents of the letter, had refused the gentleman entry to his home – Mr Jackson arrived a half-hour early to wait outside the meeting house at Dean Street on Sunday morning. Maria was invariably heard before she was seen, but not on this morrow – she came from the corner of the street, quite silently, on her cousin's arm. Mr Jackson had rehearsed a hundred different encounters in his mind, saw his wife ignore him, upbraid him, and cry at him; never did he expect to see her smile and lift her hand into a delicate little wave. Maria sent Ralph ahead, who proffered a fiercely forbidding look to his old friend before entering the church. By the time his wife had approached, entirely vanished was Mr Jackson's nerve to speak.

'Hello, Sidney,' said she with a weak smile.

'Sidney, since when do you call me that?' he answered in astonishment.

'It is what you would like me to call you, is it not?'

He knew not, at first, how to respond. While he thought, Maria, usually such a happy filler of any silence, said nothing more and continued to look at him, though her sight appeared fixed on nothing at all.

'Did you hear me, Maria?' Mr Jackson began for the second time. 'You look cold. Would you like my jacket?'

'I am not cold!' How unexpectedly cheery was her voice as she now beheld him with her gaze as well as her eyes. 'But you are kind to worry. Shall we go inside?

'May I sit with you, Maria?'

'Of course, where else would you sit? It is an odd man who does not sit beside his wife at church!'

His courage to speak the words of one of his many prepared declarations returned, and Mr Jackson took Maria's arm, holding her back before she reached the door:

'The letter, Maria, hear me, please. I cannot deny those were my vulgar words, but you must know that they are entirely irreconcilable with my thoughts towards you now. Even as I wrote them, they were more pomposity than anything else. Like a fool, I sought to diminish your value because I knew, the moment I saw you, that you were too good for a man like me. I knew you could never prefer one such as me, not if I came clean about my lies. I made a game of my affections, Maria, to cure them.'

'There is really no need for such hyperbole. No more of your nimble-tongued eloquence, sir. You are forgiven. There is nothing more to say of it.'

'Maria, you cannot suppose to forgive me already.'

With her more serious smile, the lady replied, 'Upon my word, my honour, I shall even say, upon my soul, sir – and you know I would not speak such a thing lightly – I promise that I have forgiven you. Would not half the wives in England be forever broken-hearted if they were to judge their husband's character on the letters he wrote before they were married? I am only sorry I saw it, but as I cannot unsee it, then I shall forgive it. Believe me, will you not, Sidney? You are forgiven.'

Oh, how she wounded him, how she cut him to the soul, by her exalted generosity!

Might we here briefly turn our attention to *Le Bonheur* – the pairing in which both parts found utter contentment simply existing in the same world as the other. Penny and her doctor (oh, let us call him '*her doctor*' for he truly was) had visited Mr Carrey after the service. His ailments grew worse, now unable to enjoy sitting by the fire; this bedbound elderly man had not the money for even the worst apothecary in London and was entirely reliant on the charity of Dr Paterson to improve his comfort. While the doctor spoke with Mr Carrey in the bedroom, Penny, in a most gay and lovely new bonnet, was shewing young Caroline a selection of pretty ribbons she had no longer need for and wished to gift to her.

'You must allow me, Miss Stuart, to pay you something for the clothes and the ribbons,' said Mrs Stephens as she looked over a heap of fabric.

'I most certainly shall not,' replied Penny softly. 'It is not charity, my dear, but the simple act of sharing between friends. Half my things are castoffs from Maria's closet, and I tried to give these to Joanna, but she said they were too garish for her! Queer creature she is!'

Blushingly and somewhat reluctantly, Mrs Stephens accepted the refusal with her bewitching smile – so easy it was to see why her brother was in love with this lady. After some simmering silence, broken only by young Caroline's admiration of her new ribbons, Dr Paterson entered the sitting-room and declared Mr Carrey ready for visitors. Penny, finding in this elderly gentleman a connection to her own father, eagerly took up the invitation and left her doctor with the others.

It had not been a week since last Penny had seen Mr Carrey, but he seemed to have aged years in that time. Despite the most diligent care from his daughter, his body was nearing its natural end; his eyes milky, his hands weak with fingers knotted together; just as Penny's dear papa had been. The gentleman, though, was determined still to learn more of the boy at The Egyptian Hall.

'Boy Friday. That was his name,' Penny said, answering his question.

'Boy Friday?' Mr Carrey replied, sounding a little saddened. 'That is what they named him? Like, *my man Friday* – I suppose – the savage manservant in Robinson Crusoe. They gave the child a joke for a name.'

He was not wrong. The lady affirmed it with an unhappy nod. For all the variant and ranging sentiments he held alongside the memories of his own boyhood, this was the first Mr Carrey had reflected with gratitude that his patron had given him the name of a man and not a pet.

'Here,' Penny said, taking a piece of paper from a black velvet reticule, 'it is a sketch Joanna did of the boy from the portrait at Foston Abbey. She is very handy with a pencil, and Mr Jackson agrees he is depicted almost entirely as in the original.'

The gentleman took the drawing from her and clutched it in his shaking, frail hands. For a moment, his failing vision was entirely consumed with the face of this child, and when it seemed as if tears might break from his tired eyes, Mr Carrey put down the drawing on his bed and remarked, 'I say – it is very quiet through there. Is not Mrs Jackson with you?'

'No, she is not. She returned home after the service…with her husband.'

A curious brow was raised by Mr Carrey. 'I am glad to hear it. Too long she has been hiding away with her cousin. You know I am very fond of the girl, but she has always been a flighty creature, and I have heard nothing but good recommendations of her husband's character. I tell you – young women these days are always running from their husbands the moment the novelty wears thin, and the toil of a wife really begins–'

Penny attempted a yielding smile, but the corners of her mouth were unmovable at the thought of the man's poor daughter. '*No,*' she thought to herself, '*he could not be including in that grouping Mrs Stephens. Her situation had been very different from Maria's.*'

'…and now they are reconciled, perhaps Mrs Jackson will influence her husband to take up the issue in Parliament.'

'In Parliament!' Penny almost choked on the words. 'It is an abomination, Mr Carrey, but what will Parliament care for it; there are far greater injustices they are in no great hurry to end.'

'If you ask not, dear madam, then you shall never know.'

CHAPTER TWENTY

IN WHICH SOMETHING AND NOTHING HAPPENS.

Mr Jackson was very glad to have Maria returned to Russell Square. Though, really, he could not understand *why* she had returned with him after church. For the first week, he quite expected any small inconvenience to his wife or slight misdeed on his part would bring forth an eruption of the symptoms of the hurt his letter must have caused. Such a release never came. A brief sob was had when Maria knocked over her bottle of hair oil; she threw her brush at the wall, lamenting on the floor for ten minutes. That was, till Mr Jackson picked her up, sat her on the bed, and promised to buy a replacement on his way home. She was then perfectly contented once again; nothing out of the ordinary at all.

The second Monday after Maria's return, Mr Jackson arrived home, late in the afternoon, to find her in his study; always, he found her in his study. Sitting on the couch, her gaze at the book in her hands was only temporarily broken by a happy smile and greeting to her husband. 'Hello, Sidney!' On the little table next to Maria's side of the couch, was a book open, with a passage underlined. It was her Kempis. Maria's third favourite book. The first being the Bible, the second, of course, *Clarissa*, and the third, *The Imitation of Christ* by Thomas à Kempis. With his wife staring intently at a different book, Mr Jackson took a moment to glance at the passage she had marked out:

What would become of patience, what of forgiving and forbearing one another for Christ's sake, if there were no provocations to try our temper? And such there could not be, if every man were perfect and did his duty. But as the present condition of the world is ordered, God hath furnished us with constant occasions of bearing one another's burthens. For there is no man lives without his failings.

After some moments of contemplating these words, Mr Jackson closed the book. Maria had not looked up from her own reading. She also had not turned a single page since his coming into the room. Her finger rested still in the same spot it had been when first she had greeted him.

'What are you reading, dear Maria?'

It took a moment for her to hear him, but when she did, Mr Jackson's wife turned to him and looked as if she was close to laughter. 'Oh, pray, do not mock me too much! It is a domestic index. I am going to choose us something to have for dinner to-morrow. What do you think to *that*?'

'I think that depends on what you will choose,' said he with a smile.

'That is a good answer,' she laughed. '*Pigeons au Poires*? – No, I shall not fuel your vengeance against our dear friend at the window. Soup, what do you think to soup?'

'It is a meal I might bear if I am at a dinner party or a ball.'

'Yes, you are quite right – soup is an odd meal to have for a dinner at home.' She flicked through a few pages more. 'Ham braised – or is that a little boring?'

'It sounds wonderful, Maria.'

'Ham braised it is then,' she declared, closing the book with purpose. 'I shall go to inform Mrs Heeley and leave you to read your letters.' Before the lady could leave, he called her name, causing a smile of confusion to appear upon her face. 'Yes, Sidney?' she answered. Maria had taken to speaking Mr Jackson's name so happily and so sweetly, it pained him immeasurably, and for a reason the gentleman could not at all understand. 'Oh – before I forget,' said she, moving closer and taking his hand earnestly in hers. 'Mr Carrey believes we should petition Parliament on behalf of that poor little boy at The Egyptian Hall. Perhaps, when you have a moment, you might give the matter a fraction of time in your thoughts and tell me your conclusions later.' Or, at least, that is what Maria thought herself to have said; her words had come to an abrupt end after, '*perhaps*', and not a thing more was spoken.

'Perhaps *what*, Maria?' Mr Jackson prompted after beholding his wife gazing blankly at him for some moments. *Lord, those beautiful, mournful eyes!*

She hemmed a quiet noise of bewilderment. 'I beg your pardon. My mind drifted for a moment. What were you saying, Sidney?'

'I was not saying anything, Maria. You were. Are you feeling unwell?'

'No! I am very well. Thank you, sir, for asking. What a kind husband you are,' smiled she, and with a sudden gust of remembrance, she declared, 'Ham braised! That is what we had decided upon. I shall go now to tell Mrs Heeley and leave you to read your letters. You have quite the heap. What a man in demand you must be!'

A letter written by Maria Jackson to her grandfather – two o'clock the following morning:

'Do you speak with our Lord, sir? Can you speak to him? Excuse me, I must put down my pen for a moment. My heart flutters too much to keep a steady hand, and I see Mr Jackson is threatening to stir from his slumber.'

'I feel much improved for an hour of sleep. What I was speaking of when I began before, I do not remember. The answers to those questions you could not reveal to me, of course, you could not; such knowledge is not for we mortals. I had a dream just now that pierced my aching heart – Oh – I did not believe it could weep anymore! In this dream, Mr Jackson and I visited my mamma, and as we stepped into her little parlour, she cried out to me, "Ah, dear Maria, there you are, my child!" What a familiar gaze she gifted me with her pretty, dark eyes – and what happy eyes they were. I have never before dreamt that she remembers me. What meaning becomes this? Come to me and tell me if you can. I miss you terribly.'

'Though I have said it again and again in my prayers, might you inform Him that I am humbled? My dear Clarissa says it better than I might ever do: "My calamities have humbled me enough to make me turn my gaudy eye inward; to make me look into myself. And what have I discovered there? Why, my dear friend, more secret pride and vanity than I could have

130

thought lain in my unexamined heart." How many times we might read words but not understand their meaning.'

'I had thought myself too much for my God and His plans; too clever, too witty, and too proud. I have judged my husband so severely for his sinning and been myself an obstinate sinner all the while. If my father's cruelty was by design divine or demonic, I shall surely never know in this life. Nobody could force from my lips that lifelong oath, though done sorrowfully, it was said willingly – and since the moment those words were uttered by me before God, it behoves me to bear with all that this oath might bring.'

'Is that right? Do I have it right, sir? What else could be meant by the words of that letter being put before my eyes? I shall ask Thomas on Tuesday evening – no mortal in the world understands the workings of Him better than dear Thomas.

Always, am I, your, Maria.'

Maria did not ask Thomas this on Tuesday. Not owing to any forgetfulness, nor a change in her own thoughts – but because she was quite preoccupied with lambasting his name for utter betrayal. Thomas Stuart was to be married. That in itself did not injure Maria. For a few moments, she did reflect upon her former flame for the gentleman, but it had long since dwindled back to nought but familial affection. The treachery came in the new knowledge that Thomas had been secretly engaged for two years to the daughter of a freeborn man from Spanish Town.

The young couple had met on his first day in Jamaica, and the gentleman could bear to live apart from her no longer. Thomas Stuart was to leave London forever and move to a distant corner of the world. Spanish Town might well have been on another world altogether to Maria's mind – Penny was affected in much the same way – what great tears of anguish and grief did the meeting house witness that evening! And, as if to rub salt into the open wounds upon their hearts, Ralph had known of it all the entire time. As he came to leave the meeting, Dr Paterson was accosted by his least favourite old friend, who appeared in a state of grave apprehension.

'Maria – do you think she is well? I find her acting strangely and not like herself.'

131

'In what way?' replied Ralph, intrigued enough to hear the man.

'Daydreaming – always daydreaming – more than he had ever known. A half-laugh declared her compliant, oddly obliging – tractable he would vouch to say – she might agree with anything he said. The letter to her grandfather – he had not meant to read it – but Maria had left it open on the desk – and once he had begun reading, he found he could not stop… what did it mean? What had her father's cruelty been? She would not say, she would never say – What had he done to force Maria's acceptance? Why would she write to her dead grandfather about her duty to her husband?'

'For God's sake, man,' Ralph whispered harshly. 'Calm down! You are sounding quite deranged. She has always written to our grandfather since his passing. She makes no secret of it. Maria is always telling me of her letters to him. And every so often, will emerge my martyr cousin, declaring how she should have loved nothing more than to have been a nun and wants for nothing but to give her life to God. She will read nought but her devotions, spend her days quantifying her sins and then flagellate herself with rigid observance of her Christian duty.' With a sour eye, he added, 'The last time she did such was soon after your encounter with her in July. I dare say you are the cause of resurfacing her penchant for penance this time also.'

Swallowing his shame, Mr Jackson replied, 'How can you speak with such flippancy? Do not you worry for her?'

'I *always* worry for Maria. But as she has, in the past hour, admonished me for being a Judas, and named me the very worst of all cousins, who she will hate for the entirety of this life and the next – declared how she has never in her whole life been so wretchedly used – asked my pardon for her calling me Judas, then told me that she forgives me for my secrecy and how dearly she loves me; Maria seems very much like herself to me – I believe you just do not know her very well, Jackson.'

Thomas would not be leaving London for six months, enough time for Maria to forgive him a hundred times over and again. Really, he had been acquitted of his treachery before she had returned to Russell Square. Taking in the dark streets through the carriage window, she was silent on their return home. *'How?'* Maria considered, *'How could Thomas bear to burden a broken heart with such a cheerful countenance for two years?'* How could he have borne her many lengthy lamentations, as self-indulgent as they were frequent, when all the while, his heart struggled for each beat with its bruised and broken flesh. Oh, to be loved by a man who would cling to your letters for two years, abandon his life, and sail across the world for you.

With that last thought, Maria looked briefly at Mr Jackson, and arresting his gaze, she smiled. He was not wrong. Her manners were too open for anyone's liking. A passing link-boy might well know the contents of her heart. *It is a very unlikeable trait, Maria; it is a wonder Mr Jackson can see beyond it at all. He would love you better if you could learn to command your lips from constantly bestrewing the workings of your heart.*

'May I sleep in your bed to-night, Sidney?'

'Of course, dear Maria.'

CHAPTER TWENTY-ONE

CONTINUING MR CARREY'S TALE.

Penny was not so willing to forgive Dr Paterson, and she certainly was not willing to speak to him. Maria's silence, Ralph could always burden, because it was a very noisy sort of silence; what with all the slamming, huffing, lamented sighing and sobbing, and it was certain to never last longer than an hour. Penny's silence, well, that the doctor had never experienced before, and now he had endured an entire week of being completely ignored by the woman whose storytelling brought him endless joy.

Penny went about her work with all the usual care but with none of its usual spirit. There was only a frigid void where the song and dance of her employment should be. A shame for a great many reasons, but particularly so because the lady had so very much she should like to tell her doctor. Dr Paterson's office was her little slice of the world in which she could share that which weighed upon her thoughts. When her father had died, that very morning, she wanted for no place but that ill-lit room, nobody but her doctor, and what a comfort he had then been.

James too had been kept in the dark about his brother's engagement; Penny knew, as did Maria, that, soon to be the only man in his home, he would give up all hopes of marrying Mr Carrey's daughter. Mr Carrey's condition was rapidly worsening, a fact revealed to Dr Paterson by the study of the gentleman's person and a fact revealed to Penny by the study of his words. Just as her father had been, Mr Carrey cared little for his present and focused upon the future of his daughter and his own history. In a quiet moment alone a few days earlier, the elderly gentleman had cried to Penny and said himself to be damned:

'You, sir, damned? I cannot think of anyone who will be more welcomed in the Kingdom of God!'

But she did not know his shame, not till he told her of it. Fear, he declared, is the basis of all poor decisions, and it had been the cause of his choosing the life of an overseer instead of a return to chains. Three days after leaving Madagascar, he stood at the ship's edge, quite determined he would jump into the embrace of the ocean. But he had made somebody a promise, and he so hated to break a promise. She had come aboard the ship with two children, and now she had not one. We will not repeat the scenes that poor woman had been forced to witness.

She could speak only a little English but knew enough to string together a plea of three small words of the greatest consequence. He went to her when she would be sleeping, with a rag to hold over her nose and mouth – he did not want her to know a thing of it, and she did not. A young woman in chains caught the young Mr Carrey's gaze in a glimmer of moonlight, at first fearing he was come for what so many of the brutish crew sought in the women's holding, but seeing his intention, she lay down her head. Penny did not think Mr Carrey damned, and she told him such. It was a circumstance of great complexity, one that no person would wish to find themselves in, one she was glad to never have faced.

'...but, truth be told, Mr Carrey, I believe I would have done exactly as you did. It seems, to me, to have been the path of greatest kindness. It might not have felt very kind, but it was the kindest thing within your power – God will see that, and he will forgive you. How could there be a God who is just and all-knowing and send you to the same fate as that demonic captain? – there could not be. The guilt you have lived with was punishment enough. Believe me, will you not? God will forgive you, sir.'

'I am not certain I want God to forgive me.'

Dr Paterson was the only person she wanted to speak with about this. Not to confess Mr Carrey's secret – no, she would never tell a soul of that – but the idea in its abstract. As a doctor and a Methodist, how much she wished to know his opinion on the matter and talk with him of hers. If someone is in such abject suffering, with no prospect of relief, is not it the kindest thing to attend their pleas if they wished to die? She was not sure her doctor would agree with her. In fact, knowing him as she did, she was almost certain he would not, but he would have talked to her about it, and not with judgement or pretension. How many things this pair had disagreed upon in this little office, and yet never had the course of their conversation veered from the most pleasant amiability.

135

'Do you think Maria is acting oddly?' The doctor said, watching the belle make her melancholy journey about the room.

She gazed at him severely. 'Yes, a little.'

A three-word answer was better than he had hoped for. The best before that was the '*thank you*' she had begrudgingly bestowed when he had given Penny a bouquet of the very finest flowers that an English spring and the London flower markets could offer.

'Jackson seems concerned with her passiveness and dreaminess, though I have tried to tell him that is just her nature; for all her fierce words and threatenings, she is a very accepting and forgiving creature, too forgiving. And she has never concentrated very well. Ever since those wretched, near-fatal fits she suffered as a child, I am sure her mind has not been quite right. Sometimes she seems not to notice a thing that is said to her, and other times engages in conversation with great avidity, only to remember not a word she said nor who she said it to. But it is not that which worries me: when I visited her yesterday, she poured scalding hot tea on herself and did not notice till I insisted on seeing to her hand! I am, Penny, I will own, quite distracted with worry for her.'

Penny gave a serious little look before answering, 'I shall write a letter to her. You know she will always respond to my letters.'

A letter to Mrs Maria Jackson from Miss Penny Stuart:

'What a treat you must think it for me to write to you when you had only seen me yesterday. I think it is always a right and proper thing for a woman of means to treat her friends! I suppose I have now forgiven Thomas and your cousin, though I shall not tell either of them yet, or they shall not think their actions as wicked as they were. James says he is not at all wounded by the deception, but I know he is lying. He is not very good at lying – which I think is to his credit. Do you remember when he was utterly smitten with you, years ago, and you had only to look at him once before you declared, "Oh, no, James, do not tell me you are now in love with me? That will not do at all! What a dreadful pair we would make." I think you absolutely broke his heart, my dear, but you were correct: you would have made a dreadful pair.'

'But he and Mrs Stephens, I do not think I have known a better pairing in all my life. Both of such rational and steady tempers, I cannot see they would argue over a thing a day of their lives. And though they might never be very rich, with James' ample wages and cautious economising, they should never want for anything, even if they had a dozen children! Though, I rather believe it is my brother's cautious economising that will be his undoing; he is absolutely insistent that he would not entertain any thoughts of marriage till Joanna and I are both wed! By then, Mrs Stephens shall be long gone. When last I visited Mr Carrey, she told me she plans to move to live with her cousin in Manchester once her father is no longer of this life. And then, poor James will be heartbroken all over again!'

'Will you permit me to impart a little unwanted advice, my dear? Begin writing a little play – you are, once again, lost entirely in one of your worlds – writing is always the best balm. I am quite bored ignoring your cousin, so be pleased to send me as many pages of your reflections as you are able. Do reply quickly to your,

Penelope St.'

The first two pages of a six-page letter to Miss Penelope Stuart from Mrs Maria Jackson:

'Command me to write another play, will you! If only it were so simple as all that, my love. I have not, as I have told you, had a single thought of writing ever again since burning all my plays. Besides, I have not the time to write any plays. Of a morning, if I awake early enough, I sit with Mr Jackson while he has breakfast, then, if I am not helping Thomas with distributing food and clothing, I am always to my cousin's home (and would you have me no longer visit his office before lunch, as I have always done?). I am then home for something to eat, speak with Mrs Heeley about whatever little things she requires my opinion on, and then I wait in the study for Mr Jackson to come home.'

'And I know what you shall say – and no, I cannot write while I wait for him. Though sometimes he is home much later than expected, and I might write a great deal in that time, his coming home would only disturb my writing, and what an awful thing it would be for me to resent his homecoming simply because I have made myself too busy to miss him. I much prefer to be in happy anticipation for his arrival, even if I am waiting a very long time. You know me better than to think I do so to gratify Mr Jackson, though I think he is never sad to return to me waiting for him. Enough of that, my love, I begin to feel as though I am chiding you, and I love you too well to do that.'

'Oh, dear thing, how you cut my remembering soul! Do you really suppose I broke poor James' heart? What a puffed-up proud creature I was at that age. Though I cannot say my mind is much changed in respect to what an awful pairing we should have made. Allow me, if you will, to speak with James on the matter of Mrs Stephens – I shall say no more, yet. As to my little reflections, la, have I anything to tell you, Penny, my love? I think not.'

CHAPTER TWENTY-TWO

CONTAINING THAT WHICH NOBODY, NOT EVEN MARIA, KNEW HOW TO EXPLAIN.

When Mr Jackson arrived home the following afternoon, he did not find Maria waiting with eager anticipation in his study. He got not so far as the study, as he was told by the butler that the lady was taken ill in her parlour and attended by her friend James Stuart. On her favourite black couch lay a sleeping Maria, still wearing the sad little smile she had been directing at James ten minutes earlier.

'What on earth has happened?!' Mr Jackson demanded of James, who was sitting on a chair at the lady's side.

'We were speaking and, well… then she fainted. Only a few moments ago, I am sure she shall come round in a minute or two.'

'What did you say to her!'

Ah! With that question, James understood Mr Jackson must be familiar with Maria's talent. In absolute truth, his last words to Maria had been very pleasant, but, of course, the sequence of events had been a little more complex than all that. A vague and demanding note had been received by the younger Mr Stuart that morning, informing him he absolutely must visit Maria at his earliest convenience; James had never been much skilled in shirking Maria's instruction and found himself at Russell Square some hours later.

'You are quite ridiculous, James, do you know that?' had been the lady's starting remarks.

When he could not guess at the reason for such a declaration, she continued, 'How few people have the opportunity to marry the person they love? And you, *you*, would throw away such a gift in the name of economy!

140

Are you really so determined that your brother's happiness must signify a forfeit of your own?'

Long accustomed to Maria's dramatic verse, James' temper was not inflamed by being so rebuked and spoke only to restate the same he had said to his sister: he would not marry till he could be reasonably sure that to do so would not put either of his sisters at risk of financial calamity – 'La!' was the lady's response.

'Do not – *La!* – me, Maria. When has my opinion ever changed on this matter? If I can witness your fickleness without passing comment, I should hope you could give my consistency the same grace.'

'Oh, indeed I shall – *La!* – you, James. Will you really see the woman you love go off thousands of miles away?'

'Manchester is two hundred miles away, Maria.'

'La! To your wretched facts, what little good they will do you! Will you really let slip through your fingers the chance at happiness simply for the pleasure of being known consistent? What is consistency in comparison to love?'

James would not be drawn in and simply repeated his stance on the matter and sought to change the subject altogether. Equally as tenacious as her conversation partner, Maria then offered to remove the object that he would place in the way of his happiness.

'No, Maria.'

'What do you mean – *no*? Why not?'

'I thank you greatly for the offer, but I do not want your money, Maria.'

'Why? If your want of money is the cause of your heartbreak, and if – having so much of the wretched stuff myself – it is in my power to remove that concern, why would you not allow me to do so?'

Some time passed before his answer would come, and in that time, Maria found her own. How her lungs could be shredded by the fits of her wailing heart. It thrashed about her chest, a drowning man clinging at straw. She had always inserted herself a little too enthusiastically into the Stuart family. Penny would not hear a word of it, but the others thought it, even if they did not say it aloud. They hated her, but they tolerated her because they were good people; Maria was not a good person. She was only good at pretending to be good. *That's true, isn't it, Maria?* In any room – any room in which Maria was comfortable to be more than just a smiling shell – the airs would inevitably change upon her appearance; she felt it, as much as anyone, perhaps more acutely than any other. *How good they are to tolerate you.* The collision with her own blind self-regard cut through the soft flesh of her belly; her innards were ugly.

How profoundly irritating you are, Maria. Always supposing yourself to be doing good things, believing yourself some Samaritan, when truly, you must know you do it only so your downfallen neighbour will be your friend. What is good in that? It is quite wicked behaviour, really. 'Forget it, please,' said she just as James began his reply. 'It is none of my business, truly. Though, should you change your mind, the offer shall always stand.'

'You are upset, Maria.'

'No, I am not.'

'You are crying, Maria.'

There you go, with your deceiving crocodile tears again. See how he panders to you, poor man! 'La! I cry over nothing and everything, James. You have said so yourself many times! I am quite fine, really. I am just a little tired. Perhaps I shall go to bed.'

'Heavens, Maria! It is only two o'clock in the afternoon. You will not change my mind, but it was a very kind offer, and I am thankful to know you care so much for my happiness,' said he, but Maria heard not a thing at all. Quickly he realised her determination but could do nothing to stop it; all he might do was catch her.

'I see,' was the response of Mr Jackson when he understood the particulars of the conversation. And those he understood very well, but why such a conversation had led to Maria forcing herself into a fit of fainting was entirely beyond his comprehension.

'And that was all – all that was said between you?'

'Yes, that is all that was said.' Seeing the man's confusion, James continued to add, 'She had done one of her little staring turns shortly beforehand, and I often find after those that if Maria cannot quickly be coaxed from the edge of despair, this is the inevitable end.' The last word was punctuated with a nod towards slumbering Maria.

You should wake up, Maria. They are talking about you. Or perhaps that is what you want them to do; is that why you perform these little turns? How do they all endure you?

An hour or so after James left, Maria awoke, much to Mr Jackson's relief. And to his absolute astonishment, when she did awake, his wife appeared as if nothing had happened. Maria smiled and chatted, as she was always in the habit of doing. Her presentation of contentment was not even disfigured by the further encroachment of their dinner plans that evening. 'Sidney?' How that name was thrown about, accompanied by such sincere smiles! 'Which gown do you think I should wear? Really, I cannot decide at all! You gave a very pretty compliment to the hairstyle of Mrs Phillips last we were at a party. Would you like me to do my hair in that style this evening?'

'By God, I hope we are spared the presence of Mrs Phillips this evening! I only complimented her hair because she kept pressing me for my thoughts on it. I like your hair as you usually wear it.'

'Very well, Sidney,' she smiled, 'I shall wear it as I usually do.'

'If that is how *you* would like to wear it, dear Maria.'

She only replied with her serious sort of smile.

Twice he had attempted to understand her part in the conversation with James and what, among the words exchanged, could have led to her forcing the appearance of a fainting spell. 'Oh, you know how I can be,' had been Maria's reply, though not her first. The lady's initial response to such questioning was to fly into a most sincere apology for offering such a thing without having first asked Mr Jackson's permission. In an effort to disperse a newly breached flood of tears, the gentleman had declared, 'Oh, dear Maria, I am not cross with you! Pray, you do not think that. It is your money as much as mine, more so, in fact. You need not ask my permission to do anything, though, in future, I would prefer if you mentioned, at least in passing, such plans when they first come to your mind.'

'And if I had mentioned it to you, what would you have said?'

'I would have said that I should not think James Stuart would accept your offer.'

'Well – that is very easy for you to say with the wisdom of hindsight – I neither thought he would accept the offer, Sidney, but–'

Interrupting his wife, the gentleman said with a sorry smile, 'You have not once called me Mr Jackson since returning home. Will you always now call me Sidney?'

A little laugh escaped her smile. 'And to think, it is my sex who are accused of contrariness! What a fuss was created when I did not call you Sidney, and now you charge me with saying it too often. Prescribe me your required ratio of *Mister Jacksons* to *Sidneys*, and I shall make it my duty to satisfy you!' Preventing his immediate response, Maria smiled quite wickedly and said, while making a seat of his knee, 'Or perhaps you believe I would make a prettier picture of a good Christian wife to be a Pamela and call you only *my master*?'

How intently he gazed at her, remaining silent for a hard minute before himself affecting a mischievous face, 'Lord, Maria! How, with such a cunning smile, do you always have me sound like such a tyrant of a husband? I only mean to say, that after becoming accustomed to being your *Mister Jackson*, Sidney appears such a dull name.'

Would he prefer to be known, by Maria, as Sidney or Mr Jackson? That was the pertinent question. He would prefer – the gentleman declared with an undoing sincerity – to be called whatever Maria liked best to call him. Why Maria liked so much to call her husband Mr Jackson, even when they were entirely alone and in the most intimate of circumstances – well, she did not know *why*, exactly. Those four syllables always brought a skip of childlike glee to her heart; what complacency would the intimacy of a Sidney bring, or – God forbid – a Sid.

'Very well – though how odd a thing it is that you tie your preference so strongly to my own – I shall call you, from now on, and till the day I die, *Mister Jackson*, Mr Jackson.'

Maria and her Mr Jackson passed the afternoon much as they so often did; he answered some letters, she distracting him all the while. At one juncture, when the spelling of *sacrilegious* had inexplicably and temporarily escaped him, Mr Jackson turned to discover Maria strewn across the floor before the fireplace. The lady was holding a silver pheasant

144

above her face with an outstretched arm, musing aloud how long it might take for her body to be found if he bludgeoned her to death in that spot. 'Good God, Maria. You queer, morbid creature!' (Ah, but could he help himself from smiling?) Mr Jackson chose an activity: playing a brief game of piquet. Maria then chose an activity. It was not a game of piquet.

After the most worrisome period of Maria speaking only when spoken to – and even then, she often did not reply – and wearing perpetually the strangest and most unconvincing of smiles upon her face; she was now quite returned to her usual state of being – or at least, usual as Mr Jackson knew it.

CHAPTER TWENTY-THREE

A SHORT AND TRANSITIONAL CHAPTER.

A letter from Maria Harrington to her grandfather, written at 2 o'clock the following morning:

'Why do you not come to my dreams any longer? When first you left me, these little welcome visits would occur with such regularity that I would wish the night come as soon as morning was broken. Every night I ask you, and yet you do not come. What have I done, and how might I remedy it? Do not forget me, please.'

'Somebody asked me about you to-night. How my heart quakes when a friend of my Mr Jackson asks me any question, for I have never any clever reply. At this, my heart did quake for another reason, "Where in India was your grandfather from, Mrs Jackson?" – I replied, of course, with the answer I knew to be true, "Nagpur, I believe." It was not this question that felt to be a dagger in my side, but the onslaught of further curiosities (these people forever have questions), "Have I visited? – Would not I wish to? – Do I have family still in the area? Which ships did you sail on? How many years did you serve? Did not they ban East Indians from serving in the East India Company? What year did you arrive in England?" - "I do not know." – my answer to each and every one. How can I have known you my entire life and not seem to know a single thing about you? – I am being disturbed. Forgive me.'

'It was Mr Jackson. He is asleep now. How very tired he appears all the time, always up so early and often to bed so late. I worry for him greatly. There is a fellow MP he is becoming quite chummy with; he is so often the cause of my husband's tiredness. He stays long after all the other men have taken their fill of cards and drink, and I hear them talking in great passions about Newgate prison. This man – Buxton, I think he is called – knows that dear angel Mrs Fry. Sometimes I stay with them as they talk; it is far more interesting than the general conversation amongst my husband's friends.

For very clever men, they do regularly talk like uneducated imps. Lord, what awfulness it is mothers and their children are subjected to in the gaols!'

'Such a thought brings my mind to another. I begin to know why, when I sought you to tell me how I might prevent my marrying Mr Jackson, you did not. He and Thomas are going to organise the church to raise a petition for that poor boy in The Egyptian Hall. Dear little Boy Friday – I wonder what his true mother named him? Joanna suggested we call him Cuffee; it is James' middle name, its meaning is something related to Friday – I cannot remember entirely. Ah! What a disagreement this brought about between the Stuarts – I shall not relate it to you; I am sure you remember how Thomas and Joanna could be. Had I found some way to avoid marrying Mr Jackson – as I had been so wishful to do – we would not now have a member of Parliament to take up the cause. Though I am glad to have married him for more than only his usefulness in that respect.'

'A surge of tiredness overcomes me – I shall finish this later.'

'It has taken me two days to return to this letter, and in that time, dear Mr Carrey has joined you.'

On the day of Mr Carrey's burial, Penny spoke hardly a word to Ralph. Not because she was ignoring him. That trick had been thrown off the morning the two were called to Mr Carrey's lodgings in a desperate urgency. He was gone before they had arrived. How Dr Paterson's office had been filled with tears and lamentations since that day. What was there to say at a time such as this? Even Maria could conjure little more than a few contrite *hellos*. James gave his condolences to Mrs Stephens in the same manner that any of the others did. Save for uttering a benediction, Maria and Penny did all they might to urge the man to throw off his caution and pride, to seek out the woman he loved and who it was clear loved him also. When first pressed, James repeated his consistent rejection of the idea, then he declared it quite unthinkable to confess affections to a grieving woman, and then he was too busy. Eventually, he gave no answer at all. That was till the morning after Mr Carrey's burial, when Penny, anxious of Mrs Stephens leaving for Manchester the following day, pressed him again.

'Good Heavens! Are you truly incapable of keeping your opinions from where they are not wanted? If you desire so much a declaration of love, why do you not confess yourself to your doctor? Oh, *prudence*, that is

147

what you shall claim the motive for your inaction. But mine, you would decry cowardice. What a broken heart you say I shall suffer when I hear of Mrs Stephens having married another. Not half the broken heart you shall endure being underfoot of Mrs Paterson when the good doctor finds himself a wife. Fling not your disapprobation at me, when you would be as good to aim it at yourself!'

After this raving fit, Penny spoke not another word on the matter, and soon Mrs Stephens was gone to Manchester having heard no confession from the man she so much admired. James did not even seek her out to say goodbye before she left. Mr Carrey's passing – his having been so affected by the boy at the Egyptian Hall – gave a new impetus for the friends at Dean Street to resolve some way of changing the poor child's fate. Mr Carrey had spoken fondly of pamphleting Parliament as the MPs were leaving, but with Maria's familial connection to not one but *two* politicians, there was every hope that a petition could be brought to Parliament very soon. Mr Richard Jackson's reply had been a polite negative when asked by Maria, a less polite negative when his youngest brother made the same request. Against every word of advice from Richard and the other politicians in his circle, Mr Jackson was swayed to take up the cause.

CHAPTER TWENTY-FOUR

A LONG, PRIMARILY EPISTOLARY CHAPTER.

If there is one thing that can always be relied upon, it is the temporary breaking of Parliament to ensure the rest of those honest, humble, and selfless servants of the people designated to represent the citizens of Great Britain. Maria's husband was that peculiar breed of creature not especially fond of his own repose and – had not his person been committed elsewhere – would have been very happy to begin the preparations for the petition as soon as the plan had been agreed upon. It was to be soon Jane's thirtieth birthday and her fifteenth wedding anniversary – yes, really. The eldest Mr Jackson had settled on the plan of a ball in his wife's honour at the family home a few miles from Windsor. All the Jacksons would be required to attend for the entire two weeks of the planned stay – including Maria.

Hurlough Place – a monster of a home constructed on an ancient plot of Jackson land, and somewhere Maria had never any desire to visit. Not for any contrariness of her own, no. If ever the place came up in conversation, Mr Jackson was quick to withdraw, and when Maria would suggest their going there, he would always reply, 'No, I would be happy to never see that house another day of my life.' It had been his childhood home; that was all Maria really knew of it – and perhaps that is all she needed to know to understand her husband's reluctance to spend his time there again. Protestation upon protestation was given by the youngest Jackson brother, all to no effect. They would all remain there for two weeks – including Gilly, who rarely had shewn a single objection to any plan as long as Maria had known him – eventually, Mr Jackson accepted defeat with a despondent sigh.

'Where is Mr Jackson?' Maria asked, finding Richard and Gilly in the summer breakfast parlour.

'Why, I am right here, Maria,' replied Richard.

'And I here,' said Gilly with a little teasing smile.

'Yes, very funny.' A pert, half-smile was offered in response. 'Have you seen him this morning or not?'

'He is taking a walk.'

'A walk!' Maria exclaimed, taking a seat at the table with an air of hopelessness that brought a look of amusement to the face of her companions. 'Then I suppose I shall have to wait till he returns.'

'You look a little lost there, Maria, sitting only on a chair and not my brother's lap. I almost do not recognise you.' A strange, sour joke to come from Richard, as he was so often in the habit of speaking very kindly with Maria. But then she had never before passed more than a few hours in his company, and they had now been at Hurlough Place for almost a week.

'You can sit on my lap if you like, dear Maria, till Sidney returns,' came forth an offer from Gilly.

'Would to Heaven you would not make such comments, Gilly!' she responded with a delicate smile.

Gilly had long been forgiven for his transgressions, along with his brother. Why he had shewed the letter to Maria, she still could not truly answer, but when she would not speak with him the first morning of their stay at Hurlough, at the next opportunity of a private interview, a great flooding apology came forth. How she melted him like wax – came his declaration – when she so quickly forgave him. The two were friends again, and the brothers returned to their bemusing appearance of being concurrently the closest of allies and the worst of enemies. Always one was trying to best the other, unless Richard was present, in which case, their efforts were united in irritating him. All, though, behaved themselves well enough. It was Jane's birthday after all, and nobody would be forgiven for spoiling it. The day of the ball quickly arrived, and while Jane was kept busy ensuring all was as it should be, the Jackson men spent their afternoon drinking and playing at cards.

'How much longer will you be? You said that you would read to me before the ball. You absolutely promised it, Mr Jackson!' said Maria, tears already filling her eyes when she, at last, found her husband.

'Here,' said Gilly, answering before his brother could and taking the book from Maria's hands, 'I shall read to you, dear Maria. Good God, queer creature! What do you have my brother reading to you? *The Fable of a Woman Barbarously Murdered at Islington by Her Two Lovers!*'

'Be very careful with it, Gilly, will you not?' She gave a little pleading smile. 'That book is over eighty years old. Really, I would rather Mr Jackson read it to me, but if he is determined to break my heart with his false promises, then I will allow you to take his place.'

'False promises? Dear Maria, I have not yet had the chance to speak, and I shall certainly not have Gilly taking my place! I shall read your book to you if you allow me to finish this game. Where will I find you waiting for me?'

'Where would you like to find me waiting for you, Mr Jackson?'

This exchange garnered a few curious looks between the gentleman's brothers. Mr Jackson's apartment was the answer given. Very well, she would wait for him there. And with the conclusion of a parting and unnecessarily prolonged kiss, the lady was gone from the room.

'And that,' exclaimed Richard, pointing at the door, 'that is why you have taken up this ridiculous petition! A warning never to marry a charmer if ever there was one, no matter how rich she is. What your *breweress* will not get from you with her *Mister Jacksons* and pouting pleas for your instruction! I do not believe I have once been at your home for cards and not witnessed you scurrying off upstairs as soon as she demands it. We need to find you a pretty little distraction, Sidney, before you make a complete disaster of your career.'

'Oh, happily I would take that charge!' answered Gilly. 'If only because Sidney knows the moment he betrays Maria, I shall gladly tell his wife the whole of it and spend every moment he is off snaking about convincing her to betray him in return. I think Maria could have me commit treason in exchange for her pouting pleas for instruction and making me her *Mister Jackson*. Certainly, I would never leave her waiting while I played at cards!'

Mr Jackson gave Gilly an admonishing glare before extinguishing his cigar in his brother's drink. 'Well, as amusing as this conversation is, I think I shall be off to my apartment now.'

Oh dear, a proper ball; an enormous room filled with faces Maria did not recognise, excepting her husband's family and his friends, none who seemed to care for her very much. What an awful combination of noises occurred at such events; the music, the chattering, the laughter, the clanging of dishes, and the stomping of feet – how does anyone find enjoyment in such a place? She could little hear the words of the conversation happening as she held onto her husband's arm, and what she could hear she could not concentrate upon.

'Will you step outside with me for a moment, Mr Jackson?' she asked.

'In a moment, Maria,' came his answer. The same answer came when she asked him ten minutes later, and on the third time of her asking, he replied to say, 'Why do not you go outside by yourself? You do not need me to go everywhere with you.' No, she did not. Though she wanted him to go with her everywhere. *How irksome that must be for him. What a petulant child you are, Maria.*

He was busy and happy in conversation with a young woman who he seemed to know very well and who appeared to know very much about him. Maria was being a nuisance, probably an embarrassment too; she had very little to say for herself when engaged in conversation, not a single clever thought to share, not a pursuit or talent to talk of, and everybody always asked what business her father was in – it was as if they already knew the answer; never before had she felt mortified by her beginnings, but these people had such a particular way of asking that made her feel she ought to be humiliated to say the word *brewer*. Mr Jackson had a talent for redirecting this conversation by mentioning the irony of Maria's being teetotal, which was always a diverting fact to everybody they met – though she was never sure if he did this to spare her discomfort or his. Not really wanting to stand outside alone, but wishing not to bother Mr Jackson further, the lady pressed hard her nails in the soft flesh of her palm to command her composure for long enough to make the significant journey from the room.

'I thought that I had seen you come out here. Good God, you are crying! Why are you crying, dear Maria?' Gilly had found her standing alone in the courtyard. Maria shared with him her troubled thoughts.

'Embarrassing! In what world could you, Maria, be an embarrassment to any man? If you were my wife, I would carry you into every ball on my shoulders so that everyone there should see how much above them all you are! Sidney cares too much for being liked. He is a fool to put their conversation above your happiness.'

'What a great mystery then is his marrying me if he cares so much for being liked. I have not yet met a single friend or acquaintance of his who appears to like me.'

'His marrying you is not a mystery to me, Maria. I like you very much.' And there it was, that devilish Jackson smile.

'I know you are only here for the purpose of upsetting your brother. But I am not in the humour for it, Gilly. Whatever horrible things you have to say about him, you may keep to yourself. Whatever it is shall not make me love him any less.'

'And what an angel you are to love such an undeserving man so well.'

Mr Jackson's being deserving or undeserving of her unalterable admiration was immaterial to Maria; she loved him so well because she had long since decided to – but, at present, his happiness would be greater without her presence as an obstacle. Gilly wanted very much to make himself of service to Maria's amusement, and though – never being sure how serious his declarations to her were – she would keep his ideas firmly within the realm of the brotherly, she could not refuse his offer to take her for a walk of the park. At first, Maria sought to turn the conversation to Gilly's own past misdeeds – it seemed only fair that if he would so willingly share those of his brother, he must share some of his own – he replied with only this, 'Promise you would forgive me it all and say you will be mine, dear Maria, and I would reveal the entirety of my rotting soul to you in an instant.'

Maria would pursue that branch of conversation no further and instead insisted her *brother* (she would remind him keenly he was now her brother) balance his former mischief by sharing some pleasanter parts of her husband's past of which she did not know.

'Lord! Very well, but only because *you* have asked me, I would not say a kind thing about Sidney for any other but you, dear Maria.'

154

'Oh, you do lay on thick this sycophantic lapdoggery, Gilly. You are just like your brother in that respect. You will conjure the most ridiculous declarations of devotion when the motivation strikes. I am sure I always know his motivation, but what is yours in saying such things to me, I do not know – you must stop with this. Next, you shall be saying to me that you would lie face down in manure just so you could know how it feels for me to walk over you!'

He laughed. 'That is a good one, Maria. I shall have to add it to my collection.' Then he turned with a seriousness that plunged her into the icy waters of guilt for opening such a conversation. 'You know why I say such things to you, Maria. If I could change things and make it *me* who had stumbled across you in that meeting house last July – I would sell my soul to make it so. I make no secret of it to my brother. He did not see your true value when first he encountered you, and he does not see it now.'

'Heavens! What is it with you Jackson men and these artful declarations? Will you stop it, Gilly, or I shall insist on finishing this walk by myself. What a great sin it is to covet your brother's wife!'

'It would hardly be my worst sin, Maria. But as you have asked me to stop, I shall. Now – I must wrack my brain to think of something good to say about Sidney!'

A letter to Miss Penny Stuart from Mrs Maria Jackson. To avoid the repetition of particulars, some pages have been omitted:

'You have my permission to acquit me or charge me as you see fit, my love. Do you think I was wrong to continue walking with my brother-in-law after he said such a thing? Though he did not speak of it again after I had instructed him away from such words, I did further declare to him that – though I was sorry if it injured him – for as long as I shall live, and in my next life too, I shall belong to none other than my Mr Jackson. Despite insisting it would be a great strife for him to think of anything good to say about Sidney, he shared a great many stories that made me love his brother only more, and for that, I think all the better of Gilly. I shall not relate them all to you now, but one in particular shewed a great tenderness in Mr Jackson's nature. When their mother was very ill, in complete defiance of their father, Gilly and Mr Jackson refused to return to school (one being thirteen and the other eleven). He said their father beat them terribly for it, but still, they would not go. And every day, my dear Mr Jackson would sit and read for hours to his mamma and sleep every evening on a little couch in her room, attending to her every need throughout the night. Gilly said his brother barely left her side for the entire two months before she died.'

'Mr Jackson has never once spoken to me of his mother. To own the truth, I was not entirely sure that she was dead, but Gilly seemed not to mind speaking of her. The more I learn of their father, the gladder I am to have never met the man. Apparently, because my Mr Jackson would not stop his crying, his father went for him twice as furiously, causing the cane to snap off and quite impale his son in the shoulder! I have seen the scar myself, but he has always told me it was from fencing. It is little wonder he seems entirely incapable of raising even one tiny tear to his eye – I really think I could die in front of him, and his face would remain unchanged – poor man, my heart breaks at the thought of it! I have found myself unthinkingly planting kisses on that shoulder throughout the day. How odd Mr Jackson must think me. La! Surely no odder than before he thought me to be.'

'What a change was to come after this very serious conversation, for we then happened across a lake. I asked Gilly if he could swim, and he answered in the affirmative (how is it that all these men know how to swim?). Of course, I responded that I could not and that I had never been in any water deeper than a bath. The next thing I know, he had jumped into the lake to shew me it did not come up any higher than his chest, and then he made me jump in with him. Perhaps, given his earlier conversation, I ought not to have done so, but I have always wanted to jump into a lake, and now I can say that I have! It was awfully cold, and my gown came out quite muddy. As Gilly is very tall (the tallest of all the Jacksons), what came to his chest was sloshing about my chin even when standing on my toes, I really thought I would drown, and I screamed dreadfully for him to get me out – all this he found very amusing.'

'As you know, I run very hot and rarely feel the cold air. I had not taken a shawl out with me; Gilly insisted I take his jacket to keep me warm on our long return to the house. If he were not so insistent on his being infatuated with me and a little kinder to his brother, I would really love Gilly's company very well, for his freeness of character makes him a most amusing walking companion. Soon we returned to find Mr Jackson looking for me in the courtyard, and there I was, drenched to the bone, arm-in-arm with Gilly, and wearing his brother's jacket. Mr Jackson looked absolutely furious and told me to go inside to change. I did not – I waited unseen by the door. I could not hear what Gilly said, for he is much softer spoken than his brother, but Mr Jackson shouted at him vehemently. I was quite terrified that he would be similarly cross with me and come to me shouting and shoving. To my disappointment, he was not cross at all. I have told you what exquisite tremors of terror it brings over me when he shouts, and what a labour it is to convince him to direct even a little of his pretty anger towards me. He declares it is not in his nature to shout at a woman. La! Wives are renowned for changing the nature of their husbands, are they not?'

'Did I ever tell you – once in a fit of rage at a letter he had received, Mr Jackson threw his letter opener furiously to the floor, and so I said to him, "Oh, to be a letter opener! I wish you would fling me onto the floor like that, Mr Jackson!" He laughed at me and remarked what odd things I said sometimes. Well, instantly, I was brought to tears, and I sobbed for a full five minutes before I was able to make any sense. "Odd, Mr Jackson, do you think me odd? What an awful thing it is for a wife to hear from her husband that he thinks her an odd creature!" He replied to confirm that he did think I was odd but that he would sooner have me and my oddities than any normal sort of wife.'

'Anyway, I have become distracted with that little recollection – he was not cross with me, and I think Gilly must have told him of my upset, for he declared how very sorry he was (in that dramatic, artful way he employs) and that he did not think I was an embarrassment at all. "What," asked he, "could he do to remedy his transgression?" Well, I shall not repeat what I said, but he laughed at me as he always does and said with a very handsome smile on his face, "Lord, Maria, again? What a satyr I have married! Will you never simply ask me for some new jewels or a better carriage? And no, I will not shout at you – strange creature!" Really, he would not, not even a little – what a cruel trick of our Lord to pair me with a man with such a provoking and beautiful shout but form his mind so that I should so rarely hear it.'

–

'Forgive me, my dear, for writing you another letter before I have even sent my last. Writing a letter to you is a very good excuse for remaining away from the Jacksons and Miss Rose. What a pretty surname, and what a pretty rose she is. Miss Rose is a particular friend of Jane. I had awoken very late and was engaged in a little tête-à-tête with Sarah, who insisted my stays would not pull any tighter, they would, and did – you know how I get hungry in the mornings if they are not laced very tightly – I do not know why she was being so awkward this morning – but while we were having this conversation, I spotted Mr Jackson walking in the park with Jane and another young woman.'

'I am not the jealous sort; you know I am not. I would sooner lay my naked flesh to sleep upon a bed of hot coals every night than allow the seed of that sin to flourish in my heart, but I learn she is to remain a guest here for our entire visit. I am being disturbed, my love. I shall finish the rest later.'

-

'Sorry to cut off, my love, I was distracted by Gilly. He said he is certain Richard and Jane have invited Miss Rose to stay for his benefit; apparently, they have quite the idea in mind of his marrying her. What unwanted conversation this opened, for, as seemed natural to do, I asked Gilly what he thinks of Miss Rose – I must have told you he abandoned his suit on Miss Cosway (much to that lady's disappointment) – well, then he replied, "I think nothing of her, Maria, I can think nothing of any other woman while you walk this earth." I rebuked him very sternly for saying such a thing, especially as his brother has said that precise, artful phrase to me before – what an odd pair they are! I really think they must sit down and write these lines together.'

'As I could not implore Gilly to leave me be, I decided it was best to join with the others, although I would much rather have been by myself. Gilly and I entered one of the sitting parlours, and what should I happen upon, but my Mr Jackson reading to Miss Rose, reading to her! He will probably tell me he was reading to the room, but Richard was occupied with his newspaper, and Jane was fiddling about in the corner with some flowers. Lord, I am being disturbed again! Can there be no peace in this house?'

-

'I am returned! I shall be fortunate if I am allowed enough peace to finish this letter within a se'nnight! And now I have entirely forgotten what I had been recalling earlier.'

'A very odd conversation was had over dinner. Richard was rather obviously attempting to engage Miss Rose on the topic of marriage and her views on the subject. Gilly, always one to cause trouble, said something to Miss Rose to the effect of asking why any young woman would want to get married, to trade in their freedom for becoming a maid and mother to their husband. Jane replied with a very pretty declaration about how it was a source of pride and gratification for a wife to care for her husband; Miss Rose agreed, as much as a single woman might. "What do you think, dear Maria?" he asked me – fiend! You know I do not like to contradict my own sex for the amusement of the other, but you must also know I could not agree with the sentiment. "I am sure there are a great many women who would concur with such a statement." I tried then to move the conversation onto a pretty reflection about the park, but my handsome tormentor would not have it.'

'He replied, "But not you, dear Maria, do you mean to say? Does it not gratify you to tend to the care of your husband?" The mischievous man wanted a mischievous answer, so I gave him one: "No, not at all. As his wife, I shall do any reasonable thing he asks, but I would only be satisfied in performing those little tasks that no mother nor maid could do, and he knows better than to ask anything of me that does not please me supremely." I do not think Miss Rose understood what I meant by that, as she seemed unphased, but Jane went quite scarlet. "Though there are a great many things he could do for me that I would find very gratifying." As this last phrase passed my lips, I exchanged my 'to' with a 'for', not wanting to shock them too much, though I gather Mr Jackson knew just my meaning from the devil smile on his face. Gilly found it very amusing and gave a charming laugh. God help Miss Rose if they are to be married; she seemed to be utterly clueless to it all – but I suppose, was not I once upon a time?'

'Richard did not find my answer amusing at all and glared at me most furiously and told Gilly and me to be quiet if we could think of nothing sensible to say. I think Jane was quite cross with me too because she would not speak to me at all when we separated after dinner. Fortunately, Miss Rose – who I now rather regret feeling so put out by – was a very pleasant companion. What a charming creature she is. She has this wonderful raspy little voice. If I were Gilly, I would be taken in by every word she says, for all is spoken with a pretty and perfectly plump pout – the female species are far more beautiful than the male, do you not agree, my love? I am so rarely struck by the handsomeness of any man, but I find myself continually distracted by the faces of pretty women. How many

159

times have I been lost in conversation for gazing at your beauty and airs? You are so beautiful, Penny, and what is most beautiful about you is the lack of any affectation of false modesty; you are a woman who smiles and laughs with the knowledge of her own divine perfection. Many claim there is nothing more attracting than a woman who knows not her own beauty, but I disagree; there is nothing more pleasing to my spirit than a woman who knows herself to be a goddess.'

'I would not make a very good man for a multitude of reasons, but none more than because there are simply too many beautiful women, I could never choose who to marry – and what a choice I would have had as the sole heir to my father's fortune. I should not give up being a woman for a thousand thousand worlds. Mr Jackson may keep my money and his authority, and I shall happily keep my right to insist on being carried home whenever I tire of walking. Remember this for when you are married, my love – they may at first say they will not carry you, but if you sit down and refuse to walk, they will give up their point very quickly. When first I asked this of Mr Jackson, it was soon after we were married, the second day of visiting my mamma. He was quite bemused and said no, for it was a very long walk. I set myself a seat at the base of a tree and refused to move. He stormed off in a very pleasing rage but returned some minutes later, still very handsomely cross, and without a word, he picked me up and carried me over his shoulder back to our inn – the rest of that tale I shall spare you. Now I barely need ask him, and he shall happily carry me from one room of the house to another – never will these men know the gratification of being contrary.'

Disturbed once again from writing her letter, Maria considered she would never speak to Gilly again if it were him knocking now at her bedroom door. It was not Gilly, nor Mr Jackson.

'Oh, hello, Richard. I shall be down for cards and the like in a few moments. I am just finishing that letter to my friend Penny,' she smiled, wondering if he was still cross with her. He was. He was also drunk. Oh, why could it never be her husband barging into her bedroom with a cross face? Richard Jackson did not reply and sat himself on a chair a short distance from her writing desk. Maria asked if all was well. Again, he answered her not at all and leant forward in his seat, eyeing her the whole time. 'Goodness, Richard, you are scaring me! Is something the matter?'

This time he did respond, but it was an ugly vulgarity not worth repeating. Perhaps Maria's first impression of him had been the correct one. Quite startled, she stood and instructed him to leave her room. He stood but would not leave. He only came closer.

'You can drop the terrified lamb charade, Maria.'

'What do you want, Richard?'

Though she had often thought his furious glare to be very handsome, Maria now learnt there was nothing pleasant about this man's anger. It was not like that of his brother; Mr Jackson's warm fury came always when sufficient provocation brought a short lapse in his usually steady temper. There was something pleasingly visceral about it. Richard's anger was cold, creeping and vicious.

'I am sending you back to London. To-night.'

'And what does Mr Jackson say to this?'

'You can give up this *Mister Jackson* nonsense too.' He prodded at her chest as he spoke. '*I* am Mr Jackson in this family, Maria. I am sure it is part of some titillating little act of yours to never call my brother by his name, but he will be Sidney when you are talking to me. Is that clear?' She did not answer. He prodded at her chest again. 'Is that clear, Maria?' She only nodded. 'You will tell him that you have decided to return to London and that you would like him to stay here.'

'No! I will do no such thing!'

She would; he told her she would as he shoved her so hard that she fell backwards into the window seat situated behind her.

'Why – why do you want me to go?'

She might have ruined Sidney's marriage prospects, but she would not do the same to Gilly. How far that dalliance had gone and how many times, he cared not, she would not *Jezebel* her way between this match, she would leave; to-night. 'Do you think you are funny? Hmm – scattering your little sluttish hints at the dining table to procure the smiles of two men? Were you hoping I would smile at you too?' He grabbed the lady by her face. 'Hmm – did you think you could drop to your marrow bones and have me at your beck and call like my brothers, Maria?' Such a strange smile he gave her; that devil smile, but with nothing of its charm.

161

'What accusations, sir,' said she, finding he had drained all the power from her voice. 'And how crudely and freely you speak to me. I have nothing but sisterly affection for Gilly, and I have certainly never *Jezebelled* myself between any match. And as to you, sir, I would sooner be stripped naked and stoned to death in the street than even contemplate such a thing.'

He looked so angry that Maria really thought he might kill her. 'Your crying will not work on me, Maria, so you can stop your crocodile tears.'

How she hated that phrase. They were not crocodile tears; they were real. *Were they not, Maria? They are real, are they not? Or are they not? Maybe you are only crying to get your own way. Hold your breath, Maria. Hold your breath, and he will be gone soon.* Lord, how he angered her with those words! But before she could make this wretch disappear, he caught wind of her plotting. Seeing her chest had paused its heaving, and her lips were quite blue, Richard Jackson hit her hard across the face, causing Maria to gasp for breath as she was propelled head-first into the writing desk.

'By God! You are not terribly injured, are you Maria?' he said, looking panicked, lifting her so that her back rested against the desk and mopping under her nose with his handkerchief. 'You feel well, do not you? You are not seriously harmed?'

She gave a little shake of the head.

He fetched a bowl of water and cleaned her face once the bleeding had stopped. He had not meant to hit her so hard. She knew that, did not she? If that is what he said, that is what she would believe. She should not hold her breath like that. She could hurt herself. Maria agreed. He decided it was best not to tell Sidney the truth; he would not understand and had such a delicate temper when it came to matters concerning Maria. He could do something very rash, career ruining even. 'You could not wish Sidney to throw away his career when it has only just begun? Could you, Maria?'

'No, indeed, I could not.'

'We shall say that you tripped on the stairs, and I found you. Hmm?'

'If that is what you think is best.'

'Yes, Maria, it is for the best.'

Mr Jackson did not appear overly convinced at the story but said nothing more to her in front of the others in the drawing-room. He was playing at whist with Gilly and Miss Rose; Maria set herself upon his lap and draped her head over his shoulder. She was tired, and her face hurt, and she wanted to hug him, and she did not want to look at Richard. Gilly very clearly did not believe the story and remarked, 'How fortunate that you should have been there at the precise moment of her fall, Richard. What were you doing on the upper landing anyway? I thought you left to have a piss?'

'Really, Gilly, do not speak that way in front of Miss Rose and Maria, or myself for that matter!' exclaimed Jane.

Maria did not remain in the drawing-room for long. Returning to her bedroom alone at first, she locked the door behind her and burnt the pages of the letters she had written to Penny. One she retained only long enough to copy out the lines of a new letter:

'You are so beautiful, Penny, and what is most beautiful about you is the lack of any affectation of false modesty; you are a woman who smiles and laughs with the knowledge of her own divine perfection. Many claim there is nothing more attracting than a woman who knows not her own beauty, but I disagree; there is nothing more pleasing to my spirit than a woman who knows herself to be a goddess.

Yours always, Maria Jackson.'

CHAPTER TWENTY-FIVE

A STRANGE CHAPTER IN WHICH THE WIND APPEARS TO BE PERSONIFIED.

It sprung to life with an elastic vigour, as if summoned from the calid innards of the earth by utterations of Latin upon a diabolical tongue. *Devil wind*, Maria named it, though with the same air of delighted bewitchment in which the lady would damn her husband's *devil voice*. What an enchanting display the devil created with his screeching winds. The frontier blossoms were stripped from their branches and forced to dance low circles about the ground in their convocations, dropping – every so often – to the earth in their weariness. He rapped at windows and knocked upon the entrances, calling Maria out-of-doors to feel his wrath upon her skin. Mr Jackson took up the point of dissuading his wife from answering these callings; it was very almost dark, and he was half-certain she would be blown over and do herself an injury should she go outside.

'When did we see last such winds as these? Such frenzied tossings and turnings of the invisible strings that control our world. Will you really stop me from going out there, Mr Jackson? What a sour mood you will put me in all evening if you force me to remain indoors.'

'It is advice, dear Maria, not instruction.'

The approacher crept ever more forcefully at a nearby window with a vengeance growing in furiousness. Mr Jackson was cognisant that his advice to Maria was as good as an instruction. His acquiescence was not what the lady required, nor only his approbation; what she wanted was her desire to be his directive. Strange creature she was. *Lord, those beautiful, mournful eyes!* The vermillion staining was gone from her nose, but her puffy, broken lips made the lacerations brought by Maria's sad little smile all the more penetrating.

'Do you really not want for me to go out there?'

164

'Does it matter what I want, dear Maria? I do not believe it a good idea, but I will not prohibit you from going out there if it is what you truly wish to do.'

If he thought it a bad idea, that was enough for Maria to think the same — with what haste the notion was cast from her heart. The devil, though, would not drop his point so readily; the winds tumefied to a vociferous crescendo, clawing at the sandstone in order to reach the lambish one seated at the window so late into the night. The sound of breaking glass was to jolt Mr Jackson from his slumber.

'Maria? What has happened?'

'Oh, nothing really. Everything is quite fine. Only, some of the windowpanes have broken.'

'Broken? Good God! How?'

'Something hit the window in front of me. It must have been the wind.'

She remained seated by the window. The old serpent's whistling song was carried upon a frigid breeze, forking — like an icy stream — as it met with the man who came to Maria's aid. Having reignited a candle in the fire, Mr Jackson approached his wife till a contraction of horror temporarily disallowed his feet from moving any closer. Maria's cherub-like face wore a crown of crimson across her brow; it had begun to trickle downwards, meandering to avert from her eyes — creating the effect of a bloody masquerade.

'Mother of Christ! Maria, there is a shard of glass in your neck!' There was, and a fairly large one at that.

With an extraordinary sedateness, the lady arrested his gaze with a smile that threatened at any moment to become a laugh and said, 'Is there really? What a strange thing to happen! I do wish you would not speak in such a way, Mr Jackson. Must you really drag the name of our Lord *and* his mother into your exclamations?' Drawing her hands to her neck, Maria tenderly traced the glistening spear gouged into the delicate flesh of her throat. Producing still her amused smile, she asked, 'Do you think I am going to die?'

A letter from Mr Sidney Jackson to Dr Ralph Paterson. Sent at one o'clock that same morning:

'I can only hope this finds you with haste. Maria is injured, though I believe not very seriously. There is a shard of glass (no more than half an inch across) wedged in the lower left side of her neck. I believe it sits only in the muscle. She will have nobody but yourself see to it – and is threatening to travel back to London with the thing still impaled in her if you will not come. I have attached the address below, and you have a chaise and six at your disposal.

Yours &c., S. Jack.'

An excerpt of a letter from Mr Sidney Jackson to Mr Gilly Jackson from July the year previous, currently in the possession of Mr Richard Jackson, who had read it many times over, and who was presently reading it again by candlelight while his wife slept in the bed beside him:

'O - how I recall her supine splendour! What a creature is this Miss Harrington, who, with no coaxing at all, would doff her pretty gown for me - what it concealed was not just pretty, Brother, it blistered my eyes. The gentleman that I am, I shall give you only this hint: I am yet to be proven wrong about these praying girls and their kneeling. How I now pray to lose this contest next week. If my old friend chance would turn his back upon me, and I am to win the seat, I surely must drop the girl lest her cousin discovers my closeness to her. I cannot bring Mr King along with me to Parliament, or I fear our father will cut me off as he so loves to threaten. But if I lose this challenge, then I shall have paid my debt to Richard and may have this lamb under my crook again.'

'There is a way about her I can barely describe; she is all tremors and boldness at once. Tell me, what do you make of this: Before even she had shed her muslins, I could see the tremble of her watering eyes and I, much like yourself, am not such a rogue as some other rakes we know that I could charge ahead if I believed one of their sex to be truly unhappy at the prospect. Resigning myself that I should lose the girl and five pounds to you, I promoted her returning to the party if she was distressed. I said to her that she looked terrified of me; I felt an utter monster in her gaze.'

'Hear, Brother, with what she replied, "Oh, you see how I tremble, sir! It is true. I am absolutely terrified of you and your plans, Mr King. But I shall not go downstairs, not for the world. For I am very fond of being made to feel afraid." Now you must see why I would make this devilish innocent my mistress for at least a twelvemonth. Have not I yet convinced you about these religious beauties? God lose us that seat, or I shall know he has truly forsaken me! If I do win this farcical contest, and I am forced to burden that dreary existence and the parade of equally dreary spouses Jane has in line for me, do not you think of going to find this girl for yourself when you return from Venice! I shall have her again one way or another, and you know I will not share that to which I rightly have a sole claim. Once mine, always mine, till I decide otherwise. Promise me you will not, upon your honour, sir!'

Dr Paterson arrived at four o'clock that morning. Though Maria had wanted desperately to sleep, Mr Jackson, quite sagely, had not allowed her to do so till the arrival of the only man she would trust to unimpale her. Maria's trusting her cousin did not preclude her from screaming murder as he sought to, in his frustrated fatigue, perform the delicate manoeuvre; after a few moments of struggle, he insisted Mr Jackson hold his wife's arms by her side.

'You will stay for the day, will you not, Ralph?' Maria asked over breakfast the following morning. When he did not, at first, reply, and the others only stared at her, she exclaimed, 'Oh, must you all look at me as if I am a dying horse! It is only but a few scratches upon my face. La!'

'Oh, yes. You must remain here with us for the day, Dr Paterson. You cannot leave already. You have only just arrived!' sounded a raspy encouragement from Miss Rose, eliciting an odd look from Maria.

'Yes, stay, will not you,' Jane began. 'The men will be taking the hounds out this morning for some hare coursing. You must join them!'

'I beg you do not, Ralph!' exclaimed Maria. 'How reprehensible and cruel I shall think you if you stroll through those fields to make the death of an innocent creature your entertainment!'

Dr Paterson had never once in his life hunted, neither bird nor mammal, and he had no interest in beginning that morning. He said so in the matter-of-fact way he habitually spoke. Causing a flutter of confusion in everybody, Miss Rose subsequently declared her thoughts on the sport of hunting – they were very much in the good doctor's favour. Richard was most perturbed by this and decried that it was best if everybody remained home that morning.

'Absolutely not! I only agreed to come so that I could take the new dogs out coursing! No slight meant to you, of course, Jane.' Gilly's response resulted in a stern glare from Richard that left Maria feeling rather unwell, even though it was not directed at her. She had not shared their secret, not even when Ralph bombarded her with questions about the bruising to her face and her swollen lip. Yet, in this moment, Maria felt a wild little inclination to tease her bully while she was safe at the side of her husband and cousin.

'What do you think, *Mister Jackson*?' Maria said, looking at the youngest of the three brothers. 'Do I not always declare that you have Solomon's wisdom? I am sure no woman in England could claim a husband of such good judgement! You ought to have the final say on what the Jackson men should do with their morning.' Richard looked suitably displeased. But Mr Jackson found it very amusing and could hardly help expelling a laugh at this. Maria did often tell him he had the wisdom of Solomon, commonly when she crossed paths with a decision she had no wish to make. This was almost every decision across which Maria came. Still, he seriously gave his answer, 'I really think you cannot disappoint Gilly – the two of you should go out with the dogs, and *I*… I am going for a walk with my dear Maria.'

Miss Rose wanted too for a walk and invited Dr Paterson to be her strolling companion. *Damn her pretty, raspy voice!*

'Really, dear Maria, I do not think you need wear a veil on your bonnet. We are hardly likely to come across anyone but a few servants.'

'I want to wear it; it makes me feel mysterious.' She smiled at her husband through the white lace covering her face. Truly Maria did not want anyone beyond the house to see her face, not for any vanity, but for fear of what wretched assumptions and conclusions might be made. She wore it for Mr Jackson's benefit, not her own. Though she would not tell him as much.

'No, really, Maria. I cannot speak seriously with you while you wear that thing dangling over your face.'

'Well, if you want me to take it off, you will have to command it a little more severely than that! There is no good hinting in these roundabout ways. You are sounding very placid, Mr Jackson, a quality not very becoming in a husband. Next, you will be stammering and hemming with, *"sorries"* and *"if it pleases you, madams"*, and allowing me to do anything at all I should want. A very strange way of carrying on!'

Mr Jackson allowed himself to smile only inwardly and replied, 'Take it off, Maria.' Though, not wanting to please his wife too much, his voice did not rise beyond a most ordinary severity. Dr Paterson and Miss Rose walked at the rear, arm-in-arm. Her cousin, Maria considered, looked most charmed, and why should he not be? Miss Rose was a very charming creature. When the couples were sufficiently far apart, Maria said to her husband, 'Tell me – Mr Jackson, what do you make of Miss Rose?'

'Miss Rose?' he replied quietly. 'She is reasonably pleasant company and quite a pretty sort of girl.'

'*Quite pretty*? Quite pretty! You and Gilly are forever of the same artifice! Why do you both dampen her appearance so? To my eyes, she is supremely pretty. Very beautiful, I would vouch to say. I thought so the moment I saw her. I am sure I barely notice you when Miss Rose is in the room! If it is fear of my jealousy that makes you speak so blandly of her, then I beg you would stop. When has a jealous wife ever prevented a husband's eye from wandering? You did not – I recall – vow never to see another woman's beauty when you married me.'

A laugh preceded Mr Jackson's reply. 'Very well. I will concede there is a beauty to her but a very ordinary one. It is a forgettable beauty, I believe. Not as yours, Maria, there is something not of this earth about your beauty.'

'La! Officious, forever scheming man!' Maria replied with a contented smile. 'This is not a coy hunt for compliments. I am musing how much my cousin's heart is in danger with the girl.'

Mr Jackson too had noticed the admiration swelling in young Miss Rose and was in perfect agreement with his wife when she asserted that Gilly's ignorance towards the lady gave her good cause to look elsewhere. Her cousin, she declared, was too modest to have noticed the distinction. His mild spirit would surely lead him to acquiescing to such a beautiful creature as Miss Rose if she made her affections known more boldly.

169

'I believe your cousin is not so modest nor mild spirited as you would have him, Maria. He seems to be very sensible to the distinction if you ask me. And should it matter if he does acquiesce? Have you not just sung the lady's praises to me? It would be a very advantageous match on his side.'

'Miss Rose is a creature of such delicate airs and divine beauty that she should make any gentleman a fine wife even had she not a penny to her name. Any gentleman, that is, excepting my cousin. His heart is designed for another.'

'If he is promised to another, then what grounds have you to worry for his acquiescing to Miss Rose?'

'Because he does not yet know he is promised to another. I have in mind the most perfect woman for his marrying, far superior to any creature for a thousand thousand worlds. And when the time is right, I shall suggest her name to him, and I am certain he will be all agreement. He surely cannot marry her if he is to engage himself with Miss Rose.'

Another laugh ensued. 'Why then, if you are so fearful of his being married to a woman not of your approval, do not you whisper your suggested name to him already? Your cousin is of the age and situation in which most men would think of marrying – time is not on your side.'

'Because the lady herself will not yet be convinced to share her affections for him.'

'You mean to say your friend Penny?'

'How did you guess?'

'Ah, dear Maria,' he answered with a voice intentionally charming, 'I have eyes well adjusted for reading the hearts of young women.'

Now it was Maria's turn to laugh. 'There, I had thought that was the talent of only your good friend Mr King!'

Still with a smile, Mr Jackson said, 'By Christ Maria, I do wish you would not speak that name!' Since forgiving Mr Jackson (né King) for his duplicitousness, Maria was not, or at least did not appear to be, any longer injured by the cunning designs her husband had once plotted against her. Much to her husband's amusement, she seemed to find it all very much an event worth mulling over.

170

'You might command me not to speak of it, Mr Jackson, but you can hardly command I do not think of it. And very often do I reflect on that evening. Lord! With what regularity do I mortify myself remembering what a fool I was to follow you into that room. How possessive you men are once you have a helpless young creature in your sights. I was entirely, entirely at your mercy, was I not, Mr Jackson? Good Heavens! My blood curdles to think of it! I could really weep with mortification and regret! It is so very easy for a young woman whose heart is so engaged to make a false step... really, you might have done all manner of wretched, devilish things to me. You very easily could have forced yourself upon me like a violent, handsome, wicked, charming brute, and I would have had no power at all to have stopped you!' The breathless excitement of Maria's voice somewhat contradicted her multiple professions of mortification.

A look of stifled amusement from Mr Jackson was all that was required for Maria's words to pour forth again. 'I simply cannot help thinking of what good fortune I tumbled into in spite of my foolish, *foolish* errors. For had you been a different sort of man, that night could very well have been my end. I am sure over the noise of Violet's party, you might have subjected me to all manner of churlish, lecherous butchery, and not a soul should have heard me scream out!' At this declaration and seeing the sparkling look upon Maria's face, her husband could withhold his laughter no longer.

The walk was soon coming to its natural conclusion, and he was very much in the hopes of writing a letter or two before receiving his afternoon invitation to Maria's bedroom. So, Mr Jackson, to distract from his lady's ruminations on what debasing and lewd thoughts he might have once had for her, offered to enquire with Dr Paterson his impression of Miss Rose.

'Oh yes. What a good idea that is! He is always making himself such a clam to me and his thoughts such treasured pearls. But he might be convinced to speak to you about it.'

There was one condition Mr Jackson put upon his promised prying: Maria must tell him the truth of her injury the other night. Gilly had asked around the staff, and a housemaid had happened to be on the landing at just the time of Maria's supposed fall. She had seen no fall but had heard a great deal of shouting. After some gentle reassurances that her confession would remain entirely anonymous, she said it to have sounded very much like Mr Richard Jackson's voice, coming from the apartment of Mrs Sidney Jackson.

Maria found herself quite unable to lie at this direct questioning. *Damn his handsome devil voice!* But for Mr Jackson's sake, she would omit that which would give him the greatest fury. 'Richard had come to her room and had shouted at her and told her to leave, and in her anger, she had committed her mind to a fitting spell, only her fall was broken by the writing desk.' It would have been a good and believable homogenisation of the absolute truth and a few careful omissions had not Mr Jackson relayed this information in his later conversation with Dr Paterson, who would remark,

'How could such a thing be true? Maria always faints backwards. I have never once in my life seen her faint forwards! Any which way she stood, in any spot near that desk, never would she have injured her face simply by fainting. She is lying.'

There were guests at Hurlough Place that evening – more guests that was – and owing to this, Maria had remained upstairs, not wanting anybody to see her face. Mr Jackson went to his wife and pleaded to know the truth of the matter. She really would not say and fell into a fit of great despair when he pressed each time a little further. Ralph did not need to ask his cousin to determine the truth; he could surmise who she was protecting and for what reasons. It was owing to this that caused Ralph to act very rashly when he overheard Mr Richard Jackson remark to a friend, 'Sidney's wife? Oh, yes, she is a very pretty little thing. The face of a lamb, but the heart of a rake. I tell you – if you witness her in Gilly's company, you shall understand my conviction that she is determined to have offspring who are siblings and cousins alike.'

This quip brought forth a furious laugh from his nearby friend, a laugh that ended quite suddenly when Dr Paterson took to punching Richard square in the face. And *that* was the end of Dr Paterson's visit to Hurlough Place.

Not a chapter, but a letter.

A letter to Mr Gilly Jackson from his friend Mr Alexander Friedman-Rothshorn Esq:

'Guilielmus, thou old drab, what have I to inform thee of since thy departure for Hurlough Place (or as Sidney calls it, Hurlough Prison). Thou must rememberest Miss Clay, how couldst thou not; that pretty young peony with whom thy younger brother got himself into a paternal scrape when she was visiting an aunt and uncle in Cheapside — well, her gloomy father might have been convinced to drop his threats of litigation by Dickie Jackson and the rustle of crisp pounds; but her sunburnt sailor brother now demands satisfaction of a different kind. The man, probably still deluded from rum and seasickness, parades himself about town, puffing his chest like an emboldened pigeon, harping to any man who might listen that he is come to London to fight Sidney Jackson MP.'

'No doubt he is after a pursefull, just like his father. I have it that the man is staying at the Blue Bear — wouldst thou have me pay off the gawky fellow, or perhaps thou wouldst have Richard's brutes educate this unlicked cub and send him on his way? Whatever thou wouldst decidest, I wager thou ought to act with haste. Though he be presently flapping his white glove about in the lower rungs of the city, knowing the connections of Sidney's comely breweress, I doubt it would be long before she hears of the affair. Besides, thou knowest at what exponential speed these tales make their way to ballrooms and dinner tables.'

'Another thing before I break off — thou hadst not said that thy thespian charmer now calls thy home her own. Beaumont informed me he has seen her coming and going all the while thou hast been gone. Cohabiting with the pretty dear is an enviable scheme. But to do so not in lodgings and instead in THY HOME, allowing her to remain whilst thou thyself were gone as if the girl was thy wife… devil take me… what am I to make of this, sir?!

Ever thy faithful companion, A. F. R.'

CHAPTER TWENTY-SIX

IN WHICH MARIA CONTEMPLATES WHAT MIGHT HAVE OTHERWISE BEEN.

James Stuart offered his arm for Maria to take, through politeness and courtesy but not because Maria would chide him if he did not. Maria seemed not in a humour to chide anybody. She and Mr Jackson had been returned to London for two weeks; her face had mostly healed in that time, and he had been very busy, so busy that Maria had hardly seen her husband. They had left Hurlough Place in a great hurry four mornings before their intended departure, some emergency of a political nature. All was much as it always was, excepting Mr Jackson's being unusually busy and absent. Still, every day Maria would sit with Mr Jackson while he had breakfast, help Thomas at the church, visit Penny and Ralph, return home to speak with Mrs Heeley about whatever little things she required an opinion on, and then wait in the study for Mr Jackson to come home; only, he had never once been home till after seven.

Everybody spoke – of course they did, what an obvious thing to say – but really they said nothing at all, nothing that did not concern the petition, and what a lot there was to say about that. Well, perhaps that is a slight fib. Penny had remarked to Maria upon their first rencontre:

'Do you know, my love, that when I had first seen the measly length of your letter to me, I had felt quite sour with you. But on seeing your message, I thought to myself that I could not have wished for a more wonderful letter for all the world. I hoped that the unusual briefness of your correspondence was owing to your having such a pleasant time.' At this, Maria understood that Ralph had told Penny nothing of either Maria's run-in with Richard or his. She answered only to say that it had been, *'a very sedate trip, with nothing of any interest coming to pass.'*

'What did you think of the proposals for the petition?' James asked Maria as they walked. They were walking nowhere in particular, strolling after the Sunday sermon, a revenant of their former promenades to Mr Carrey's home.

'La! Me? Why, I do not know at all what to think of it. What do you think, James?'

He smiled at her, at that glimmer of her *Marianess*, but she did not see. 'Not even Joanna's outburst? Neither Thomas nor your husband shall be in her prayers for quite some time! Do you take their side?'

'Heavens, no! I am all in agreement with Joanna! She is my friend, and a woman moreover, and what a traitor I would be if I did not agree with her. No, James!' she exclaimed archly, accosting a look she did not much like. 'Do not ask me another question, or really I shall scream so loudly that everybody in the street shall look at us. And then what shall you do? You are a wretched tease always supposing to want my opinion on matters I so little understand. It is a good thing you are so handsome with arms built just for holding a lady upright because you would be a very tiresome walking companion otherwise!'

James had very much missed Maria while she had been away.

'Well,' he began after a moment of smiling at her, 'I think my sister is both right and wrong. She is right that it is not fair to have a petition that can only be signed by men, but she has become distracted from one cause by another. That fellow whom your husband brought along to the meeting, Buxton, was it? He explained it well enough; the petition will be taken more seriously with the absence of female signatures. An unfortunate fact, but a fact all the same. I can only hope she will drop her point before the next meeting, but her being Joanna, I am inclined to expect otherwise.'

Quite without meaning to, the two had waltzed through the filth of London's less respected streets to a stop at their familiar destination: Mr Carrey's home. It was always James who steered their direction, for Maria always insisted he did so, claiming – in spite of living in London her entire life and walking out on her own frequently since her marriage – to remember nothing of the route anywhere. And this day, he had been distracted by the increased requirement upon his conversation.

'That is a plaguy sad look upon your face, dear James,' she said when he would say nothing. When he said nothing once again, the lady began to say, 'Really, James, I–' Maria was stopped before she could hardly begin by the objecting protestations of a man who had no want to be reminded of the woman who had once lived in this tired boarding house.

'Would to Heaven I could finish a sentence before you rush to chide me! What an eager talker you can be, James Stuart! I wonder that young women do not give up the notion of talking altogether, the way we are bullied by men from concluding any sentence we begin!' In a much calmer and sweeter voice, Maria shortly continued, 'I was going to say… I rather think, had life been different, and you and I had married, that you would have made me a very good husband. Do you think I would have made you a happy man, James?' said she with her serious sort of smile.

'You would have made me many things, Maria, I am sure.' Maria insisted on an elaboration of that particular point. 'You would have made me a very rich man and a very tired man, that is for certain.'

'Teasing wretch! You loved me once, did you not? Do you not think I would have made you a good wife should we have married then?'

'For pity's sake, I was seventeen, Maria – forever will I regret confessing my heart to my loose-tongued sister – and you could not have made anybody a good wife at sixteen. Which girl could?'

'Jane was married at *fifteen*, and Richard always says what a good wife she is and has always been.' James Stuart had only met Richard Jackson once, and he did not like the man at all. He had really no reply to Maria's remark. 'You know,' she said, in an attempt to coax back his freer disposition, 'I really think I must have loved you at least a hundred days in my life. I cannot say they were consecutive because you can be of a very changeable temperament sometimes, and inconsistency in the object will beget inconsistency in the admirer. Really, I am sure there have been a hundred days passed in my life when I should have liked nobody in this world more than you and allowed a little fancy of *Mrs James Stuart* to skip across my heart. There, now that has brought a smile to your solemn face!'

'I hope you did not say it only to humour me, Maria.'

'Indeed I did not! But it did make you smile, and I am happy for that. You know, truly you would have made her a very good husband.'

A short reflection reminded Maria this was not a conversation to be entered into, and walking about a great while longer, go ing nowhere in particular, the two amused themselves with what disastrously calamitous newlyweds would they have made as two implacable and stubborn juveniles.

Walking together in a very different part of town were the estranged friends Mr Jackson and Dr Paterson. They walked swiftly to avoid anybody overhearing the particulars of their conversation for more than a passing moment. Both having a predisposition for concern that their conversations might be listened to, and both with good reason to avoid being overheard, these fast-walking conversations had been a habit adopted in their first acquaintance.

'Can you say we have heard the last of this?' Dr Paterson asked.

'My father has been roped into the matter. You can sleep with the peace of a mind unobstructed by this issue any longer. I am assured it is dealt with.'

'*How* has it been dealt with? Are you quite certain this will not be a recurrent problem? If Maria were to learn a thing of it–'

'As it was Richard who wrote to my father, I cannot say exactly what has been done. You had trusted my father well enough before to solve your little problem. If he says it has been dealt with, then it has been dealt with.'

Unfortunately, even with the cover of their walking conversation, this was as explicitly as the gentlemen were willing to talk. Something more *might* be surmised from this letter written by Gilly in response to his friend's:

'Devil take thee indeed, man. And may he take me too! About two months or so ago, nature and the corporeal functions of my dear acting girl conspired to have us both believe I might soon be the proud father to another handsome Jackson child. Thou knowest I am always washed over with sentimentality at the prospect, and I should really like to have another girl; in this giddy state of progenitor's pride, and she being in such a state of distress, I invited the charmer to live with me till she was brought to bed. Well – but a week later, and over her distress was. Only then, having been previously so nervously fraught and dread-filled at the notion, the contrary creature was in fits, utterly grief-stricken, and soon declared there was nothing that would make her happier than a child of mine – and so at my home, she remains.'

'Tell me, which man would answer in the negative to such a request from a face so pretty and manners so gentle? There is nothing that swells my heart as does fatherdom, and nothing that has ever bloated my pride such as a declaration from this beauty that she must needs be mother to my child. Now take pity upon my board-treader, Xander, for I have been reconciled with the Redeemer's angel herself, Maria Divine! I returned to town soon after receiving thy letter and found in the collar of my jacket a long black strand of angel hair. This forgotten strand brought to me more joy than anything another woman has gifted me – how now everything my poor actress does irks me terribly, for her every breath I compare to that of a Maria.'

'I have made no scruple to disguise my adoration for this goddess-woman from the day I first saw her. Did I not write thee a lengthy narrative of my venture to her little church last October? Did I not describe to thee this apparition of absolute divinity my brother had cast aside? Why then, Xander, dost thou persist in dishonouring her with such toying names? The ass that thou art, I ought to flay thy hide should thou name her anything in my presence but MARIA DIVINE! Should my brother ever be a fool enough to lose this angel to an early death, readily would I be the Henry to his Arthur and meet at the alter his widowed bride. And when – if Sidney be not a brother enough to die young – he tires of her perfection (and both we know that he will tire of it), mine shall be the steadfast shoulders for her to weep upon, and the lap where might rest her sweet desponding head.'

'I am convinced, in matters concerning the fairer sex (and other matters besides), Sidney will ever be a varlet and compulsive deceiver, but yet it is my elder and not younger brother who makes himself a villain to the best of all God's creatures. He is and has always been a caitiff and a hypocrite – with what scorning lectures does he set himself above Sidney and me. Yet the illest behaviour of any member of our confraternity is not half as wicked as Richard's history with the sex. All we have ever done is for love of women; all he does is for hate of them. And now, dear Maria's sweet face sports the latest decoration of his unstable tempers.'

'What a short memory Richard must have, for though he is the eldest, he is by far the weakest; Sidney and I have seldom been unified so well as when we have reason to lay *cane* upon Abel. Fie! My actress has found out my newest hiding spot. Best I break off – the longer I ignore her, the louder the dear despondent becomes.'

House of Commons

Wednesday, 14th June

[Petition from London for the release of a body held at The Egyptian Hall]
Mr Sidney Jackson presented the petition from the members of the
Wesleyan church on Dean Street, who claim the preserved body of a boy
slave is being unlawfully held and exhibited for profit at the aforementioned
premises. The petitioners expressed their great hope that the issue would
be taken into the consideration of the House on grounds of both legal and
moral interest. The hon. member trusted in the good judgement of the
God-fearing men elected to serve in Parliament to end this indignity and
see the boy buried in consecrated ground.

Mr Fowell Buxton thought profiteering from the prevention of a child's
Christian burial for the purpose of nothing more than entertaining the
masses was objectionable and saw no reason why a short bill could not be
introduced to at least prevent the continuation of this profiteering.

Mr John Ashby and Mr Richard Jackson objected to the petition presented
by the hon. member; the latter stating that he was a strong defender of the
right to petition Parliament but believed that it would be imprudent to
waste parliamentary resources for such a comparatively trifling matter. Mr
Ashby contested that there was good reason to doubt the quality of the
signatories and that he had received a hint that most of the names signed
to this petition were of vagabonds and paupers, bribed for their support,
who neither cared nor knew to what they put their name. The House was
much in agreement with the objections.

Petition Withdrawn.

CHAPTER TWENTY-SEVEN

CONTAINING SOME HINTS ABOUT THE PROGRESS OF THE PETITION, A PARTY, AND TALK OF RADICALS.

Henceforth tensions amongst the congregation at Dean Street escalated so unreservedly that, within a week, Thomas Stuart had lost the interest of half the bodies that filled his pews, losing command of nearly every woman who attended the church. After Mr Jackson's defeat at Parliament, talk between him and Thomas quickly turned to improving both the quantity and quality of signatories. Joanna's suggestion was that any perceived deficit in the credibility of the offices of signatories could surely be overcome by a significant increase in the quantity.

'…if you were not so exclusive in who should be allowed to sign the petition, it would not take half so long to find suitable persons to sign it – if it were open to persons of all sex, education and occupation, then we might put a copy in every shop, inn, coffee house, and bathhouse in the vicinage–'

There she was stopped by her brother, who ought to have known better than to allow her request to give a short sermon the following Sunday. Joanna's sermon was less of a theological persuasion and rather an impassioned speech imploring the female congregation to abstain from any but the most necessary dialogue with any man of this church till *all* people were permitted to sign the petition. In spite of the contrary protestations of Thomas, and to the surprise of even Joanna herself, the women of Dean Street were most placable in this solicitation – including Maria, who was quite amused at the prospect.

There was some great amusement to be had also for Mr Jackson, who found himself now able to say anything he liked to his wife, knowing she could only castigate him as quickly as she might write, and Gilly found himself unexpectedly blessed as the only man whom Maria sought out for conversation. Where there was a diverting cause for amusement, there was also a cause for some great strain upon Mr Jackson, who was desirous that his first petition to Parliament should not be an abject failure. This strain led the young gentleman to seek the interference of a person whom he wished so little to further his reliance upon: Maria's father. If there were two facts about Mr Harrington that had remained steadfast since his youth, it was that he liked to spend money on parties, and he liked to feel important amongst important people.

A letter from Mr Harrington to his son-in-law Mr Sidney Jackson:

'What a pleasure that you should be desirous of the assistance of your much-obliged father-in-law on this head. Indeed I am in possession of acquaintance with a great many men of very respectable professions who (with the assistance of portwine and champagne) could be convinced to sign their names to this venerable cause. I shall make enquiries and soon name you the date best for such a short-noticed affair. All this will be gladly put into motion if I may be assured that I can depend upon the attendance of my daughter, your honourable brothers (who I am yet so in want of meeting) and your intimate friends.

Your most humbly obliged and ever obedient servant,

A. Harrington Esq.'

'Maria, must you really insist upon writing letters at a party?' asked Penny, who sat in a forgotten corner of the room with her strange friend.

'I am not writing a letter. It is a note.'

'If you are going to be a pedant, my dear, then I shall happily leave you to go sit with Joanna and your cousin at the card table.'

Maria lifted herself above the screen before them with a look of no insignificant perturbation. 'Since when does Joanna play at cards? She has always told me what a poor use of time it is. And what could Ralph mean, sitting beside Gilly and across from my Mr Jackson, when he continues to make it so abundantly clear how very much he dislikes them both!' Turning to Penny with ardent confusion in her gaze, and taking her seat once more on the couch, Maria continued, 'Really, I do not understand why any of you have put yourselves through the torment of one of my father's parties; it was only *I* who was forced to accept the invitation despite my greatest protestations!'

'The petition, Maria! We are all here to find support for the petition. Really, I am quite sick of perching myself at the edge of the room with you, most especially as you have committed half your attention to writing little scribbles to Mr Jackson all evening.' The petition. Of course, Penny was right; that was why they were here. *Self-interested as ever, Maria!* 'Truly, I have only stayed beside you for so long because I have a secret I should like to tell you.'

These words excited such intrigue in Maria that her note to Mr Jackson was immediately forgotten, Mr Jackson himself was forgotten. A secret, there was nothing for all the world more worthy of her attention than a secret belonging to Penny Stuart.

'Good Heavens! Penny, why did you not snatch the paper from my ignorant fingers? What a very bad friend my sulking has made me, you must tell me, good Lord, you must tell me immediately!' Maria crumpled in her hand the following unfinished note:

'Would you oblige me in quitting the card table immediately? Do you remember where sits my old apartment? You need not remember such in any case, as I shall wait in the hallway beyond the door of Pearl's parlour for you.

Your horrendously bored wife, Maria.'

'P.S. – I beg you do not roll another cigarette for our venture upstairs if you will be pleased to come. I am quite furious with Gilly for convincing you to throw off cigars. You may tell me all you like that they are a tenth of the sin, but what does this signify if you are ready rolling the next while–'

Penny would tell Maria, but only on the condition that afterwards, Maria would join her in walking about the room to talk to people about the petition. 'Oh, Lord! Yes, of course, I will walk about the room with you, of course I will. You needn't even ask, but you must, *you must* tell me this secret.' The two young ladies set about a scheme of quitting this room for another.

'Maria?' Penny tried again shaking her dreaming friend who was now gazing at the clock in Pearl's little parlour. 'Maria, if you are not listening, then I shall return to the drawing-room without so much as a hint!' The threat was successful in procuring Maria's attention. The succeeding scene was a crossfire of cracking gasps, elated squealing and a procession of words that came from her mouth so quickly that Maria's tongue nearly failed to keep pace with its owner; and is, therefore, best summarised in one sentence: Ralph Paterson had asked Penny Stuart to marry him.

'Elope! Why in the name of all that is sacred in matrimony would you elope? You have nothing to expect but resounding approval from all your friends. Why would you rip from us the joy of witnessing your happy day with an elopement? Lord, how could my wretched cousin consider such a thing? Upon my faith, I always consider it to be a very ill thing in a man if he thinks to elope with the woman he means to marry! What honour can there be in an elopement?' Maria had always been certain everyone should be as delighted as she would be at the prospect of her cousin marrying her favourite friend. Penny did not share her confidence.

'The elopement would be at my insistence, Maria, not your cousin's.' A sigh followed. A sigh Maria mistook for silence. A mistake that begat another mistake: continuing the pursuit of deterring her friend from an elopement. 'It was not right, it was not proper, it was such a strange giddy way to go about marrying. It was the practice of ill-bred schoolgirls and soon-to-be mothers.' The more she thought on it, the more Maria resented the idea, and one exclamation was soon followed by another. 'It was a very selfish business. Maria never had in all her life attended a wedding apart from her own. And poor Joanna, to not be a bridesmaid at the wedding of her only sister!'

'Good God! Maria! Can you not just be happy for me? I thought of all the people in the world I might have told, you would be the last to judge me so wretchedly!'

Penny left feeling very affronted and hurt. Maria remained feeling very sorry and wishing she could unsay all her unkind, childish rantings. *You really are an awful friend, Maria. Hiding away all evening, allowing the others to do all*

185

the work. And utterly spoiling the happiest instance of Penny's entire life. Maria left to return penitently to her friend in the drawing-room but was stopped on her way by Mr Ashby, Richard's horrible friend, who lingered in the hallway.

'You dropped this, I believe,' he said, giving Maria the piece of paper she had crumpled some moments prior. If his knowing it belonged to her had not revealed the truth that he had read the note, his strange smile would have done so. Maria had never anything to say to Mr Ashby, who was, my reader might be reminded, the horrible fellow who had once berated dear Maria at Richard's home. This gentleman frequented Russell Square often for card games and had proved himself to be somehow less amiable upon their every acquaintance. So, she said nothing, and after taking the note, she sought to return to the rest of the party.

'I am curious for *your* thoughts on this petition, Mrs Jackson. Do you believe I should support your husband's campaign?'

A long stare accompanied Maria's unwillingness to remain alone with the man. 'Very much so, sir. Now, if you would excuse me.'

'Come, have you nothing more you might say to convince me? If I were to back Sidney's petition, I should think a fair few would follow suit.'

'Then why do you not support it, sir?'

'Because I remain wholly unconvinced that it is a necessary use of parliamentary resources. Do you truly have no further thoughts on the matter? Is it not your purpose this evening to gather support for–'

Before he could finish, Maria replied, 'Forgive my candour, but might I ask why you should care to learn my opinion on the matter, Mr Ashby? I suspect because I am an easy target for your mockery. You have made it quite plain you think very little of me, and surely by extension, anything I might have to say on the matter.'

'On the contrary, madam. I think very highly of you.' A cautionary pause lingered between his words. 'And so very often.'

Oh, Lord! There came the smile again. But an Ashby smile was not a quarter so charming as a Jackson smile, leaving Maria to feel the totality of the indignity of such an address and not an ounce of the flattery. After years of encountering champagne-soaked gentlemen at her father's parties, Maria knew better than to refuse to feign any semblance of flattery. 'Really, sir, you must know you do a great dishonour to my husband by telling me such! Though, as I am sensible to the distinction of your address, if you say not a word more of it, I shall spare Mr Jackson knowledge of our little conversation here.'

'Tell Sidney if you please; I am sure he has guessed at my thoughts long before now. Say you will sit and speak with me this evening, and I shall promise not to utter any such hints again.'

'Sit and speak with you?! I have taken pains to speak with you upon many occasions, sir, and every time I have been met with nothing but contempt and derision.'

He was sorry. He was very sorry. But his sorry had not the vivacity and charm of her husband's, nor Gilly's, and Maria agreed to return to the drawing-room and sit with him only to bring an end to this private audience. '…but do not follow me immediately into the room. You will take a turn of the house before rejoining the party.'

Re-entering the drawing-room, Maria made a line directly for Penny – who was now at the card table – but was stopped just shy of her destination by her father. Mr Harrington had placed himself and three friends as an admiring audience to the gentlemen who this butcher's son could now call his family. 'Sit with your old papa, will you not?' he said, not waiting for her answer and forcing with a great deal of bruising might the objecting and reluctant Maria to sit upon the edge of his knee. The first minutes of conversation were not so much with Maria, but *about* Maria. When one of her father's friends asked how she did, Mr Harrington replied, 'She does very well, sir, very well indeed. Do you not say that the nuptial state has been very agreeable upon her countenance?' The man agreed and remarked that she must be well suited to marriage.

'Very well suited!' replied Maria's father. Maria, who was still, with a degree of subtlety, attempting to free herself, stopped listening at the phrase, 'Obedience is a superiorly desirable quality in a wife.' And instead turned her ear to the conversations at the card table, which were harder to hear but infinitely more interesting. Penny was speaking with Gilly and would not return Maria's smile. Mr Jackson was with Ralph recommending, Maria thought she heard, a play they had seen a few days ago. While she could not be with her friends, Maria was intent on hearing what they spoke of without her, but no conversation held her interest more than that between Joanna and Richard. Richard was smiling, but in that manner he employed when he was irritated, Maria attempted to pick out their words from the flurry of conversations about her.

Oh dear, Maria had made out the word *radicals* from Joanna's lips, followed by *unjust*, *setup*, and *brutal beheading*. Having heard Joanna's speeches on this charge of treason several times before, Maria unglued her arms from her father's firm grip by exclaiming, 'Really, Papa, I have hardly seen my husband all night, you must allow me to go sit by Mr Jackson!' Mr Jackson was, as professed by his father-in-law, a man of such superiority in every respect that the old brewer could never be brought to disapprove of his daughter's open and ardent attachment to her husband, let it be quite improper for a young lady to behave with infatuation in public. 'To be sure, I could never upbraid the dear child for it! Off you go, dear Maria, on your way now!'

Maria took the spare seat beside her husband and instinctively and rather urgently taking his hand in hers, turned her head towards Joanna and whispered earnestly, 'You must stop. You must stop this talk immediately.' Joanna began a repudiation, but Maria would not allow it. 'No. Joanna, truly, you must not say another word of this man or his co-conspirators.'

'They were not conspirators, Maria. They were tricked.'

Maria lowered her voice further, hoping Joanna would follow suit, 'Whatever they were, you must stop defending them to my brother-in-law, who is one of the men they would have gladly killed. I think you do not understand of what you speak and with whom. You must stop, or you must leave, Joanna.' There was to be no further argumentation on the matter, and Joanna did not like being forbidden to speak of anything, certainly not by Maria. Thus, at no great length, she left the party and took Penny with her.

CHAPTER TWENTY-EIGHT

DESCRIBING SOMETHING QUITE HORRID.

'I s Jane not at home?' Maria asked to make conversation. Richard had spoken not a word to her in the several minutes since she had entered his study.

'She is in Harrogate visiting her sister.'

'Well, that sounds very pleasant, the weather is nice for–' but before Maria could finish, she was interrupted.

'Be quiet, Maria.'

The lady eyed her brother-in-law's chaotic desk; she had never before noticed it in such disorder. Her husband always kept a very tidy desk. He was most skilled in returning things to their proper place, and because she was not, Maria admired Mr Jackson very much for it. She noted that she must tell her husband of this peculiar admiration when she could, at last, speak to him.

'You know, I have finished reading *Frankenstein* at long last, and, in fact, I quite lik–'

'I said, *be quiet*, Maria.'

Richard was writing a letter. Mr Jackson did not like to be talked to while he wrote letters either. A note received that morning had instructed Maria to attend Richard immediately. Richard's unpleasant mien and half-empty glass of something strong-smelling told her it was unlikely to be a happy visit. She was not wrong. Once he did start speaking, Richard did not relent, and within fifteen minutes of his upbraiding, Maria could barely answer through her sobbing.

'Upon my soul, I swear it, Richard, the Stuarts are not radicals, far from it, they are extremely good, God-fearing people. Joanna is not a radical. She is just young and incensed at the brutality of the executions!'

Richard watched in a cold silence as Maria continued to cry and plead the case for her friends, till he broke her off abruptly with a shout that was neither handsome nor pleasing. 'Be quiet, Maria!'

His voice softened, but his tone did not. 'From the moment I saw you in that church, Maria, I knew you would bring nothing but trouble my brother's way. His good name might survive your vulgar lineage and the criminal conversation in which you engage yourself with other men. But one whiff of your associating with radicals will rot away not just his career, but mine and my father's too, and rust over what might remain of our distinguished family. Are you truly so stupid, Maria, that you do not realise how catastrophic such an association could be?'

'Of course! The moment I heard Joanna speak of it, I begged she—'

'As Sidney is clearly incapable of being lawmaker of his own house, I find I must do it for him: you will stop going to that confounded dissenting church, you will convince Sidney to leave off this petition, and you will stop associating with this damned, radical, black family!'

'I do not see what need there is to particularly mention their being bl—'

'Be quiet, Maria,' he said, clasping her jaw firmly in his hand.

Lord, how angry he made her, doing that again. 'No!' Maria exclaimed, shaking his grasp off – failing to shake his grasp off, he gripped her only harder. 'I will not stop associating with the Stuarts, they are as dear to me as family, and very soon they *shall* be my family, as we are to be joined by the marriage of my cousin to Penny!'

'Pray, be telling fibs, you stupid girl.'

He was so close to her now. His angry breath clung to her mouth, suffocating any words Maria attempted to conjure at first. 'It is true. They are to be married,' she replied eventually, with an air of lofty defiance that felt instantly foolish.

'Tell me you are lying, Maria.' How calm he sounded, quite in contrast to his wild eyes.

'I cannot.'

A knock at the door brought a moment of relief. Short-lived relief. Richard instructed Maria to remain in her seat as he made his way to the door. It was a servant, asking a question the lady could not make out, but it was answered only very briefly before he shut the door once more and locked it. The key was removed and placed far back atop the bookcase. Maria knew she would not reach it without the help of a chair. Richard must have known that also. Acting upon the command of instinct, the lady rose from her seat and stepped away from the table.

'Tell me you are lying, Maria.' A twitching flicker of rage was companion to Richard's words.

'I cannot,' she barely answered.

'You stupid, simple whore, say you are lying!'

What an ugly voice he had. She had never before noticed it, and when she had, how she then missed the timbre of Mr Jackson's voice. Maybe, if she concentrated very hard, Maria considered, just maybe Mr Jackson might sense her distress. Richard's desk, which was located in the furthest corner of the room, was the extent of Maria's escape. Shortly, by her hips, he had her fixed against it. Mr Jackson could not hear her pleading thoughts; his wife was entirely alone, waiting for the worst to begin.

'Do not cry, dear Maria.' He took her jaw in his hands again. Far more tenderly than his last. *Would to Heaven he would not call me that with his ugly, wretched voice!* 'All will be well. Do not worry.' His anger had transformed quite suddenly into something else. 'You need not look scared, Maria.' Something no less unpleasant. 'Though I know you are very fond of being afraid.' There it was, that devilish Jackson smile, except, somehow, Richard managed to strip it of all its handsomeness. Here he kissed her. 'By God, you are an exceptionally pretty creature; before I had read Sidney's letters, I could never have guessed at the thoughts you hide behind those little, black lamb-eyes.' He kissed her again.

'Richard, you are hurting my arm!'

He apologised, but his grip did nought but tighten. As his unwelcome, bruising affections began, Maria begged they cease – he apologised, and he kissed her, and he apologised again – but they did not stop. She ought to have fought him off; Maria knew she ought to be furiously resisting every touch, for she wanted nothing more than for him to stop. *What yielding consent is this, Maria? Where there is not a positive rejection, there can only be a positive encouragement.* But Maria could not form another word; her tongue was as lead-like as her limbs. Our poor heroine could not move nor speak to resist Richard's advances. *What dishonour you do to Mr Jackson.*

'*Oh, what was the Psalm Joanna had read the other night?*' Maria said only into the darkness of her mind. '*It was a very good one. Strength – it had been about strength. Lord, if thou be silent unto me, I become… what do I become… I cannot remember it now at all. Oh, why must he grab at my body so invasively? And my wrist! Why must he suffocate my wrist with that demonic grasp? I become… I become like those who go down to the pit. Yes, that was it! Hear the voice of my supplications when I cry unto—*'

To redirect Richard's impassioned bussing away from her mouth, Maria wrenched herself loose from the tangled grip he had upon her hair, leading his notice to her neck. Maria's prayer was stopped when she saw the discrete hand of Providence: a folding knife, open on his desk! Fortuitously, the arm he imprisoned was not the one of which she was in need. The knife was reached with little effort, and the man was too occupied with his horrendously gentle attentions to Maria's neck to notice. It lay heavily in her grasp as Maria summoned the courage of her dear Clarissa. At last, she lifted her hand so that Richard could see what she had found. To her surprise, he laughed.

'Oh, Maria,' he said with a smile, kissing her brow with a cold softness. 'Miss Pious. You will not even have a glass of wine for fear of your God. I know you would not injure me.'

She smiled in return. 'You are quite right. I would not injure you.'

Richard's amusement quickly dissolved when Maria pressed the sharp end of the knife against her own throat. 'If you do not let me free, then I shall do it. My God shall forgive me; I am sure of it. In fact, why do you not do it, Brother? For I would rather you killed me than continue to press yourself upon me in this manner. Go on! It would only take a moment.'

He released her arm and eyed the lady most severely. 'Put it down, Maria.'

A mad smile appeared on Maria's face, and she released a little laugh. 'Oh, you are no fun, Richard! Will you really not do it?' Not cognisant to how forcefully she was pressing upon her flesh, Maria was surprised by his sudden backing away, till was felt a trickle of blood across her clavicle.

'Sidney was right about you,' he said, shaking his head in disbelief, 'you truly are unhinged, Maria.'

'You are a liar,' she half-whispered, 'Mr Jackson would not say that about me.'

A coruscate of amusement came over his eyes as another trickle brushed down Maria's neck. Richard took the opportunity of her surprise to take the knife from Maria's hand and throw it across the room. 'Oh, indeed, he did. After you had thrown a book of his into the fire in a fit of rage. Do not lament, dear, pretty Maria.' Richard encroached closer and, seeing that she had no response, retook her arm in a hold even more fervent than before. 'I think no man could have declared himself so happy in his choice of wife. How rare a trick Sidney has said it to be, to happen upon such willing young game in the nuptial state; a pretty, simple little wife who could not be more eager to please if he'd picked her from a brothel. And if that were not enough, with an abundance of filthy lucre to be gambled away.'

'Mr Jackson would not speak about me in such a way!'

'Oh, *he would*. I have heard it all. I shall not use you as boasting fodder, dear Maria, no matter what you do for me.'

'I shall do nothing for you, so you should never have anything to boast of, *Brother*.'

Before Richard could reply, another knock rung out at the door. It was Mr Ashby. 'Unlock the door, Jackson. You queer fellow!' he called out, twisting the handle from the other side. Richard instructed his friend away.

'No, do not go, please, Mr Ashby! I beg you do not go!' Maria shouted before her last word was cut off by Richard's callous palm smothering her mouth.

'By Christ, Jackson! What in God's name are you doing?'

'Maria and I are just having a private conversation…' Richard pulled Maria along towards the door. He now squeezed her arm with such vigour that Maria was quite confident at any moment she would hear the crack of the bone snapping in two.

'It does not sound much like a conversation to me, Jackson. Damn it! Open the door, man!' The handle now twisted frantically.

Maria tried to speak, but her efforts amounted to nothing more than muffled nonsense. There was only one thing to be done, and he would not stop her this time, no matter how hard he might hit her. *Hold your breath, Maria! Hold your breath, and this will all go away.*

CHAPTER TWENTY-NINE

TAKING PLACE CHIEFLY IN THE UGLY DRAWING-ROOM AND MR JACKSON'S STUDY.

T he neck of her gown was torn, her skin stained with a little meandering river of crimson that pooled upon the white lace-trim, and her uncovered arm sported already the huge, swelling pattern of Richard's ferocious grip. Maria awoke from her forced spell of fainting in a carriage opposite Mr Ashby. 'You are awake!' he said, with a smile of great relief. Maria felt not much like smiling nor talking; she did neither. He asked questions, none of which she would answer. She simply stared beyond the window into the passing streets, allowing the shuddering of the carriage to produce her only movements.

'May I help you inside, madam?' he asked when they arrived at Russell Square.

Maria replied with a brusque negative. Realising her sharpness, she cast a rheumy-eyed smile in his direction and added, 'Thank you, Mr Ashby.'

Maria took the servants' entrance for fear of Mr Jackson being home and seeing her in this way. She was right to suspect her husband might have arrived home early; he had. Mrs Heeley informed her the gentleman was in his study. Fortuitously, in this servant-parlour was only the housekeeper herself and Sarah, Maria's maid. Neither need ask *what* had happened, but only *who*. Richard had been a visitor at Russell Square enough times that both knew well who Maria spoke of; when she could, at last, through her crying, speak his name. 'Do you think I ought to tell Mr Jackson?' Maria's companions answered with the silent shaking of their heads. A bath was drawn in the housekeeper's apartment, Richard's touch washed from her skin, and his caressing brushed from her hair. Plaited, prettied and in a fresh, long-sleeved day-dress, Mrs Jackson presented herself very cheerily to her husband in his study.

'Hello, dear Maria, I did not hear you come home,' he smiled before spotting the one trace of her ordeal that could not be concealed. 'What have you done to your neck?'

With a happy smile, she pushed a finger to her lips before mouthing, 'I am not speaking to you, remember?'

Before he could protest and further press the matter, Maria threw upon his lap a cushion, swiftly followed by her head. He needn't ask if she would like him to read to her. Her answer would always be a positive. The lady liked little the book in his hand but was too pleased to hear his voice to care what he read. A few dwindling embers of hurt subsisted, and Maria felt she was obliged to question her husband on what Richard had told her. She could break her promise to quiz him. That, though, would surely give rise to questions she had no want to answer, and besides, she knew asking Mr Jackson would be of no consequence at all, whatever his reply; her forgiveness for him was infinite and incurable. He was half-absolved already.

Her catechism was turned inwards. What an ugly thing it was for her to lie to her husband. *Poor Mr Jackson.* Maria reflected how little she had done to release herself from Richard's unwanted attentions. *Why did you not do more to stop him, Maria?* How she then pitied her husband. If she had not, in her petty spite, told Richard about Penny and Ralph, if she had been not so yielding to Richard's attempt. *Where there is not a positive rejection, there can only be a positive encouragement.* She knew well of Richard's temper and yet chose to provoke him with her obstinance. *Good God! Poor Mr Jackson. What a fool you have made of him!* Mr Jackson began to play with her hair. Maria liked it when he did that. She would always get cross if he refused. Undoubtedly, she would forgive her husband, but how could she expect he would ever forgive her?

Having closed her eyes, Maria soon found herself resting upon only the couch in Mr Jackson's study and not Mr Jackson himself. It was seven o'clock. However had she slept for so long? There was some significant commotion coming from the ugly drawing-room, and when Maria was close enough to the half-open door, the lingering smoke and raucous laughter told her it was a card game.

'Maria?' Mr Jackson called.

Damn these echoing hallways!

Maria entered the room, and there he was, her eldest brother-in-law, the finely dressed brute, bold as brass, fiddling with a little box of chewing tobacco. Mr Jackson beckoned her in, 'Sit with me, will not you, dear Maria?' he said, smiling and leading her onto his lap. He had been smoking those thin little cigarettes again. The stench of it was cohabiting sinfully with the odour of whatever brown liquid was in his glass.

Damn his handsome devil voice!

Mr Jackson often invited Maria to sit with him during his card games. After two or three drinks, constant would become his brushing against the décolleté of her dress. Sometimes she would tell him off for it; more often, she would not. It was rude, really, for him to do that with his friends present, but then, Maria thought they were all quite rude themselves. Not half of them would stand when she came into the room, one of them never acknowledged her at all, and all of them would happily continue their lewd conversations regardless of her presence. The only one she was ever happy to see was Gilly. Clearly, Mr Jackson must have been already on his third drink because his activity began immediately and signified a little more determination than usual.

Richard cast Maria a contrite look. She turned her gaze immediately to look only at her husband before announcing she would leave to fetch herself a glass of water. 'Why do not you ask your husband to fetch you a glass of something stronger, Sister?' the villain said.

'You know very well I am not speaking to him,' Maria answered, heart fluttering frantically beneath her smile. The lady imparted her glance solely at her husband whose face she now held in her hands and, having boldly kissed Mr Jackson, she turned to Richard to add, 'And I have told you all many times that I do not drink.'

One of the men made an unoriginal and humourless quip about wishing his wife would stop speaking to him; it amused the others sufficiently.

'Not even a little glass of wine, Maria?' Richard pressed.

'No.' Maria was beginning to sound quite vexed.

Richard was prevented from provoking Maria again when another gentleman at the table decried, 'For the love of Christ, Jackson! Will you settle down or carry her off upstairs and be done with it? Nobody desires your obscene little *shew* with our game!' It was the man who had continually refused to acknowledge Maria's existence and only ever referred to the lady as *she* or *her*. Not everyone was in agreement. Gilly particularly noted, after admonishing the fellow with some unsavoury vulgarities, that he wished very much for Mrs Jackson to remain. Maria was in no humour for Gilly's spectacle of adorations and feigned little more than a half-smile in response. Rescuing Maria from any further distress came Mrs Heeley, who insisted most adamantly that she needed to speak with the mistress of the house, in spite of Mr Jackson's uninhibited pleas that she would not take from him his lady.

'What is it you need to speak with me about?' Maria asked once their voices were clear of the room.

'Nothing at all, madam. I thought only that you might not wish to remain in the room with the *other* gentleman.'

'Thank you,' Maria said, in a devoted voice she reserved usually only for her mother, taking the lady by surprise with a hug.

Free now, to do as she pleased for the evening, Maria wished to return to Mr Jackson's study; she liked reading in there. Removing her shoes so that she would not be heard, for she absolutely would not be called upon to return to that uncomfortable scene, Maria walked by the door of the ugly drawing-room again. And as she did, she overheard a conversation that caused her steps to pause.

'Why do not you go chase after your little *breweress*, Jackson?' said the gentleman who did not like Maria.

'I have told you all never to call her that wretched name!' Mr Jackson replied sharply. 'And you only want rid of me because I am winning.'

'Calm down, Sidney,' came Richard's voice, 'are not you the originator of that term of endearment for dear Maria?'

Maria would not – could not – linger to hear his response and instead continued towards Mr Jackson's study. Why had hearing such upset her so much, she did not know. *Breweress*, there were far worse things he might call her. Only, it was so supercilious, so conceited. Though her husband was so often surrounded by friends with such arrogant airs, Maria had never once considered Mr Jackson to think himself above her. Unable to fix her mind on a book, the lady rested herself once again upon the spot in which she had awoken earlier. Her arm hurt, much more now than before, and her heart returned to its familiar heavy aching. How long she passed in this state, the lady knew not.

'Maria? Dear Maria, why did not you return?' He pulled her from the couch and embraced her as he ever did when he was drunk. 'Come back with me, please?' She could not speak to him, so she kissed him. She kissed him again, and again, and again. After some moments of this employment, he stopped and said, 'Maria, you are crying, why are you crying?' She did not answer and instead kissed him again. 'No.' He drew back. 'Maria, you must speak to me. Why are you crying?'

'I am not crying,' she, at last, answered, 'now will you carry on, please?'

'No, I will not,' he said in a disbelieving laugh. 'You *are* crying. I am watching you cry! Why are you crying, Maria?'

'Did you create that name for me?' said she softly after a short lull.

'What name, Maria?'

'Your little *breweress*. Is that what you call me to your friends?'

A humbling countenance of discomfort overcame the gentleman, who extricated himself from this once impassioned moment and sat down on the couch. Maria remained standing. 'No, Maria, that is not what I call you. Once. I said it *once*, a long time ago when I was far more of a fool and stupidly drunk.'

Her tears had not yet stemmed. 'Did you call me mad? And tell your friends that I am unhinged? And about that dratted book I had burnt?' Seeing his face, she could only exclaim, 'Oh, you did, Mr Jackson! You said it all. Good God, you have talked about me like I was a deranged, half-witted whore!'

He had. Oh, how it crushed his pride to think on those words now! Always it had been when he took to the drink; what a poor excuse he declared that to be. Forever he was being incensed by the disparaging of his choice of wife, he would not repeat what they had said. Everybody was so certain he had been induced to marry her only for the money.

'I will not lie and say it was not a very pleasant byproduct of our union, and I will admit to encouraging your father – preying on his desperation – to agree to terms that were far more generous than they ought to have been. But the money was not why I wanted to marry you, Maria.' His wife beheld him with a faint and silent smile. 'By God, perhaps the real reason is worse!' Here he thrust his head into his hands. 'When I met your father and heard the name Maria, I could not banish you from my mind. I wanted to have you again, but moreover, I did not want anyone else to, *ever*. I could not bear the thought of any man but me making you a wife. I convinced myself that I had a claim to you, Maria, that you were already, in effect, mine. Once mine, *always* mine. And when my friends would taunt me for marrying – in their opinion – so far beneath my potential, I would boast of my talent for both subduing and inflaming the passions of the most charmingly innocent harlot in the world. I must confess, I did, when first we were married, speak about you very crudely to inspire the jealousy of my friends.' After several moments, he continued at last, 'Say something to me, Maria.' She would not. 'Hit me, shout at me, anything you want. Just not that sad little smile. Please, Maria.'

'I need a little time to think and to pray before I can forg–'

'No!' he half-shouted. 'No, do not just forgive me again, Maria.'

With a smile, she came closer and gave Mr Jackson her hand. 'You call me your *forgiving angel*, do you not? Just like Clarissa.'

Kissing her hand, he replied, 'I do not want you to be like Clarissa. She forgave the vilest of men for his wretched treatment of her and died of her misery. I want you to be like Maria.' Many moments passed, and the lady would not speak another word; she was crying again. 'You should divorce me, Maria,' he said, looking away from her.

'Oh, Heaven help me! Is *that* what you want, a divorce!?' Maria was entirely undone by his words.

'By Christ, no!' He clasped her hand tightly. 'There is nothing I could want less, but if it would make you happy to be free of me, dear Maria, I would agree to it.'

'I have no grounds to divorce you, Mr Jackson.'

'Say whatever you must. You may drag my name through the mud, paint me as the vilest and most violent husband in England. Say whatever you need to sufficiently sully my character, I would bear it all if it is what would make you happy!'

'What artifice is this, sir? You need not contrive such professions to me. These are a drunk man's words.'

'No artifice, Maria. Believe me, please. I had it in my power to put an end to your misery when first you told me of it. I might have had the marriage annulled or dissolved, and yet I did not.'

'I never once suggested that you ought to end our marriage.'

'No, but *I* should have suggested it. Only for motives entirely selfish, I did not. With wretched swollen pride, I sought to recapture your heart, and once I had, I knew not what to do with it.' Maria beheld him with silent, overflowing eyes. 'Dear Maria, you have heard with what impoliteness I once spoke of you, and you must remember with what impatience I spoke *to* you when first we were married. I thought myself entirely indifferent, except when I was inspired by jealousy or lust. Oh, but when you left, Maria, how the pain of your absence near killed me! And with what horror I reflect, that had not your cousin made himself such an interferer, my pride might have lost you forever. I have made myself undeserving of you over and over again, and I see what wretched misery I bring you – if you wish to be free of me, then allow me to remedy all my dishonourable words and deeds by putting it in your power to emancipate yourself of me forever.'

'You are very drunk, Mr Jackson. You must be very drunk! The shackles that bind me to you could not be undone by Parliament or any court in the land. What a waste of time and money would a divorce be.'

'It would not be a waste, not if it was what you wanted.'

'Absolutely it would be a waste,' she replied, setting herself upon his lap. 'Even if I *could* divorce you, I would only remarry you afterwards, and then what fools we would look! La! In a thousand thousand lifetimes, I would choose to marry you every time. I love you, Mr Jackson. Why do I feel as if you never believe me when I tell you?'

'You could stop loving me, Maria. I would rather see you happy.'

It was not he who made Maria so unhappy. She told him so with the greatest reassurance. 'Really, will you believe me, please, Mr Jackson? I could be made no happier by any other. You are not the cause of my misery. Will you believe me, and prevent my being pushed into further misery by dropping this wretched talk of divorce?'

'If it is not me who makes you so miserable, then who, or *what*? Tell me, dear Maria, so I might make you happy again – you know how I hate to see you in such a despondent way.'

'It is nothing worth discussing. Here, let us return to your friends. They shall all be wondering where you have got to.'

'By Christ, dear Maria, you are crying again. You must tell me what has upset you so!'

'It is nothing, Mr Jackson, will you believe me? You know how I am. I cry sometimes for no reason at all.'

'Maria, there is always some reason.' She kissed him. She kissed him again, and agai– 'No, Maria! Tell me, will you, what has upset you so?'

She clasped her hands to her heart. 'Lord! Would you stop pestering me for an answer, Mr Jackson! It is nothing. Nothing at all worth mentioning.'

'Maria… Maria, what are you doing?' It was a moment before the penny dropped. 'No, Maria, stop it – for God's sake, stop it! You are going to harm yourself one day doing this. Maria…'

By now, Maria had forced shut her eyes and clamped tightly her hands over her ears so that Mr Jackson could not disturb her before she could obliviate herself from this scene.

CHAPTER THIRTY

CONTAINING A BRIEF ACKNOWLEDGEMENT OF SOME UNEXPECTED INFORMATION.

A note from Mr Jackson left on the table at his wife's bedside:

'My Sweet Terrifyer, If you awake and I am gone, know that I am only downstairs taking breakfast. I did not wish to disturb you with servants clattering dishes and cups about – although why I am concerned, I know not, for nothing ever seems to charm you from your dream state except your own will. Call for me immediately if you wish. Yes, you have been without consciousness the entire night! When an hour had passed, and I could still stir you not, I called for your dear Ralph to be brought to your side. He could wake you neither, though seemed wholly less concerned than I had been.'

'It appears as if you travel to another realm when you sleep, one where we cannot reach you, and one from which you appear very reluctant to return – I cannot blame you for that, Maria. When I see you have awoken this morning, I shall be the happiest man alive.

As you would have me, Mister Jackson.'

At Dr Paterson's office, the contentment of its residents was little reduced by Penny's vow of silence. Not as it had been the last time she would not speak to him. For, while her lips produced no words, the lady smiled at her doctor near constantly and found no contravention of her pledge in laughing with him when he spoke to her. But that morning, there was a bleak air over all their proceedings. For Ralph by reason of having had so little sleep, and for Penny because she was still avoiding Maria. Though, her present unhappiness with her friend did not preclude her horror at hearing the doctor had been called out in the night to attend

Maria. Dr Paterson was not concerned for his cousin. Jackson, he declared, had been in quite a state, beside himself convinced that Maria was half-dead. Ralph had witnessed Maria sleep for an entire day after such a turn. If she did not wake by nine the next morning, then Mr Jackson should send for assistance again.

'There – see, it is ten o'clock, and he has not called for me; she must be fine. "How do I prevent her from doing it?" he asked me. Well, if I knew the answer to that, I would not have spent an entire summer at our grandfather's home watching Maria faint every time I beat her at a game of backgammon. If it was going to harm her, I think it would have done so a long time ago!' Penny was leaning over his desk, looking very earnest, not willing to say a word. To make his lady smile, the doctor continued, 'Do you remember when she did it because James refused to take her arm while we were walking to the theatre? And then when she came round, James was forgiven, took her arm and somehow we still made it to our seats in time. Oh, Maria! What a determined creature she is!'

Penny did remember. She remembered all the faults and follies of her friend most fondly. The doctor took her hands in his and said, in a very kind, reassuring tone, 'You will be friends again, I am very sure of it.' All of a sudden, a strange air began to invade the space betwixt our two betrothed; his easy and cheerful humour subjugated by the unpleasant pangs of guilt. He clung to her hands as if he could not bear for the lady to return to her work, and after hemming a few false starts and looking paler than ever she had seen him before, Dr Paterson began on another thought, 'There is something I should like to tell you, Penny. Really, I think I ought to have confessed it a very long time ago...'

Thanks to her vow of silence, the lady was not obliged to respond immediately to the subsequent confession. After taking many painfully silent minutes to understand what he had said, she did break her vow and replied, 'A daughter. You have a daughter! Good Heavens! How old is she?'

While some penetrating slice of dear Penny's mind, neatly plated and served to my charming reader, must be here expected, I am afraid to say I have very little to offer. Penny was never as free in giving her thoughts to me as Maria, and there have been a great many times when I could but only guess at what the dear thing was musing. Though I could not profess it has caused no difficulties in the retelling of this tale, Penny has every right to her privacy, and I believe we are best not to play at blind man's bluff with her emotions.

'She turned nine in December.' Dr Paterson could not quell his rebelling features from forming a doting smile. 'Her name is Eliza.'

'Nine... nine? Heavens! Nine years is a very–' here Penny shook free her smothered hands, 'it is a very long time. And Maria, does she know?'

'No, I told nobody but my grandfather and Jackson.'

'*Jackson?*' she answered with wide, horrified eyes. 'Do you mean to say Maria's Mr Jackson?'

He replied with a nod. Mr Jackson had been Ralph's first friend at Cambridge, and Ralph Paterson discovered his news not long after he had arrived. He offered to marry the girl. Her father would not agree, thinking Ralph below their aspirations for her. The child would be given away. Ralph no sooner learnt he had a daughter than he was told he would never in his life meet her. Of course, he could not stomach such a fate. Mr Jackson had long been the main confidant in this matter, and his elder – but not eldest – brother had recently had his status elevated to that of a father himself. Mr Sidney Jackson Senior had, apparently, long ago accepted the funding of illegitimate grandchildren as a natural consequence of having three handsome sons. Young Mr Jackson asked his father to loan his friend the money to have the child cared for till he could afford to do so himself.

'I paid him back all the money, of course. She is at a school now in Surrey. For all the reasons I have to hate Jackson, if it were not for him, I would likely never have met my daughter at all.'

'Do you visit her?'

'As often as I can, though not as often as I would like to.'

A note handed to Mr Jackson by Maria, who had since resumed her vow of silence:

'As you are on a little holiday from your work, I would like to go away. I have organised the first night of our stay, and we shall leave this afternoon. Do not bother objecting to the scheme on account of my health.

You have had me confined to my bed for three days, and as I cannot speak to you, and you have adopted the sensibilities of a nun in this time, I am becoming very bored. Really – you cannot expect me to be satisfied with only listening to you read all day long. We shall return whenever you need to, but we must go this afternoon. I cannot stand any longer being confined to my room, and I shall hate you horribly if you do not agree to the plan. Though I never thought I could tire of you reading to me, I have absolutely no intention of seeing you with a book in your hands at any juncture of this trip.

Your, perfectly well, and horrendously bored, Maria.'

Mr Jackson could only but laugh as he read this note sat at the side of his wife's bed. 'Well, I am not sure that I can give a negative to such a plan, Maria. But I will only agree to it if you promise there shall be none of your little fainting fits while we are away.' She released a contented smile of acquiescence. 'No,' he said seriously. 'You must say it, you must promise me. And then you may return to not speaking to me.'

'I promise, Mr Jackson.'

Mr Jackson was utterly astounded when their carriage came to a stop at Maria's carefully plotted destination. Despite having refused his bringing any form of entertainment for the journey, she held him off till their arrival. As she gazed at the passing scenes, he made himself content beholding her heaving heart, which was perpetually bounding in thanks to the motions of the carriage. Had he been asked to guess, this location would be quite possibly the very last place on earth that the gentleman would think to suggest: the inn where Violet had held her birthday party the previous summer. And his disbelief was propelled into absolute bewilderment when his wife said to the innkeeper, 'We should have an apartment put aside for the night. Under the name of King.' Maria's wickedest smile appeared upon her face as her husband and 'Mrs King' were led to their abode for the evening.

Maria had assumed the name before this moment. A lifetime of unwavering commitment to the tenets of her faith was undone in just a few moments of conversation outside an inn. Mr Jackson (King) had then set his nimble tongue to convincing the innkeeper his *wife* was taken most ill and needed a room to rest in – he would pay for an entire night upfront –

money would not be an issue at all. When reflecting on this happening in the months following, Maria had considered that Mr King had appeared very well practised at such a speech. Her self-enforced penance had been a lengthy affair. But returning to this spot a year later, Maria the Martyr was nowhere to be seen.

CHAPTER THIRTY-ONE

CONTAINING SOME LETTERS AND OMITTING OTHERS.

A letter to Mrs Maria Jackson from Miss Penny Stuart, forwarded from Russell Square:

'I have been sitting for ten minutes thinking of what to say to you, my love. I am truly sorry and penitent for having behaved so coolly towards you. When you are deserving of scorn, you know I would never spare you, but in this affair, I have been far from faultless, and I have blamed you too severely for your part. Write to say we are friends once again?'

'It is not that upon which my hand jams in writing but the business of your cousin's letter that you will have found in the same packet as mine. Our engagement is not cast off, but I was so surprised by his confession that when he has asked me if I would still like to marry him, I have not been able to give him an absolutely positive answer. I do not know what to make of him or myself. The past three mornings, he had been drenched with that odour one happens upon when walking by the open door of an especially lowly inn.'

'I am broken-hearted for you that he has chosen to tell you by a letter (of only a single sheet no less!) – he is not himself, allow that to be a balm to your wounds – he is not, at all, himself. Your cousin has told me very little of Eliza. He will absolutely say nothing of the child's mother except that she is alive but has never met the girl. He will not look at me in the eye when he talks and takes all his letters and papers to another room – I have barely seen him. When he told me that he had written to you, I insisted I must send an accompanying letter, how betrayed you must feel, my love, and how justified you would be in that feeling. I cannot fathom why he has not told you in all this time.'

'If I know you as I believe I do, I think you will be just as betrayed by your grandfather and Mr Jackson. But I really think the blame must only lie with your cousin. The man himself awaits my finishing this letter; he is very agitated to send you his news. I shall pray for you, my dear, for I know what pains it shall bring you.

Yours, always, Penny Stuart.'

It would require only a most basal imagination to conceive how Maria and Mr Jackson had been spending their time since last we looked in on their trip. Maria certainly had not been talking with her husband, and she had not left the room once. They had been five days as 'Mr and Mrs King' and offering the gentleman some much-welcomed repose, though causing the lady's greatest displeasure, came an invitation of near insistence from the innkeeper's wife that the young couple join a little private ball they would be holding that evening. Mr Jackson had not danced with Maria at Violet's party; he was careful of maintaining the appearance of being entirely insensible to her till he spotted an opportunity for a private interview. How pleased the gentleman was to have his dance with Maria in this hall now. Only for the interruption of a letter being brought to his lady did he give her up.

'You are all such wretched deceivers,' Maria half-whispered through a sob as she dropped her letter to the floor. Her lamentations were causing such chaos with the eager-to-overhear dancers that Mr Jackson hurried her gently upstairs to their room.

'Who has deceived you?' he asked, feeling reasonably sure it was not himself to blame.

'All of you! Dear God, all of you have been at it. You, Ralph and even, good God, even my grandpapa!'

Not one of them was without this unnameable disease. This disease that allowed them all to speak to her with such betraying smiles and forked tongues. And whose deception was worse, she could not conceive, for all three she adulated so much that Maria sometimes quite feared she risked her soul in the act of idolatry. Her dear grandpapa, did she not commit half of all her prayers in his name? Had she not confided her every thought to him before and after he had left her? Mr Jackson, in spite of every good reason she had to blame and resent him, did she not forgive him and love him with such perseverance? Had she not abandoned herself in mind, body and heart to his ascendency, as a wife ought to do? And Ralph, her dear, dear Ralph, a death burning at the stake she would have risked pledging that he would never keep a secret such as this from her. And now he confessed it in a one-sheet letter. Maria sobbed, as ever she did, and confronted her husband for his role in this treachery.

'It was not my secret to tell, Maria,' he answered once she had put upon him sufficient blame and condemnation.

'After we were married, did you ever encourage him to tell me? Did you underline the fault in his deceit and have him ignore your pleas?'

'No, Maria, it was not my place to encourage him so.'

'*Not your place*? If it be not the place of my husband to counteract such a wilful deceit against me, then whose place could it be?'

'I really think you are overreacting a little, Maria. All men are entitled to some secrets, and I am certain he had his reasons for not telling you till now. He surely does not know everything you have ever done.'

'He surely does! And it is not a *deed* he has disguised from me, but a person, a child, *his child*!' A fit of despondency overtook her for some moments before she could continue her vexed thoughts. 'You astound me, sir, with your composure! Perhaps you speak to soften the blow for when you shall reveal your own hidden children. Who am I to learn myself a stepmother to? A son, a daughter? Or perhaps there is a whole band of your brood!'

Mr Jackson glared at Maria quite seriously, a look she could not decipher. Causing her to ask, 'Do you? Do you, Mr Jackson, have any children?'

'I have no children, Maria.'

'Do you swear it?' As she said this, Mr Jackson's face unfolded from stiffness to one of great hurt. Maria was too blinded by her sense of his treachery to notice this and leapt to her next thought in an ever more bitter tone, 'Ralph did not tell me, and I have far fewer reasons to distrust him than I do you! *You* who made such a game of leading vestal young women to ruin! How? *How* could a man like yourself possibly claim such a thing with any certainty? Or was I the only girl who you completely abandoned after you had won your little wager with Gilly?' At this last utterance, Maria fell onto the bed, choked by a train of heaving tears that would allow her to do nothing more than gasp for air and hit – with great vigour – the pillow beside her head.

'I understand you are angry, Maria.'

Mr Jackson waited till the greatest severity of her upset subsided before reaching out a hand to lift her from the bed. The effect of his touch upon her still inflamed and bruised arm caused her to cry out in pain and pull the offending limb to her chest. 'Forgive me,' two words softly spoken before the lady stumbled into a daze from which he could not pull her. *What a wretched hypocrite you have been, castigating Mr Jackson with such venom for his little deception, all the while disguising from him the lingering evidence of your own cowardice!* Mr Jackson called her name many times, took her hands, even gently shook her shoulders, but Maria would not return to him till her self-flagellation was done. And when it was, she smiled at him light-heartedly and kissed him. She kissed him again and again till he, at last, pulled away from her. 'For Christ's sake, Maria! Sometimes you act like an utter lunatic! Just as I think I am beginning to understand you, you become even more deranged.' He had not meant the words to sound so cruel, but now they had been said. *That is fine.* Mr Jackson could call her a lunatic and deranged; *after all, you probably are, Maria.* He could call her anything, so long as he did not ask about her arm. 'What is wrong with your arm, Maria? Have you hurt it?'

Damn. Damn his handsome devil voice!

'No,' she answered after having smiled pleadingly at him for several moments. Maria attempted to distract his unusual seriousness with her usual distractions. Mr Jackson had never been as powerless to her charms as she had been to his, and he politely redirected every affectionate advance before saying, 'Stop, Maria. Please, will you shew me your arm?'

Why could she never deny him anything he asked of her? He was no fool and knew no trip or fall could leave such a mark. The best she could hope for now was a sufficient mixture of the truth and a lie. 'Some awful brute of a man grabbed me on my return from Ralph's home and was trying absolutely to carry his point with me. I understand all your warnings now, and I swear, upon my faith, I shall never walk out alone again, not without your express consent!' Mr Jackson had not imagined that the truth could be so awful. He stood listening with that silent look Maria could never quite interpret. 'I did not tell you because I knew the thought of it for you must be far more painful than the reality for me. Believe me, please, Mr Jackson,' she said, taking his hand and kissing it, 'the man did no real dishonour to you. I was quite rescued from any trouble by a kind passer-by.' Still, Mr Jackson looked at her in that impenetrable way he could conjure. 'I swear, upon my soul, you have not been dishonoured. He managed nothing of any consequence. You are still the only man who—'

Before she could finish, Mr Jackson had pulled Maria into his arms and said in half astonishment, half despair, 'By Christ, Maria, do you really believe *that* is what concerns me? My being dishonoured is the furthest thought from my mind. He must have nearly broken your arm to leave such a mark upon it!'

Maria was very grateful for Penny's accompanying letter, which did much to soften the pain of Ralph's. Several sheets have been omitted from the below reply to Miss Stuart from her friend, including Maria's thoughts on her cousin's having hidden a secret daughter from her for nine years and the repetition of the same lie that she had told Mr Jackson – that she had been attacked by a stranger in the street:

'And, Lord, how glad I am to not need to wear those stuffy, long-sleeved day dresses perpetually to hide my arm. It is so hot all of a sudden, is not it? I believe I really could die from it! I have written to Sarah to send me some different clothes, till then I shall stay in our room wearing only my crepe petticoat. Though I would happily not wear even that (how I smile imagining your face as you read those words!), but Mr Jackson has it in his head that I am formed from brittle china and thinks himself very chivalrous, declaring always "I do not want to hurt you, Maria." – so I must remain covered, or he threatens to take the adjacent room for only himself.'

'There was quite a to-do between us, my dear. When first I revealed my scrape with such brutishness, I was taken aback by how upset Mr Jackson was for my sake and not his own (you know that I thought he would be very angry with me for walking out alone after he has asked me so many times not to do so). He cried, Penny, he really cried! But when he stopped crying, he was very cross, ranting and raving about finding this fellow (which I told him to be impossible), kicking things and striking his fist against the wall in a very pleasing manner and talking of "demanding satisfaction". Had the man been there, I am certain Mr Jackson would have shot him between the eyes, which he once threatened to do when an actor spilt wine on me in the green room of a theatre and did not stop to apologise.'

'You know I have such a weakness for Mr J when he is cross; what a pleasant quiver it sets upon me. Well – my quiver was not well received when I set it upon him. "I see how it is," I replied (you can imagine how I sobbed and fell to the floor), "I am ruined to you now, spoilt at the hands of this thuggish fiend!" He tried to speak, but I must needs finish a speech once I have begun; I shan't bother reciting it all, but I put a great many disparaging words about myself into his mouth.'

'After he had listened to the whole of it, I thought he might cry again. He really looked as if he would. He refuted it all and said he simply could not think of such a thing till I was recovered. I stated that he need only avoid one of my arms and not my entire person, and then he replied to say, "I do not just mean your arm, Maria." – what he meant by that I do not know for the cut on my neck is quite healed already. Then he told me that he wished I had such an appetite for food as I did for him (really, I must learn to abstain a while, or he will become too pleased with himself), and he sends the innkeeper up with a constant influx of meals for me.'

'I am talking to Mr Jackson again, as I am sure you can surmise, but I really feel it is excusable in such a case as this, as is your speaking to Ralph – let us not tell Joanna, and resume our vow when I return to London. As I have said, I am sure I shall forgive my cousin in a few days or so, though I cannot say my opinion of him is not a little coloured to know he was engaged in such unchristian dealings at only eighteen. But then did I not do the very same with Mr Jackson? I suppose, therefore, I must not cast the first stone. As you are without sin in that respect, you may cast as many stones at him as you please! If that was his only failing, I think it could be overlooked, but if he spent his years at Cambridge as it appears my husband did, then may God help you, my dear!'

'I have long been had and will now be led by the whims of this mischievous creature I call my husband till the end of days. Pray, his future be less wild than his past, unless he cares only ever for my bed, in which case, pray, he be wilder still (you really must burn this letter after reading it)! – I must leave you here. I believe by virtue of my being so occupied writing to you, Mr Jackson is feeling left out and now has a very eager look in his eye. Write to me when you have learnt more of this dear Eliza!

Always, your, Maria.'

'Postscript: I was not wrong about the look in his eye, but quickly his sensibilities returned to him, and I am now back at this wobbling desk in the corner. He has given me a little something to keep myself entertained. Did I tell you that I forbade him from bringing any books? Well – I did. And he got around this instruction by instead bringing a printed pamphlet of about thirty or so pages. What an odd thing for him to bring, you might think. I thought so too. He said that he would like for me to read it because he is very curious to know my thoughts. Penny, I rather fear I am married to a very strange sort of fellow! I have only read a couple of pages; what a queer thing it is: a man exalting a society in which it is the female sex who are the superiors in every respect, and men are called upon only when their passions are required. La! Do you think this is some humorous prod at me? For he did say, with a very becoming smile, that sometimes I make him feel like a woman of the town! What a strange thing for him to give to me!'

'Oh, by the bye, we are leaving for Brighton to-morrow morning. The further I can keep Mr J away from London, the better. I am still not convinced he has been sufficiently discouraged from his vengeful quest. I shall send details of where to send your reply.'

CHAPTER THIRTY-TWO

IN WHICH WE TRAVEL TO BRIGHTON.

'Mr Jackson,' Maria whispered, seeking her husband's attention, 'I have been given a glass of champagne. What am I to do with it?'

'Why are you asking me?' replied he, affecting the lady's own wicked smile.

'Because you are my husband. Do not play with me, sir, tell me — what should I do with it?'

Of course, Mr Jackson would have acquaintances in a town of such amusements as Brighton, and the first night of their arrival, they had found themselves invited to a supper party. Maria had never before been to any event where the only person she knew was her husband. The lady clung to his arm as if she might tumble to the centre of the earth if she had him not keeping her aground.

'How would you like me to instruct you, dear Maria. Should I tell you that it is your duty to me to drink it? Or command you to give it up to me so that I might?'

'I do not drink. You know I do not.'

'Then do not drink it.'

'Maybe I would like to drink it. It was, after all, Mr Wesley and not God who ordered this abstinence. And my duty to your word is superseded only by my duty to the word of God, so if you tell me to drink it, then I shall have to.'

He stifled a laugh, 'Very well, dear Maria. There is nothing that your husband should like more than for you to drink that champagne. But pray, drink it slowly. I do not believe supper is for another hour.'

At their little inn, Maria had found herself instigating this trip as a distraction for her husband, who was desperate to return to London. Mr Jackson's agitation had seemed only to increase at Maria's lack of agitation. She would not sanction any vengeance sought on her behalf – there was to be no fighting, certainly no duelling. Mr Jackson was forbidden also from seeking any satisfaction through the courts – Maria did not desire her attacker to be beaten, killed, nor prosecuted – she only wanted him to leave her alone.

Perhaps Maria might not have been so enamoured with embracing and enforcing her spousal duty if she was not entirely confident of being the prima donna of her husband's heart – when she had asked him to take her somewhere diverting, anywhere he liked, Mr Jackson could hardly ignore such a disarming invitation. And doubtless, the gentleman would not have been so enamoured with engaging Maria's duty if she seemed not so gratified in giving it. And how gratified was she observing, at this party, his art, his nimble-tongued eloquence, as she would put it. Long had she been lanced upon the barbs of his charming self-assurance. When first they crossed paths at Mr Garcia's talk, Mr Jackson had not introduced himself to Maria directly, instead, advancing his acquaintance on James, whose arm the lady took, and with great boldness stating, as he caught Maria's eye:

'By God! What a very pretty wife you have, sir!'

It was her reflection on this happening, and perhaps also the champagne that inspired Maria's confidence to find herself a friend in this room. When Mr Jackson introduced his wife to a young couple in his acquaintance, Maria took her part in the conversation to say, gazing only into the eyes of the lady, 'Good God! What a very pretty wife you have, Mr Attwood!'

Mrs Attwood was very pretty. In fact, Maria thought this lady was far more than just very pretty but considered it might have been a little over familiar to declare this man's wife distractingly beautiful as the first thing she said to either. The compliment had the effect Maria had hoped for, and shortly Mrs Attwood and Mrs Jackson had abandoned their husbands, contriving even to sit near to one another at supper. Less by chance, and rather because she could not hold any conversation without at least once mentioning the name *Clarissa Harlowe*, Maria discovered that her new companion was just as much a fanatic of this novel as she was. Though this young lady had very different ideas about it than Maria. 'Wasn't the villain

219

unbearable? There was nothing so ugly in a man as wanton womanising. She had been forced to pass over all the pages relating to his awful brutality with Clarissa.'

'Oh, indeed, I barely took in the words as I had read those parts myself. But those passages I did take notice of I found very provoking,' Maria answered, with only half a lie being told.

'Oh, I am sure you did. It is a very affecting novel. Upon the whole, I think the author wrote the villain too severely. It is very unbelievable that he could have been so successful in his conquest of such a significant number of women of all different ages and stations in life. He was supposed to be very charming, was not he?'

'Yes, I believe he was,' Maria said, feigning recollection.

'Well, I never saw anything charming in anything he said or wrote. Always bent down on one knee, declaring one unbelievable officious remark after another. Really, would any girl above the age of sixteen fall for such obviously designed flattery? I believe the book does a great discredit to our sex, as much as it does theirs; so many women falling into an obsessive, helpless sort of love with a man who made such a game of the virtue of young women. It would not look very good upon us if so many girls were really set on throwing their fate into the power of brutish, lewd men, even if they are handsome!'

'Oh indeed. It would be a very odd sort of young woman to want a handsome brute for a husband,' Maria replied half-heartedly, smiling at Mr Jackson as she spoke.

The two young wives talked of novels for hours with a mutual enthusiasm. Mr Jackson, for once, found himself redundant to his wife. Late into the evening, as the two ladies sat on a sofa opposite to the card table where played their two gentlemen, Mrs Attwood sloped towards Maria's ear and said, 'Your husband keeps staring at us. I hope I have not caused you to be in any trouble with him, keeping you at my side all evening?'

'Trouble?' Maria smiled, sending a little wave to Mr Jackson. 'No, he is not the possessive type. I do not believe I have even once been in trouble with Mr Jackson. That is the look he shoots my way when he has an appetite for an amusement that cannot be found at a card table.'

Mrs Attwood first answered with a laugh, 'Perhaps then I ought to allow you to say goodnight, dear madam.'

'Oh no,' Maria said, taking the lady's hand, 'for too long, he has been making himself very handsome in my company, all the while keeping me at arm's length. Let him now learn to be temperate. But we must disappear from his gaze. I shall not hold out for long with those pretty eyes upon me.' Mrs Jackson led her companion away from the drawing-room to the balcony of the adjoining parlour.

The effects of the champagne were far more apparent upon standing upright in the fresh air– was not everything a little more brilliant in this state – every face more beautiful, every joke a little funnier, every laugh a little longer – Maria could understand why her husband so regularly employed himself in this occupation. Though, what a bore she thought him, having confiscated her last drink and instructing her not to get another. Imaginably, that could be why Mrs Attwood had mistaken him for a tyrant husband. Well we know, Mr Jackson only performed the role of a tyrant when Maria urged him so charmingly.

The summer sky was slowly painting in the night, stroke by stroke obscuring the previously unblemished blue. The two women stood in silence, four eyes fixed on the horizon. It was not so much an uncomfortable silence, but there was a mystery to it; at moments, Mrs Attwood would look to her companion as if she wanted to say something, but then she would not. Each time she did, it brought a little turn of something like terror over Maria, and she did not know why.

As if he had sensed his wife's desire to be excused from this happenstance, soon came the calling of Mr Jackson looking for Maria. Any defiance of that voice would be utterly hopeless. He wanted to leave, then so did she. He did not want to take a carriage home – no, neither did she. A walk by the seafront is what he desired, and what a coincidence this was now Maria's exact desire too. What an autocrat was he, and without ever meaning to be.

Damn his handsome devil voice! How happy Maria was to be *his* marionette. To own the truth, Mr Jackson could not have denied finding this willing malleability greatly pleasing. Sometimes his wife's devotion was utterly terrifying, a fact he was reminded of upon their walk home. For his own amusement, Mr Jackson had delayed their return to the lodgings, leading them on a walk of the nearby cliffs. What a spectacular view she thought it to be – never before had Maria been to the coast. Standing a little too close to the edge, he sought to amuse her and said, 'Tell me, dear Maria, what would you say to me if I jumped off this ledge right now? Would you be so very cross with me?'

A serious smile encroached upon her face, 'Oh, yes, I would be absolutely furious with you. But I would not say anything to you at all, for I would only jump straight after you.'

'Do not say that, Maria.'

'But it is the truth, Mr Jackson. And I can think of no better answer than the truth.'

And what was he to say to *that?*

The two soon returned to their lodgings, the evening passed into the early hours, and to Maria's greatest delight, Mr Jackson very much overcame his fear of causing her any harm. Over breakfast, he announced that he had arranged for them to spend the day with the Attwoods. What an unexpected sulk came from his lady!

'Oh, what a nuisance it is to have friends!' How quickly tears drifted from her eyes to her cheeks, and her lips began to wobble. 'You shall be back to Parliament soon. This is *my* time with you, I do not want to share you, and you cannot make me! I do not care to see the Attwoods, or the beach, or the sea, how dull they all seem in comparison to staying here in this room with you!'

If Maria had seemed not so serious in her distress, Mr Jackson might have laughed at her, but settling upon only a smile and taking her hand, he replied, 'Good God, Maria, I fear I shall soon injure a muscle! Can a man not take half a day's respite? And I shall remind you of your words when you have long tired of me. You like Mrs Attwood, do not you? Surely you would be happy for her company once again.'

'Why do you say that I shall tire of you as if it is a certainty?'

'You cannot be infatuated with me in this way forever, Maria. I shall enjoy it while you are, but I do not fool myself that you shall always hold me above all others.'

'Infatuation, sir!' she replied with alarm. 'Who speaks of infatuation but to talk of little girls obsessive of a romantic fantasy? *Infatuation!* What an ugly word it is! I have not been struck with some temporary lovesickness. Lord, just because *you* will never speak of loving *me* does not behove me to pretend the same indifference.'

'I am hardly indifferent to you, Maria.'

'I will not object to the limitations of your declaration, Mr Jackson, if you will not object to the expanse of mine; I choose to make you the absolute monarch of my heart because it enriches my heart to do so. But if you make yourself undeserving – I can just as easily choose to be only *hardly indifferent* to you. Whether or not I love you in this way forever is entirely dependent on you, Mr Jackson.'

And what was he to say to *that?*

He would send a note postponing their outing till the afternoon, but only if Maria would eat something for breakfast. She would never eat breakfast, and it drove him mad. How his wife maintained such a brimming neckline on a diet that appeared to him to consist mostly of tea and emotions, Mr Jackson did not know. Whenever he pressed her for some cause of her reluctance to eat, she would always answer either to say, '*I am too happy to eat!*' or, '*I am too sad to eat!*'

Maria had not spoken entirely the truth at breakfast. She did love Mr Jackson so well and exalted him as the best among men because it pleased her to do so and because she had long felt him deserving of such love. But she could not choose to love him any less if he ever made himself any less worthy – this lesson had been taught by Mr Harrington. When he had replaced her, his daughter, the longstanding queen of his heart, with Pearl, she forgave him and loved him as well. When his view had transformed Maria from a daughter to a commodity, and all talk had turned to exchanging her for the acquisition of a better name, she had forgiven him and loved him as well. And when he had turned on the woman who had given life to his daughter, though she could not forgive him without his penitence, though she despised him for it, Maria loved him as well as she ever had. And the day Maria had forgiven Mr Jackson and returned home to Russell Square, she had obliged her heart to endure whatever happiness or misery her husband might bring her.

CHAPTER THIRTY-THREE

IN WHICH MARIA BREAKS A PROMISE.

Maria ate enough to satisfy her husband and found the morning passed much to her own satisfaction and machinations, having entirely undressed and artfully rooted herself across Mr Jackson's lap as he attempted to write his letters of that day – obligating him to be confronted with his favourite part of her person with every stroke of his pen. In spite of Maria's sulking and sullen pleading, her husband could not be convinced to falter on their arrangement with the Attwoods in the afternoon

'Really, why is it that all these men know how to swim? Can you swim, Mrs Attwood?' Maria asked her companion as they sat perched on a jetty of humongous rocks situated a little way into the sea. Mr Attwood had suggested a swim, and Mr Jackson had readily agreed to the scheme.

'No, do you know any women who can swim? They like to keep us helpless, I think.' Maria returned a laugh. 'Speaking of, and forgive my freeness, but I must speak while we are alone, my dear. I cannot help but notice you are very much ruled by Mr Jackson's opinions.'

Maria did not understand what the lady was referring to and told her such.

'Well, he takes your drink from your hand and commands you not to have another, and you did not so much as blink. In fact, I am quite certain you apologised to him. And I heard him at supper, instructing you upon what and how much you should eat. He decides everything you will do, and I see you have lost your fight; you do not ever appear to question him or have a suggestion contrary to his. Even this morning, our plans were changed because he decided he would rather stay in and finish his letters. He does not even allow you to hold your own bag!'

'Allow me! La! How you misunderstand him. Mr Jackson carries my bag because I do not like to carry it, and he does not like me being unhappy and minds not at all carrying it for me.'

'I only mean to say, Mrs Jackson, some men are quite intent on making their wives unnaturally dependent upon them.'

With a cross face, Maria replied, 'Perhaps *some men* are, but I do not comprehend what you mean in telling me such a thing! What an odd maxim it would be to do things I do not wish to do, that I would gladly have done and decided for me, simply for the gratification of an independence for which I have no desire.'

Speaking very softly and taking her new companion by the hand, Mrs Attwood answered, 'I have seen the bruises on your arm, madam, and the fresh finger marks on the side of your neck...'

'Lord!' Maria remarked to herself, *'I had thought my hair covered that perfectly well. Dratted, dratted, coastal wind!'*

'... I do not mean to pry—'

'Then do not, madam,' Maria said with a laugh, half tickled, half mortified at it all. 'You have it all wrong, I assure you. Mr Jackson is a very good sort of man. Upon my soul, there is not a better husband in the whole world.'

But Mrs Attwood continued to press and press a little more, 'Those second marks had not been there at the party. Is that why they had remained at their lodgings this morning, so that she might recover from his cruelty? Mr Attwood knew people, people who could help. Maria need not be at his mercy any longer.'

'Really, if any of what you are thinking were true, how grateful I should be for this interference. But truly, you must believe me; you have it entirely wrong. Mr Jackson is not at all a cruel husband, and I do not need nor want any help in getting away from him.'

'Mrs Jackson, *Maria*, would you really have me believe he did not do that to you?' the lady replied, glancing at Maria's neck.

Heavens! Why would this lady not just listen? *Why must she keep picking and prodding at something that had nothing to do with her?* Again, Mrs Attwood gave the offer of her husband's help.

'For God's sake, he did it because *I* asked him to! Does that satisfy the hunger of your curiosity, madam?'

Neither spoke another word.

Mrs Attwood turned her face away; she did not see what Maria was doing. Even if she had, she would not have known what she was seeing. Maria had promised Mr Jackson, she knew that she had, but she was so furious, so mortified and desirous of erasing herself from this wretched situation that she held her breath unthinkingly. Had she thought about it, she would have remembered where she was sitting and what an awful idea such a thing was in a precarious place such as this. Mrs Attwood was helpless to do anything but scream as her new companion sank into the water like a pebble. At the sound of this scream, Mr Jackson turned his head in some confusion to happen upon the surreal vision of his greatest fear come to be.

He was the nearest to her. The stronger swimmer too. He thanked God he was. No more than half a minute passed between the time of this scream and Mr Jackson reaching his wife. The water was not very deep there, but Maria had been submerged the entire time. A little crowd of walkers gathered as he lifted her hanging body onto the stony shore. She did not stir but for the outpouring of wretched foamy seawater about her nose. During one of her longwinded recollections of a conversation with her dear, dear Ralph, when first she and Mr Jackson had been married, Maria had recalled the fascinating lesson of how to revive a person drowned:

'Oh, how I hope I should never have the use for such a skill – but it is better to know it than not to know it – do you not agree, Mr Jackson? How fortunate I am to have a cousin who is such an encyclopaedia of all medical knowledge. Some people say the first thing you must do is draw a hot bath – but Ralph says that is a foolish idea because by the time it is drawn, the person shall most certainly be dead if they were not before – and he has never once known a dead body revived by a hot bath, whatever people might say! You must rub and pat the person on their chest and back, and very vigorously – it is no time for gentleness – by the words of my dear cousin. There – is that not very interesting, Mr Jackson?'

'Very interesting, Maria.'

He had not looked up from his paper. But he had heard her; he thanked God that he had heard her. Mr Jackson did all his lady had once

226

instructed him to do. Each blow a little harder than the last as he was becoming increasingly desperate. At last, Maria began to cough and purge the sea from her lungs. She was alive, and she was awake, *at first*. For the hour after her rescue, returned to the bed in their lodgings, she smiled, laughed and lied, claiming to her husband that she had simply slipped from her seat. How glad he was to see her well. Shortly, this gladness was replaced with worry when Maria began coughing, so much that it seemed she might never stop, causing herself, in some moments, to be grappling for breath. As the evening pressed on, her coughing only became worse, each of these coughing convulsions now ending only when the lady fell unconscious from her breathlessness.

A doctor was called. He could confirm nothing tangible. At eleven o'clock, Maria could not be woken for over forty minutes, her longest spell of unconsciousness since Mr Jackson had fetched her from the water. He could not rest for a moment while she slept.

A note from Mr Jackson to Dr Paterson. Written at half-past eleven:

'You must come to Brighton as soon as you are able. I shall include the address of our lodgings. Change horses as often as required to keep speed – I shall cover the expense. Maria fell into the sea this afternoon. I revived her well enough at first, but I fear she is now quite ill with an unrelenting and suffocating cough (as if that of someone in the last weeks of consumption). You need not waste any time informing her father; I shall write to him myself. She seems to grow ever worse with every passing hour, and the doctor here is nothing but a quack – hurry, will you!

Yours &c., S. Jack.'

A note from Mr Jackson to Mr Harrington. Written at eleven thirty-nine:

'I have no time for pleasantries. We are in Brighton. Maria has fallen into the sea and is becoming precariously ill – might I recommend you travel to see her? God forbid she does not recover. I have written for her cousin to attend her. The address of our lodgings is below included.

Yours &c., S. Jack.'

'She will recover, will not she, Paterson?' This was the third time that Mr Jackson had asked this question in the hour since Dr Paterson's arrival. For a third time, Maria's cousin gave the same answer:

'I do not know.'

'How can you not know! You are a doctor, are not you?'

'Yes, but he is not an oracle, Mr Jackson. Perhaps we should take a little walk outside while Dr Paterson attends Maria,' Penny answered.

Needless to say, tensions were high. Already, Dr Paterson and Mr Jackson had become engaged in a furious brawl that Penny was forced to break apart. The doctor had found, while examining his cousin, the same marks Mrs Attwood had come across and had come to her same conclusion. Penny could vouch for the truth of the marks on Maria's arm, and though she did not absolutely know the other story to be true, this lady knew enough of her friend's mind to have every cause to believe it. What an uncomfortable five minutes of silence passed after that conversation.

Brushing through Maria's long hair, Penny said, 'She will not thank any of us if she wakes up with this matted mess.' Continuing the loving preening of her friend, she fell upon a story – as Penny often did – and began to recall a tale from when Maria had first joined their church, 'How old would she have been, Dr Paterson? Six, I think, because I was eight when first we met. Oh, and Mr Jackson, it is imperative for your better imagining of this story to know that Maria could not pronounce her Rs properly till she was ten. You can imagine how Mr Harrington had her dressed, always drowning in a puffy, frilly gown with a silk sash and her hair bouncing in springing little coils.' Maria, who had been playing with Penny and her infant sister after the service, had declared with great seriousness how much she liked her playmate's hairstyle.

'…so, this little lisping doll in her giant dress walks boldly over to my father and plonks herself on his knee and asks him if she can come to our house so that he might do her hair in the same style. Of course, he told her, no. Never one to be deterred, Maria then asked if he would shew her maid how to do the style so that she might have hair to match mine every Sunday. He told her no again. His answer remained a firm no. You can imagine how Maria cried. But my father was never afraid of Maria's crying and would always say to her, "I am sorry if you are disappointed, and it is

228

perfectly natural to be upset when faced with disappointment, but you will not change my mind, Maria." After a short sob into my father's shoulder, Maria returned quite happily to playing with me and never spoke of the hairstyle again…'

A few months later, when Maria's birthday fell on a Sunday, she was invited to join the Stuarts after church for lunch at their home. 'As a present, my father plaited her hair into a special style just for her – a crown of hair, or a halo, depending on how you view it – for all the money in the world, he could not have gifted her a better thing. It is still the only gift she will accept from me on her birthday.' Always able to concentrate well on any task while in the throes of conversation, Penny had, in this time, formed that same style in Maria's hair. 'What do you think, Mr Jackson – is it a crown or a halo?'

'Both. Most certainly, both.'

Dr Paterson had a maxim he had acquired quickly while learning his craft; it was better to do nothing and cause a person no greater harm than guess blindly how to make them better. Maria was not getting any better; she would not wake, not even in the depths of her coughing convulsions. In the past half-hour, her lips had adopted a blue tinge, as had her fingernails. He assured his old friend that he had seen many people present such symptoms and recover very well. He had. But he had seen far more people die soon afterwards.

'By Christ! Her breathing has stopped. Paterson, stand up, man! Feel her hands; they are stone-cold! She is dead!' Here poor Mr Jackson tore furiously at the hair upon his own head. 'She is dead. Dear Maria is dead! My wife… good God!'

'Penny, would you fetch someone to draw a hot bath, quickly,' said the doctor after feeling Maria's hands.

'A bath! I thought you said you have never once known a hot bath to revive a dead person!' cried out the husband, almost breaking into a sob as his mouth crossed paths with the word *dead*. 'Maria is dead.' Now he did sob. 'Devil hang me! My dear Maria is dead. If I had a pistol, I would kill myself this instant, for I cannot, I *will not* live without her!'

'Good God! Will you calm down and behave like a man, Jackson! She is not dead. Dead people do not breathe, no matter how shallow, and they certainly never have a pulse!'

229

Though he could sympathise with Mr Jackson's distress, there is nothing Dr Paterson found less helpful than a flapping spouse remarking in terror over his shoulder. Once the bath was drawn and Maria had been lifted in by her cousin and husband, the doctor sent Mr Jackson on an unimportant errand downstairs. When this young husband returned, he found his haloed angel – his crowned queen – resting in a bath of dark crimson.

'What have you done to her!'

'I have not done anything to her.'

'Then what is wrong with her? What has happened!'

Dr Paterson had a suspicion. A suspicion that was given credence by a confession from Penny when Mr Jackson had been busied downstairs. A suspicion that would be proven correct in the passing of another hour.

CHAPTER THIRTY-FOUR

CONTAINING AN EVENT I TAKE NO PLEASURE IN RELATING.

'To be sure, it is always best to count your blessings; at least it was not a boy, hmm, Maria.'

Her father had not been in any particular rush to attend his daughter and had arrived five days after receiving Mr Jackson's letter. Maria had not been awake to see her, but Mr Jackson had looked upon this tiny, pinkish, wax cherub many times before saying his final farewell – she fitted perfectly in the palm of his hand, but she could not remain there, no matter how much he wished it. At this remark from his father-in-law, Mr Jackson stood up and turned his back to the room to gaze at the sea through the window. He had spoken very few words since Maria had awoken. It had been no certainty that she would awake; in fact, owing to how much blood was expelled from his cousin's body, Dr Paterson had been so sure she would die that he had insisted a priest be called for her.

'This should teach you to control your little fits of temper, Maria, shouldn't it? There are consequences to throwing yourself into the sea, young lady!'

'She has already told you, sir,' Pearl interjected in a voice of appeasement, 'she did not jump in; she fell!'

'What was it, Maria,' Mr Harrington continued, ignoring Pearl, 'did somebody make you cross? Or was Mr Jackson not paying you enough attention? You have always been just like your mother in that respect, willing to undertake any scheme to carry your point. Yes, your mother was always threatening to do this or that, till one day, the silly bitch threw herself into a river – see how that worked out for *her*, Maria. You have had a lucky escape. Selfish creature she was, doing it while Maria stood there and watched.'

232

'Heavens, sir!' cried Pearl. 'Will you stop this ranting and leave the poor girl alone!'

Here lies the water. Here stands the man. If the man goes to this water and drowns himself, it is, will he, nill he, he goes – mark you that. But if the water comes to him and drowns him, he drowns not himself.

'Stand here and hold your breath with me, like I shewed you, dear Maria,' her mother had said.

'But if I hold my breath, then I shall fall in, Mamma, and I cannot swim.'

'Oh, you are no fun, my love! Who is to say you shall fall in? If God wishes for you to remain here, in the world, then he will have you fall backwards, and if he wants you in Heaven, then he shall have you fall forwards. Will you not play the game with me, Maria?'

Maria agreed to please her mother. Her mother fell forwards, Maria fell backwards.

'Can you hear me, Maria?' Mr Jackson said, tapping her face gently. 'I have instructed your father to leave. It was a mistake asking him to come here.'

'If that is what you think is best, Mr Jackson,' she replied with a faint smile.

Maria could barely look at him, knowing what she had done. Knowing what she had done, knowing what she had known. She had not been certain of that little life, but she had suspected it, once or twice. This suspicion was absolutely forgotten in her paroxysm of mortification when speaking with Mrs Attwood. But she had promised him. She had promised Mr Jackson she would not faint on their trip abroad. She had never seen a man look so broken, and it was entirely her fault for doing the exact thing she had promised her husband she would not.

You killed his daughter, Maria; Mr Jackson will never forgive you for that. It would have been better if you had died too. That way, he would be free to choose a better wife, a woman he would actually want to be a mother to his children, a sane wife. Seeing her tears, he kissed her cheek. That only caused her to cry more.

A letter to Mrs Maria Jackson from Miss Pearl Foley. Delivered the following afternoon:

'By the time you receive this, I will be long gone. I know your father will be very angry, and I only hope he does not redirect his wrath towards you or your dear mamma. Forgive me, please, I had to leave, Maria. Since February, I have been hiding away the money your father gives me to spend on all manner of frivolities. I have plenty enough to get to my cousin's home in Swanage (I shall give you the address). Please do not tell your father where I am. I could not leave without telling you, Maria – what a dear companion you have been. I could not bear that wretched home after you left.'

'If I may give you a little parting advice, implore your Mr Jackson to take charge of your mother's care and move her somewhere your father knows not how to find her. It will enrage your father and put him entirely at odds with Mr Jackson, but it is for the best if you can convince the gentleman to do so. As all women, your mamma must be in the power of one man or another. I recommend that man be your husband and not your father, Maria. I have read over the terms of your marriage many times; Mr Jackson need not worry, there is only one circumstance in which he would not inherit the entirety of your fortune; that is if he kills you, my dear. You know I could not believe it when first I read those details, "And what," said I, "if he is terribly cruel to her? Would you not have him lose her fortune in such a case as that?" and he said to me, Maria, "I think it is far more likely she would make up such cruelty than Mr Jackson would do anything truly unforgivable to her. Her temper will do better under a firm hand, to be sure, I have told the man so myself." – how I hated him at that moment, and I have hated him more and more ever since then.'

'When you return to London, would you look in, from time to time, on how my papa is doing? I cannot tell him where I have gone, for he shall only tell Mr Harrington. If your father does come to know of my whereabouts, would you send an express to me and warn me, dear Maria? I ask so much of you and offer so little in return – and for that, I shall be forever in your debt.

Yours, Pearl Foley.'

Mr Jackson heard the slap from the hallway. He had been down to the kitchen to speak with the cook about making Maria some baked apples, without sugar – of course. He had no knowledge that Mr Harrington was still in Brighton. He certainly had no idea he was visiting Maria, not till he opened the door of her room to find his father-in-law hovering above his bedridden wife.

'What in God's name are you doing here, striking your daughter who has so narrowly escaped an early death. Leave, sir, immediately, I demand it!'

'Come off it, man, I did not hit her. A little slap was all it was.'

'Yes, it was just a little slap, Mr Jackson. You need not worry yourself,' Maria said in her father's defence.

'A little slap? Maria, you have a scarlet mark across your face! And if I am not mistaken, dear God, Maria, you have a welling of blood about your nose!' Mr Jackson replied in disbelief.

'Oh, to be sure, she has always bled and bruised very easily, have you not, dear Maria?' said Mr Harrington passing his thankful daughter a handkerchief. A smiling nod was Maria's only reply.

'The devil take me! What an objectionable scene is this, sir, a father striking his sickly daughter!'

'I would not resort to such things if she would respond to a simple question. She is being extremely obstinate and is overcome with a fit of girlish jealousy! A firm hand is the only way to provoke reason in a child sometimes.'

'I have told you. I am not jealous. I simply know nothing of where she has gone. I do not answer your question because I cannot, Papa.'

'Who has gone?' Mr Jackson enquired

'My Pearl has run off, and her last act was to have sent a letter to this madam here!' With his last words, Mr Harrington lifted and squeezed tightly the arm of Maria's that had lately suffered so much abuse. The lady screamed out unconsciously, evoking a shout from her husband so shockingly furious that she had not the wherewithal to be gratified by it.

Mr Jackson commanded his father-in-law from the room – or, with pleasure, he would give him passage to the street below via the window. Mr Harrington removed without another word to his daughter. The exchange of shouting that occurred between the two men in the hallway caused Maria to clamp her hands upon her ears, though it distorted their words, their anger permeated still, and quite without meaning to at all, Maria held her breath again.

A Letter from Mr Jackson to his brother Gilly:

'I have not the time nor will to write a long letter on this subject. I will be travelling to Swanage to pay a visit to Maria's not-stepmother, who, it turns out, is no more than a few months from her lying-in with a new sibling for Maria. The woman is determined to hide herself from Mr Harrington. I am sure, with his delightful temperament, nobody could imagine why.'

'Her cousin is gone off to a village near Dulwich to determine the whereabouts of Maria's mother on his return to London. If we are to believe Mr Harrington, his wife has been moved to a location he will not disclose till Miss Foley is returned to him. Maria does not know this fact, and given her precarious state of health, I am determined she will not know it – not till her mother is found safe.'

'Owing to a recent discovery of my father-in-law's truly brutish nature and his refusal to quit Brighton, I cannot leave for Swanage till I have secured a friend to protect dear Maria from the truth of her father's threats and his vile bullying. Come with a packet pretending to call me back to London immediately. You must absolutely refuse Maria's coming with me, regardless of any feigned submission on my part.

Yours &c., Sidney.'

'What in Christ's name is he doing here with you? If anybody actually need remain in London it is *him*!' Mr Jackson said in a serious whisper to his brother in the hallway just beyond the door behind which Maria lay.

'He was earnestly concerned with Maria's state of health. Owing, I believe, to how many occasions Jane has suffered so horribly in that way – you know she too nearly died the last few times. I absolutely could not dissuade him from joining me. Lord knows I tried, for Maria's sake.'

236

'I suppose if anyone is to threaten my father-in-law into acquiescence, it would be Richard.'

'Yes, well, exactly,' replied Gilly.

'While we are alone, and before you think the worst of me, I ought to explain that you may notice some odd bruising to Maria's right arm...'

Neither Mr Jackson nor Gilly were entirely satisfied with leaving Richard alone in a room with Maria, but when their brother had insisted he would like a moment of privacy to apologise once again to his sister-in-law – an apology they could only presume was for his offence to her at Hurlough Place – and producing a copy of *Frankenstein* declaring he would happily read to her, and Maria agreeing to his proposition, the two men were left with little choice but to wait beyond the door with pricked ears. They could hear not a thing of the conversation in the room, so whispered was it:

'When you reach the part about young William, will you skip over it? I have no want to hear that tragedy repeated. Not at present.'

'I can read a happier book if you like, Maria.'

'No. There is no comfort in happy stories. This one shall do very well.'

'Tell me, Maria, was this my fault?'

'It is amazing how young the author was when she wrote this, do you not think? I cannot remember at all what I did when I was that age, but it cannot have been of any great consequence.'

'Maria, if I had known, you must believe that I never would have... if I had known of your condition. You know, Maria, you know, do not you, that I never intended–' This gentleman could not bring himself to say the word *rape*, so settled upon, 'that I only ever intended to kiss you. You must know I never could have–' Maria gazed at him in such a way that, without her knowing, expressed her belief that his desire had been to do something far worse than kiss her against her will, 'dear God, you must think me a monster, Maria!'

'No,' she said, smiling weakly, feeling for some reason the need to reassure him. 'Is this why you bring me *Frankenstein* so that I might be reminded that monsters are simply men with broken hearts and neglectful fathers?'

'You are a clever little thing, dear Maria.' *Lord!* How she hated that name on his lips. 'I think no one gives you enough credit for your mind.'

'And you do, do you?'

'I think Sidney admires you for your passion and your devotion to him. Gilly, for your beauty and goodness. Your cousin, for your telling anybody who might listen that he is the cleverest man in England. And I admire you because you know all that and change your pretty face according to what will best please the man stood before you.'

'And here I thought you began to tempt my ego when really you speak to insult me. You have decried me a *Jezebel* once already, sir. I am not such a fool to forgive a man who thinks *this* an apology.'

'I do not mean to insult you, dear Maria.' *Lord!* How she hated it when he called her that. 'You would have made a very good politician in another life.'

'Well, you do insult me if you will insist upon saying *that.*'

'Yes,' he smiled. Maria did not return his smile. 'It is not so easy having the eyes of the nation watch your every deed and the history books at the ready to immortalise your every mistake. Christ forgive me, Maria!' He looked down at the book in his hands. 'You must know I did not mean you any harm. You are as dear to me as a sister! Stress can turn a man quite deranged. Jane has left our home for God knows how long and will not speak to me at all. I was a man unhinged with stress and undone by foul drink that I shall never again in my whole life touch – upon my honour! Believe me. Pity me. Forgive me, Maria.'

'I do,' Maria replied with a softened, blinking stare.

'You must say the words. Say you will forgive me, Maria. Have another fool indebted to your angelic mercy, your divine absolution, and say you will forgive your wretch of a brother!'

Richard differed not so much from his younger brothers as Maria had thought. Officious declarations ran blood-deep. And Maria never differed in her resignation to forgive any who asked for her mercy. Perhaps the only constancy in Maria's character, aside from her absolute inconsistency, was her willingness to resign all retribution of man to her God.

Maria gave her words of forgiveness, staring all the while at the door, hoping desperately that Mr Jackson might grow impatient and interrupt her disquiet. Richard took her chin gently between his thumb and forefinger, drawing her reluctant face towards his.

'I am so very sorry, dear Maria,' he said, leaning towards her and pressing a horrid, tender kiss to the cheek she could not withdraw quickly enough.

A little flood tumbled over the dam of Maria's blinking eyes. 'Would you please ask Mr Jackson and Gilly to return? I think I was mistaken; I am much too tired to be read to.'

As might be imagined, Maria did not take very well to the thought of Mr Jackson's quitting Brighton, and, as had been anticipated by her husband, the lady was absolutely insistent that she would attend him. Richard was far too wary of further upsetting Maria to risk taking any great pains in convincing her contrariwise. Mr Jackson took the line of pretending to be swayed by his wife's insistence that she was well enough to travel, although he could not disguise his alarm when Maria resorted to declaring,

'I do not care if I die! Even if the jolt of a single bump in the road should end my life this morning, I insist, I absolutely insist on attending Mr Jackson, for I shall surely die of grief if he leaves without me!'

Gilly alone found himself bearing the brunt of Maria's fury. What a sight at eight o'clock the following morning when Gilly was forced to utilise his body as a physical barricade to prevent Maria from entering the carriage with her husband. After crumpling into a heap of weeping, furious, rage upon the floor, and quite without another word, Maria recomposed herself and took up to leave in a hurried walk towards the seafront. Richard had long since taken himself inside, having grown restless and irritated with the crowd of onlookers Maria's one-woman tragedy had garnered. So it was Gilly who pursued the lady who walked towards the sea in her bloodied nightgown with such ardent determination. Fortunately, as was habitual for this young woman, she was wearing no shoes, which, when faced with the obstacle of a pebbled beach, caused her pace to slow significantly.

'Maria...!' he called out at the last leg of his approach.

'Go, Gilly! I do not want you here or your horrible older brother!' she ejaculated under the weight of a weary sigh, throwing a handful of small pebbles at his feet.

Dropping the collection of stones she had in her other hand, Maria burst quite suddenly into a charming laugh. Gilly laughed too. Till her laugh fell away, leaving a horrendous, heartbreaking sob. He held her, and though she closed her eyes, Maria could not fool herself. Gilly's embrace could never be confused for that of Mr Jackson. Gilly was, for one, taller and of a much slighter frame – his arms enrapt too loosely about her, as if he were afraid to break her. Sometimes Mr Jackson would hold Maria so tightly that she felt as if all the sorrow might be squeezed from her body.

'Do not leave me alone with him, promise you will not?' she said in little more than a whisper.

'Who, Maria? *Richard*? What in God's name has he done to you now?'

'Promise me you will not?' she said, and this was all she would say to each repetition of this question.

CHAPTER THIRTY-FIVE

A BRIEF RETURN TO PENNY AND DR PATERSON.

'That is an exceptionally short letter to come from such a thick packet. It is Maria's hand. I know it is. What does she say?' Dr Paterson demanded of Penny as the lady began reading the letter that had, just moments prior, been passed into her hand.

'It is Maria. She says very little, except to ask we return to Brighton, and if we are unable to oblige her in that manner, she asks that you send a letter declaring her well enough to come home to her husband.'

Dr Paterson's answer was, at first, only a tumble in his countenance. He could not attend Maria, and he could not for anything allow Maria to attend her husband, especially as he was in the opposite direction she would have expected to find him. Having sought the assistance of a friend, Dr Paterson had faced no rebuke nor retribution for his being gone from his office for so many days: a favour he had hoped to reserve for a honeymoon with Penny. By the good grace of God she still somehow endeavoured to marry him; in spite of his absolute and recurrent lies, and in spite of his abominable cowardice in communicating the existence of his daughter to Maria in a drunken letter, and in spite of his foul temper on their journey to and from Brighton.

'Does she give any indication that she knows of her mother's predicament?'

'No, none at all,' Penny sighed regretfully. 'It feels a very cruel thing that so many people should lie to her so concurrently and so constantly.'

Whether this was a dive at the good doctor, the man himself knew not. He replied to say that in this particular circumstance, deception was a lesser evil than honesty. Though he acknowledged dishonesty, in general, to be a hurtful and foul practice worthy of any good woman's scorning.

There was a look of defeat on Penny's face. A look that had made itself at home there ever since her discovering the deception of the man who engaged both her heart and her future felicity. Maria's ready forgiveness of Mr Jackson's many misgivings had bewildered Penny profoundly, a little less so now. Dr Paterson was not the man she had thought herself to know, but he was the man whom she loved. 'Have you any clue as to her poor mother's whereabouts?'

'I have not a thing more than I had two days ago.'

'Devil take that man's pride!' Penny answered.

'Devil take *him*, I dare say,' joined her doctor.

When the pair had arrived late in the evening at Mrs Harrington's cottage near Dulwich, Dr Paterson had waited for little more than half a syllable to be uttered by the door-opening half-sleeping servant before pushing past and demanding to see Maria's mother.

'Oh, but she is gone, sir.'

'Where has she gone!'

The servant surely did not know. Nobody in the cottage knew a thing of where Mrs Harrington had gone.

'Go wake Mrs Froggett for me. She must know something. If anybody knows something, it will be her!'

'Oh, but she is gone too, sir!' replied the servant, looking fearful of the young doctor's wild behaviour. 'Beg your pardon, Dr Paterson, but if anybody here might know their whereabouts, it should be you and Miss Penny. Does not Miss Maria – excuse me, sir – Mrs Jackson write to you both awful regularly?'

'What, for God's sake, would that signify!' his rage replied.

'Well, they are gone to join Miss Maria – excuse me, sir – Mrs Jackson on her holidays, are they not?'

'No, no, they are not! Who told you it was so?'

'Mrs Harrington and Mrs Froggett themselves, sir. A few days ago, a man came from Bedford Square to speak with Mrs Harrington and two hours or so later, she and Mrs Froggett were off in an open-top carriage belonging to Mr Harrington most delighted to be joining their young lady on her travels abroad.'

Neighbours had been interviewed the following morning, local innkeepers too, but nobody knew a thing, and after half a day of their investigations, Dr Paterson and Penny were forced to hand over their task to the doctor's man Phillip, who was, at present, riding about with his enquiries on the main route northbound.

'Is there not a little note or scribbled address to me within the packet?' the doctor asked Penny, who was now replacing the letter.

'No. There are a few other scribbles, as you might call them, but I am sorry to say she has only written to me, sir. When I have read them, then I shall share all I have learnt, and we might both, I hope, be assured of her promising state of health and mind.'

A selection of the aforementioned scribbles, written by Maria and sent to Penny:

'Did I tell you what an indescribable comfort it was to have your sweet face beside me in the depths of the most wretched days of my life – did I tell you that already, my dear? If I know my cousin as well as I think I do (though you must realise I do not consider myself, at present, to know him very well at all), I anticipate a negative on both counts of my other letter. Do not fear disappointing me with a reply of negatives. And if I know you as well as I think I do, my love, then I suppose you to be torn quite in two wishing to return to me in Brighton.'

'Allow this thread to sew you together again: I insist that you do not come to me, you must, you absolutely must remain with my cousin, I shall not have you attend me at all. There is no man so in need of his wife more than one who is a victim of his own misdeeds. And though you are not yet his wife, I hope very much you will soon be. Certainly, I was quite terrifyingly ill, but I heard still your confession to me that you could not bring yourself to harbour ill-will towards my cousin for his secretiveness with you. And in that, I think you are right, my love. You are, though, misguided in your loyal friendship to resent him particularly for his deception towards me. I forgive him. Be pleased to read any and all my thoughts to him, but if you do not, tell him at least that I forgive him it all.'

'I am very fatigued, my dear. I must break off for now.'

'Will you do me a little favour if you have time? Would you pay a visit to Russell Square, on pretences of whatever pleases you, and as certain how importantly occupied Mr Jackson is? I sent a man with a letter for him the day he left Brighton and have received no reply yet. If his business in town ought not to be disturbed, then I shall not. (Forgive, pray, the necessary teasing to follow) If I were to communicate to Mr Jackson the wretched misery that has followed me here, and the peculiar daily circumstances that keep me in such misery, I have not a doubt in all the world that he would ride to be with me all night without stopping once to rest. To contradict my earlier self I shall say that you should not share that last part with my cousin.'

'Cont. - I am to be gone to Crawley to-morrow, my dear. Do not tell my cousin that neither, for he will not approve. I have just this evening received a note from Mr Jackson. It speaks nothing of my (now two) letters to him and is so brief I must only surmise that he must be kept very, very busy. Poor man. To contradict myself again, I think you should not go to visit him. I want only for his permission to travel home. But, on second thinking, perhaps you might visit him still and only tell him that is all that I want.'

'This has been three days in the writing, so I shall send it off to you now, my dear. Not as thick a packet as you might hope to receive, and for that, accept the sincerest and most ardent of apologies from your,

Maria Jackson.'

CHAPTER THIRTY-SIX

IN WHICH MARIA LEARNS A GREAT DEAL ABOUT GILLY.

It is necessary to retract a little in the narrative to understand why Maria, who was, by everybody's instruction, bedbound, came to be travelling twenty miles to Crawley. The day of this plan being agreed, Mr Harrington had mistakenly been admitted entrance to visit his daughter. The young lady was, at this moment in time, most deeply asleep, and not one of the two Jackson brothers was to be found in her bedroom. Knowing his daughter to be a girl with such an unnatural affection for the sleeping state that she might have slumbered happily undisturbed through a siege of the Civil War; Mr Harrington temporarily gave up his scheme of applying pressure to his daughter's tender affections for her mother and was, instead, to be found by Mr Richard Jackson riffling through Maria's things.

Why Richard had undertaken to enter Maria's room alone, when he knew her to be sleeping, was to be accounted for, when Gilly would later question him, by the original first edition of *Clarissa* the gentleman had taken such pains in procuring, and which had, that very hour, arrived in Brighton.

'He said he came in only to put the book by my bed, and I believe him.'

'Do you really, Maria?' had answered Gilly.

She did. Richard had been extraordinarily constant in his kindness to her since his arrival in Brighton. He read to her for hours and hours every day till his voice grew hoarse, would procure any fancy or whim of her demand, and seemed, in his conduct and countenance, a very sorry man. Though, three or four times a day, he would do something wrong, something that, if asked, Maria could not have articulated why or how it was a wrong thing, but which felt to be wrong all the same. When he took her hand, he would always press a little too warmly and linger just a moment too long. Maria was certain she had seen him, on several occasions, cast a gluttonous and prurient eye over her form. And she was now secured in his vocabulary as *dear Maria*. It was not a name she could ever wish to hear from his lips. *Little Breweress* would have been insurmountably superior.

Owing to Mr Harrington's insistence that Maria was *his* daughter and *he* could question her as often as *he* liked and at whatever length *he* pleased and that *he* certainly had every right to look through her things all which were paid for with *his money*, Maria was eventually awoken by an argument between her two brothers-in-law and her father; finding the latter, unfortunately, squeezing her still tender arm tightly.

'Would you let go, Papa? You are really quite hurting my arm,' said she, not weakly but not loud enough to be heard over the various expostulations. 'Papa, you are hurting my arm!' Still, she was not heard.

'For the love of Christ, let go of her arm, man! You are hurting her!' cried Richard in the awful, terrifying shout he so often employed. Maria wondered if he felt all the irony of his words; she certainly did.

Mr Harrington would not let go. Maria was *his* daughter, and *he* could hold her arm however *he* wished. And he would not be instructed in how to handle his daughter by a man who had no claim to possession of her. Maria held her breath. Mr Harrington saw this and, without pause or consideration, hit his daughter very hard across the face. A moment passed before a trickle of blood began to fall from her nose.

Though it is of little relevance to the story, it is perhaps a particular worth briefly noting that Maria's maid Sarah had long since been sent for and was attending to the care and health of her young lady in Brighton. On the morning of their excursion to Crawley, Sarah's assistance would not satisfy, and the maid was sent to fetch Mr Gilly Jackson to aid Maria in a way in which nobody else in Brighton would be able. Gilly arrived in Maria's bedroom to find her studying a heap of gowns laid out on the bed.

'It has been so long since I have gone out of doors, I really do not know what to wear,' she began. He thought he understood what question this remark would lead to, and, preparing himself to give his opinion on the matter, Gilly was bemused to be questioned with, 'Which do you think your brother would want me to wear to-day?'

Though, upon second thought, Gilly reasoned that this was not such an unlikely thing for Maria to say. 'How should I know?' he remarked with a great deal of humour.

'Stick your head outside the window, will you? Mr Jackson always puts his head outside the window to ascertain the climate before deciding what I shall wear.'

Walking smilingly over to the window, Gilly said, 'And does he do this for you every day?'

'Regretfully, when first we were married, as I am sure you recall–' Maria spoke a little louder to compensate for Gilly's head being now situated beyond the window outside, 'Mr Jackson was not as attentive to me as he might have been. Since I returned home after our little disagreement, he has always *always* been so benevolent as to give me his judgement in this respect.'

'And how did you–' pausing that thought, Gilly called loudly, 'It is quite warm again to-day and with very little wind!' As he returned his head inside, the fellow began again, '…and how did you choose what to wear before you were married to my brother?'

'Why, of course, my papa would help me choose.'

'The spotted muslin with the rose petticoat. That would be my choice for to-day, dear Maria. And did your father always insist on choosing your outfits?'

'Insist? Whoever spoke of insisting? I feel you are trying to sink the matter to something it was not. It was a very nice thing, a very pleasant part of our day. Every evening for as long as I can remember, my papa would come to my apartment and choose for me that which I should wear the following morning. Even once he met Pearl when I was seventeen, and he had then much less time for me, *always* he would come and choose my clothes. Unless he was upset with me, or I was upset with him, or I was confined to my apartment–'

'Confined to your apartment?' he interrupted.

Entirely ignoring this, Maria continued, 'It was a nice thing. A very nice thing! Why do you try to sink it to something less pleasant and more sinister?'

'I do not try to sink it, dear Maria. If you say it was a nice thing, then I shall believe you.'

'It was. It was a very nice thing,' she replied, smiling and frowning in equal earnest. 'And when I would stay with my dear grandpapa, he would then choose for me, and my dear, sweet Ralph *he* has always been very obliging with his judgement, and now you may choose for me. It is a nice thing, is it not Gilly?'

'Well, you have, in fact, asked me to choose what I believe my brother would like best.' Seeing her face drop a little, Gilly quickly added with his most charming Jackson smile, 'But it is a very nice thing, dear Maria, a very nice thing indeed.'

Maria was very pleased with this response and, before removing to the antechamber to put on the spotted Muslin and rose petticoat, instructed Gilly towards her dressing table where he might choose his favourite of her perfumes and the bonnet that brought his heart the most joy. Though never wishing to encourage his open affections wrongly, Maria was acutely aware of the kindness of Gilly's attentiveness towards her in Brighton and the respectful brotherliness with which he treated her, despite - in his own words - being so inconsolably in love with her. She could not and would never love him as she loved his brother, but she could, for a few days or a week, at least, give him the intimate charge of her outward appearance. Maria would be, till Mr Jackson returned, a young woman of entirely Gilly's design.

They would be setting off for Crawley after some short elapse of time. That is already known. What has not been yet explained is why they were going. After Mr Harrington's last encounter with Maria, the Jackson brothers had both determined that it was imperative to remove Sidney's wife from Brighton till her father was gone, her mother was found, or their brother had returned. Gilly had a friend who lived in Crawley – well, a little more than a friend – she was mother to three of his four children. His youngest child, a red-haired absolute doll of an infant, presently resided with her mother in Venice. He wrote to this friend to explain only that – for very good reasons, but reasons he could not very well explain – he needed to trick his sister-in-law into a short trip abroad. And would she be so good as to pretend herself in desperate need of Gilly's assistance with the children for a few days.

'Do you know,' Maria remarked, rejoining him in her bedroom now dressed exactly as Gilly had desired, 'I think I have known nobody in my whole life to grow so much in my estimations over the course of our acquaintance.'

'Indeed, do my muslin choosing qualifications truly recommend me so well to you?'

'Oh, not that,' said she, mirroring his smile once she realised he had been teasing her. 'It is a very good thing that you visit your children so often and whenever their mother should be in want of your company or assistance.'

Still smiling, and now giving her the bottle of perfume he had chosen, he replied, 'Did you really think me so very base, when first we met, that I would be the sort of man to pay no notice to my children?'

'I did not imagine, when first we met, that you, being an *unmarried* man, would have any children at all, let alone *four*!' Having dabbed her skin delicately with his chosen scent, Maria regave the bottle to Gilly and continued, 'I would have judged you very severely for it then, but you must remember I was a very proud, sanctimonious, horrid little thing when first we met.'

'Far from it, Maria.'

'Well, that is how I remember myself. I was a very free and ready judger of others. But I think very well of you now, Gilly, though, for your own amusement, you would have me believe you a depraved wretch. And seeing you act such good faith by the mother of your children – it has made me think very, *very* well of you.' Maria left a silence in which Gilly might implant a joke at his own expense or hers. He did no such thing. He only looked at her, very intently and very silently. 'Come,' she said, shoving his chest to shake off this fit of seriousness, 'I am barely half-dressed, and Lord knows Richard will send up for me the moment it turns ten; and I have still no bonnet, no shoes, and I know not at all if you desire me to take a bag.'

He did desire she took a bag. And the moment they left the lodgings, Maria passed it to Gilly to hold for the entirety of their journey.

CHAPTER THIRTY-SEVEN

IN WHICH TWO OF THE JACKSON BROTHERS AND MARIA ARRIVE IN CRAWLEY.

Miss Stapleton, the mother of Gilly's children, was not how Maria had imagined her; she had expected to be greeted in Crawley by a young, giddy, hapless creature, but instead, she was introduced to a pretty gentlewoman of her middling forties who appeared sensible, steady, and intelligent. The three boys (aged ten, nine and seven) looked each so much like their father that Maria could have, and did, release a charming little laugh when first she saw them. The cottage in which this darling family lived was modest but handsome, much like Miss Stapleton herself, and with a few rearrangements and Gilly's insistence of sleeping on the couch in the sitting-room, there was room enough for the three visitors to stay.

Dinner, also at the insistence of Gilly, was taken at a private room of a local inn. They were joined by the children, perturbing Richard, who claimed it was a strange scheme. Though he had promised Maria he would never touch the stuff again, he drank a significant quantity that evening. With every glass, he grew more contemptful towards Miss Stapleton and her children. Though the young ones did make for a less relaxed and far more chaotic meal, Maria was utterly delighted with the evening. Gilly was wonderfully animated and continually silly, seeming never happier than to be in the company of his three miniatures.

A pleasant imagining filled Maria's head, and she was soon quite resolved that she, her cousin and (his new wife) Penny would take Ralph's dear Eliza to a dinner out at least once a month. Maria wondered what Ralph did when he visited Eliza, where he took her, what they talked of, if they ever talked of her, she wondered if he gave her a generous pocket-allowance – she was certain he did – and if he took much concern in her school employments – she was certain of that too. Maria had not spoken a word of Eliza to her cousin, but then, neither had he, not since his letter.

The young Mrs Jackson, despite her protestations that she would very happily share, was absolutely forced to take Miss Stapleton's bedroom alone for the duration of the stay. Retiring to her room after dinner with the excuse of wishing to write a letter, but really just wanting for a moment to herself, Maria sent down a short note to Gilly, it read as follows: '*Come, choose for me again before I join you all downstairs.*' In fewer than five minutes, he was to her door.

The nature of this scene need not be repeated, but it passed with many shared smiles, and Gilly, being more interested in the fashions, and utterly delighted by Maria's note, took to this role far quicker than his brother had done. Maria complimented his delightful children and their kind, pretty mother, finding them all absolutely charming. 'I have never, in all my life, seen a man so adoring of his children, nor children so worthy of being adored. I am sure England has never produced a happier little family!' When Maria asked why he did not marry Miss Stapleton, he answered to say, 'Because she did not wish to be married, and neither did he.' An answer not much to Maria's understanding or satisfaction. No sooner had Gilly left than Miss Stapleton herself was knocking on the door, apologising for her only maid being otherwise employed, and offering her own assistance.

'Oh Heavens, no! You needn't do a thing for me! I am quite happy to care for myself for a few days.' The lady was invited into the room by Maria, was very obliged, and was shortly asked the same question that had been asked of Gilly some twenty minutes earlier. 'Lord! I know it is mightily presumptuous, and you must, *must* forgive me for it. It is only that you seem a very happy family when you are together, and I do not understand at all why you would not marry?'

'He offered, but I did not really wish to marry him, and he did not really wish to marry me. His father would never have approved of it, which would have left us both very poor and very miserable.'

'But I am told by my husband that Gilly inherited a very good estate from their mother's bachelor uncle last year.' This was true. Gilly had been the only person of that family to continue a correspondence with the old man and was rewarded with an inheritance that made him independent enough to marry whomsoever he pleased. 'So, you might marry now with no consequence at all.'

253

Miss Stapleton explained with a patient smile that, proven by the age of their youngest child, it had been a very long time since there had been anything but the closest friendship between her and Gilly. They neither wanted to marry each other.

'And what of little Giulia's mother? The lady who lives in Italy, I have seen a miniature of her, she is very, *very* pretty, and Gilly always speaks so fondly of her. Why does he not marry her and bring them both to live with him here?'

'She is a Catholic.'

'Oh, yes, of course,' Maria replied in a feathery voice. 'Though she might repent, for the good of her soul and the happiness of her little family!'

'She is still married to somebody else.'

'Oh, dear! Yes, I see.'

Realising that she had been quite impertinent and perhaps even a little impolite in these questions, Maria sat in silence, staring at her twiddling hands.

'I was, I will admit, very pained for him when you chose to marry his brother and not him. Though I am sure you had your reasons. Sidney Jackson comes here sometimes with Gilly; he is in possession of great charm and is perhaps more careful in the opinion others should make of him.'

'Pained for who?!' Maria said, crossing her arms and sounding a jot angry – though she was only feeling very confused.

'Oh, forgive me, I did not mean to embarrass you. It is not my place to ask,' Miss Stapleton said hurriedly and with a sorry countenance, standing as if ready to remove herself from the bedroom.

'No, you mistake me,' Maria replied, pulling her companion back to her seat. 'You may ask me anything you want. I simply do not understand you. Why do you think I chose Mr Jackson over Gilly? I did not meet Gilly till at least a month after I was married.'

'Oh,' replied Miss Stapleton, colouring again rapidly and standing once more, 'perhaps I am remembering another occurrence. Forgive me. I know not what I say.'

Though Maria considered herself a fool, she was savvy enough to understand that there was something more in what Miss Stapleton had said. 'No, tell me, please,' she pleaded, pulling on the lady's arm again. 'I am not cross, nor offended, nor anything like that at all, upon my faith I am not, I only wish to understand you. What makes you say that I chose Mr Jackson over Gilly? Something must have given you that impression? And I must, *I must* understand it!'

A little further mortified conversation and the recovery of a box of letters explained it all to Maria. The following excerpts have been taken from letters addressed to Miss Stapleton from Gilly Jackson from the period of the previous October till January of that present year:

10th October:

'I have extracted from Sidney the name of this church, but he will not allow me to visit and give this Miss Harrington an address to which she might send any news of a new Jackson. Her cousin is an old college acquaintance and, he says, might easily discover where to send his correspondence should it be necessary. He forbade me going, but I shall go anyway, which he ought to expect. I am most curious to see the girl and moreover cannot understand my brother's villainy in omitting to give any hint of a means by which the poor creature could communicate with him. He is and has always been, for I am not deceived by my brotherly affection, an unfeeling varlet when it comes to women, but I have never known him to act so contrary to the most rudimentary points of decency and honour. Tell me, do you think I ought to seek this girl out?'

25th October:

'I found her with little trouble. A gentleman at the back pointed her out to me. She is a loud conversationalist, so I hear half of everything she says. She is very pretty and very affable and strangely dotes on every word of her cousin. There is no evidence of any new young Jackson, but then it is far too early for any of that. When she is not speaking, I have noticed often that she will stare aimlessly and look very sad, though smiling still – I wish I could know what thoughts troubled her mind. I have visited this church twice now, and, despite my brother's contrariwise instructions, I am resolved to give her an address should she need it.'

12th November:

'I have found myself, three times each week, at this damned church, each time resolved that I will hand her a packet with an address and a note of explanation, but three times each week I return home with the packet in my pocket. Every visit, she appears a little more lost in her own ruminations and decidedly more despondent. Her cousin was not there this evening, so I took the opportunity of sitting beside her, and I spoke with her for thirty minutes at the end of the service. I am half in love with the heavenly creature, I swear, I have never in all my life spoken to such a girl!'

20th November:

'I hear from dear Miss Harrington that her poor cousin is taken ill with a cold. Very sorry for him, but not sorry for me, who has now such an opportunity of talking with this affecting creature. She is in every respect an angel, a perfect angel. I will, as you encourage, give her the packet on my next visit. Surely by now, as so many months have concluded since that day, there would be some outward symptom if the girl were of that condition. If she has been brought to such a state by my brother and he would not own it – oh, but now I get ahead of myself! At the next, I shall give Miss Harrington the packet and inform her that she has a friend in me.'

27th November:

'I will be a day or two delayed in coming to you and the children. I have been lately driven to such distraction that half a bottle was all it took to convince my tongue to betray my heart: I confessed to my brother the whole of it a few nights ago. I am now absolutely resolved on confessing myself to Miss Harrington and, if she be not displeased, though I can hardly bear to tease and flatter myself with the notion, if she offers the least encouragement, I really would not be surprised should I set my liberty at her feet and ask for the angel's hand. Sidney is, as you might imagine, very vexed with me and appears most suddenly concerned for his paternal status with this girl, though he has not cared a jot for it these past months.'

When Maria put down the last letter, Miss Stapleton said, 'He returned to us here without having spoken to you, for Sidney had insisted that he was allowed to determine whether or not you expected a child and make some amends to you first. We heard not a thing from his brother all December, and Gilly returned to London a few days after Christmas more resolved than ever to attend one of your meetings and confess his affections to you. But see this letter here, this is the next I heard from him, to tell me that you were engaged to Sidney and that Gilly would be gone to Italy for at least a month to meet his daughter whose birth had just occurred. When he returned, he would not speak on the matter. And for many months, I assumed that you were expecting a child by Sidney, and that is why he had married you in such haste and secrecy.'

'I do not understand,' remarked Maria in a voice that was more a whisper than anything else. 'I absolutely do not remember meeting Gilly at my church. I remember very little of those months. I do not even recall Ralph's being ill. I was insupportably depressed in my spirits that winter. Perhaps, *perhaps* if I think of it, I remember speaking with an unfamiliar gentleman, young and well-dressed. But I do not at all remember it being Gilly. Good God! He must have visited Russell Square expecting to be reintroduced to a former acquaintance, but instead, I greeted him as a perfect stranger.'

'I see,' replied Miss Stapleton looking concerned and rather shocked. 'Do not you remember his address to you after Christmas? He was so determined to speak with you.'

'I would not have seen him at all after Christmas, that I know for certain. For my father never did allow me to attend my own church over Christmas time and insisted we were always at St. James's where he says every one of consequence goes to pray. I did not attend my own church again till January. I would not; I *could not* have seen Gilly in that time, I am sure of it.'

To recall the particulars of all the dialogue that occurred in this homely cottage that evening would, and *could* fill an entire book itself, so we must allow the following summary to be sufficient: at length, Miss Stapleton left Maria and, at the latter's direct request, sent up Gilly to her room. Maria was hysterical to the point of near unintelligent speech by the time Gilly entered the room. All she could say to him – as she burst explosively into sobs at the sight of him – was, 'Dear Gilly, you have truly loved me all this time and not said a thing of it!' Confused and starting a little, Gilly replied to remind Maria that he had told her of his being in love with her many, many times during the course of their friendship. The momentum of her heaving tears grew too strong, too fast; she could hardly breathe, talking was not an idea at all; all Maria could manage was to point at the heap of open letters on the bed and crumble into an elbow chair by the window. He perused the letters and, after very little time, realised at what she hinted. Gilly sat beside her and took her hand.

'It was true – he would not deny any of it – in fact, he had loved her likely before he had even set eyes on her – Sidney's affecting letters about this woman, Miss Harrington, and his unfeeling disposal of her had brought Gilly home to England early for the explicit purpose of seeking her out. He had gone to her church twice after Christmas to look for her, and just when he was resolved to seek her whereabouts elsewhere, he received a note from Sidney to say that he had settled terms with Mr Harrington and had the man's blessing to make his addresses to the daughter – it was all but a done deal.'

When she asked why he had not told her this, not spoken anything of their former acquaintance, he replied that he had at first thought she said nothing of the matter owing to embarrassment or prudence. He had wished to save her blushes or uncomfortable conversations with his brother. With the passing of time, he came to believe and accept that Maria did not, in fact, remember him at all. Every remembrance of her relationship with Gilly since marrying Mr Jackson was now, in Maria's mind, entirely changed by this knowledge. Somehow, and to the amazement of both Maria and Gilly, she regained and held composure during this conversation to the degree that could almost be called rational. A new revelation would change that:

'*Why?* I do not understand why or how he could have behaved so cruelly to you?' This was all the lady could say for a short while.

'I cannot fully blame my brother. He was not himself when first you knew him; you must understand, he was not himself, dear Maria.'

Mr Sidney Jackson had not been himself. He had, of course, not been himself in the sense that he had adopted, when it suited him, the persona of Mr King, but greater than that, he was a very bitter and a very angry man. Two months before first meeting Maria at Mr Garcia's talk on the Roman Empire, Sidney Jackson's daughter died of a fever brought on by the measles; she had been eight months, three weeks and four days old, and Sidney had met her a total of twelve times during her life. And despite, prior to her birth, swearing that he did not and would not care to do anything more than pay her mother a necessary stipend, Sidney Jackson had fallen more in love with this child every moment he passed in her presence.

'But he told me that he does not have any children.'

'He does not. Not anymore, Maria.'

258

The last day Sidney Jackson passed with his daughter was the day she died. He paid for but did not attend her funeral. He would not answer a single question about her; he would not talk of her at all. Her name had been Grace Angelica Jackson. He had not been obliged to give his daughter his name, but upon first meeting this infant, he had decided she must be a Jackson, whatever the consequences to his reputation. This had appeased the mother and the grandfather of the child, though he did not do it for their sake. He had never once visited his daughter's grave.

'He was so absolutely miserable that we all worried he might do himself some tragic mischief without intervention. Richard, believing relentless toil to be the best remedy for grief, suggested to Sidney that he could shortly find him some seat in Parliament. Of course, I never believed Sidney would agree, and he did not, at first. Richard swore that, should Sidney submit, he *personally* would pay off Sidney's forever mounting gambling debts and convince our father to increase the pitiful allowance with which he had been left. By degrees, he changed his mind. Richard came good on his promise. Our father did not. It was too late by then, for he was already Sidney Jackson MP and was more foul-tempered and hot-headed than ever.'

The outward scene which was to follow this confession should be obvious to those who have become well acquainted with Maria's despondent fits of hysteria. We shall take an interest in the scene underway in Maria's mind: she knew not what to think. Was she not guilty of being the most awful, prying wife? Forcing from a childless father tormented by grief – when she had received that letter from Ralph – the words, '*I have no children.*' How she must have shattered his heart entirely anew.

The lady could say nothing more. Her poor husband had lost two daughters in one year, and Maria was entirely and singularly to blame for the loss of the child that would have brought happiness to the broken heart of Mr Jackson. And from her own daughter, she had robbed the opportunity of having the most indulgent, the kindest and fairest father that could be found in a thousand thousand worlds. And poor, blameless Gilly had too been a victim of his brother's grief. It had been *he* who had taken pains to confirm the consequences of Mr Jackson's actions. It had been *he* who had first loved her, *he* who – without his brother's duplicity – might very well have been her husband, *her* Mr Jackson. Maria could bear it no longer. Could bear the duality of this thought no longer.

'Please, Gilly, do not try to stop me,' she whispered into his ear.

He did try but was not successful. Maria passed quickly into the oblivion of willing suffocation, and he caught her before she slumped from the chair onto the floor. Gilly put Dear Maria in Miss Stapleton's bed and sat at her side the entire night.

CHAPTER THIRTY-EIGHT

A SORT OF 'FRENCH EXIT' FROM THE AUTHOR WHO HATES GOODBYES.

The Jackson brothers and Maria only remained in Crawley a few days, for they were, two days after arriving, hurried back by a letter from Mr Jackson to say that he was returned to Brighton and very solicitous to be reassured of the health and happiness of his wife. The morning after their conversation, Gilly and Maria were quizzed at breakfast by Richard once the three were alone, 'What had he been doing in her bedroom? He had not left till the morning.'

Before Gilly could utter half a word, Maria had begun her reply, 'If Mr Jackson would like to know what we were doing, then I would be very pleased to account for every moment that passed between Gilly and me last night. But as *you* are not my husband, I really cannot see that it is any concern of yours, Richard.'

'Careful, Maria,' he replied, in a tone that was clearly intended to remind her to whom she spoke.

Maria cared nothing for his tone nor the cross face he was pulling, and said, touching Richard softly on the shoulder as she got up from the table, 'Why? What do you threaten, *Brother*? Will you hit me? Or perhaps you will almost break my arm trying to force yourself upon me again?' The two brothers sat in silence at the table, and Maria excused herself on account of having promised to go on a walk with Miss Stapleton and her boys that morning. When she returned to the house a few hours later, Richard was on his return to London.

'Do not tell Mr Jackson. I am rather afraid he will kill Richard should he ever find out,' Maria said to Gilly when the two were alone in the sitting-room that evening. He held her arm in his hand, stroking and examining the last echoes of Richard's demon grip.

262

'Oh, absolutely! Without a doubt, he will kill Richard,' Gilly replied, with the sort of smile and affecting gaze that made Maria not sure how serious he was being. 'No, truly, dear Maria. You know how many guns Sidney keeps in your house! You should not tell him, at least not when Richard is within a hundred miles of your husband.'

Maria, it seems, had known nothing of how many guns Mr Jackson kept in the house.

The return journey to Brighton was much the same distance as the outbound journey to Crawley. But it felt very much shorter to Gilly and Maria. She had, without saying a word, fashioned a pillow from his jacket, placed it upon his lap, and – laying across the seats – rested her head there the entire journey. He played with her hair while she pretended to sleep. That was the first and last carriage journey Gilly and Maria would take alone together. Before alighting, Maria took his face in her hands and, with a little flare of wildness in her eyes, said to him, 'I could have loved you very well, Gilly Jackson.' Here she paused for a moment, taking in his lovely face. 'And you must know, I *do* love you very well, Gilly.'

He looked absolutely delighted and unfathomably sad, replying only to say that if she did not mind, he would take a walk of the beach alone. Maria wanted to walk with him. She could not bear to think of him being without company and desired earnestly to ease his grief. But she could not have said a thing of any consequence; it felt as if anything she could say should only make him feel worse. And she was achingly, *achingly* desperate to see Mr Jackson. Returned to her lodgings, Maria was astounded to find Pearl and Mr Harrington in the sitting-room.

'Whatever are you doing here?' Maria asked Pearl, taking the lady's hands in her own.

'You know how you young women can be, Maria. Pearl was thrown into a little fit of hysteria with impending motherhood. To be sure, it can affect you young women very strangely. But she is returned to her senses now and–'

Interrupting her father, Maria said fiercely, 'I am sure I did not ask *you*, Papa!' Leaning towards Pearl, she continued, 'We can speak of it alone later.'

'Oh, there is no need for that, Maria,' the lady replied with her familiar watering eyes and inflexion of confusion. 'Your father is right. I was just taken with a strange humour. To be sure, these things can affect young women quite profoundly.'

'And very strangely,' added Mr Harrington

'And very strangely,' repeated Pearl with a happy smile.

'Where is Mr Jackson?' Maria said blankly after a moment of gazing in silence at her father and turning to speak with the housemaid who attended them presently. Mr Jackson was upstairs, in Maria's bedroom. She found him staring at the seafront from the window. 'I am sorry I did not come downstairs to greet you, dear Maria. Your father has already driven me absolutely–' Mr Jackson did not finish this sentence because Maria had, by now, kissed him already four times, and he had absolutely given up all hopes of continuing that thought.

After a few moments more of that, the young lady said in a voice barely audible, 'I know it all.'

'*What* do you know, Maria?' replied her husband, fearful how much Mr Harrington had said of Pearl's return or the threats Maria's father had employed to secure it.

'I despise lying to you, Mr Jackson. It eats away at all my happiness if ever I am forced to do so. I must say it all. I must before I lose my confidence.' She then fell upon a fervent and somewhat fearful speech with great rapidity, 'I know about Gilly. I know that he visited me at Dean Street. I know that he had loved me then and wanted to marry me and that you tricked him out of it. I know about your poor, *poor* daughter – forgive me speaking of her, but I must say it all. I know that you had owed thousands and thousands to men for lost card games. And I did not slip into the sea. I fell. I fell because I was holding my breath, mortified and enraged at Mrs Attwood vilifying you as some tyrant husband – I am sure I hate the woman! And Richard *did* hit me at Hurlough, and it was *he* who caused that awful bruising to my arm when he locked me in his office because I stupidly told him about Penny and Ralph, knowing it would anger him. And it did. He seemed quite determined to have me – had we not been disturbed by Mr Ashby, I believe he would have had his way. I was so terrified that for much of the ordeal, I did not a thing to stop him.' Maria's last words were so woven with little gasps and stifled sobs that they were rendered barely coherent.

Mr Jackson said nothing. He appeared entirely motionless. Recovering herself a little, Maria added, 'I have never at all understood why you married me. But I *am* always, and *will always* be very glad that you did.' The smallest absolute speck of a tear drifted into one of his eyes, causing Maria to exclaim, 'Dear God! Mr Jackson, I am terrified that I have quite broken your heart.' For a long while, for an excruciatingly long while, Mr Jackson did not say a thing. And his only motion was to raise his hand to his mouth. *Oh dear, Maria. Whatever have you said…*

'You, *Miss Contrary*,' he said, taking her hand, '*you* are singularly and entirely responsible for its repair. I know I do not say it, but I do, Maria, you must know that *I do*.'

Perplexed for only a moment, she quickly responded, 'Do you mean to say that you love me, Mr Jackson?'

'Yes,' replied he, in that implausibly will-breaking way. 'That is exactly what I mean to say.'

Damn, damn his handsome devil voice!

For the following hour, Maria was industriously employed attempting to convince Mr Jackson that she was entirely recovered from the symptoms of her recent tragic misery, and there was no need for his avoiding her bed. The gentleman's opinion was not the same as that of his wife. '*Why*,' Maria lamented to herself, '*must he be at this arrant cavilling again!*' For, you see, the fellow had once more insisted, it was not only the bodily recovery of his lady that weighed so heavy on his mind. Not for her many adoring sentiments, lamb-like trickeries, nor affecting sobs could Mr Jackson be counter-convinced. 'Oh, you must dry your tears, dear Maria. If only you knew how you inflame my hubris more with each of these wonderful despondent performances, I think you would feign a far less severe disappointment.' He had said this in the hope of making Maria smile, and that she did.

That evening, Maria suggested her husband go out with his brother. And so it was not till the following day that anything of Pearl's return was spoken. When it was spoken of, Mr Jackson, choosing to follow the good example of his wife, told the whole truth – well – almost the whole truth. Little of it needs must be explained, but the short of it is this: Mr Jackson, when he found Pearl in Swanage, had quickly reached an agreement with the lady; she would return and remain at Bedford Square if this child, whatever the sex, be promised an annuity of 500£ a year that would be theirs at the age of one-and-twenty or upon Mr Harrington's death if that event should precede. Mr Jackson had told Mr Harrington and Maria that Pearl had also insisted the terms of his and Maria's marriage be redrawn. This was to ensure that in the case of infidelity, neglect, cruelty or murder, Mr Jackson would forfeit *any* claim to Maria's inheritance. Of course, Pearl had insisted no such thing, though she would never contradict the claim.

'That is a very strange thing for her to insist upon. Very strange. But I suppose she does not know you as I do. It was very, very good of you to agree to it all, Mr Jackson. I am sure, if she could understand, my mother would be eternally thankful that you would make such an enormous concession to return her safety and comfort!'

Maria's mother had been, the entire time, at Bedford Square.

House of Commons

Wednesday, September 1st

[Petition from London for the release of a body held at The Egyptian Hall] Mr Sidney Jackson presented a new petition from the members of the Wesleyan church on Dean Street, who claim the preserved body of a boy slave is being unlawfully held and exhibited for profit at the aforementioned premises. The petitioners renewed their expressions of great hope that the issue would be taken into the consideration of the House on grounds of both legal and moral interest. The hon. member trusted in the good judgement of the God-fearing men elected to serve in Parliament to end this indignity and see the boy buried in consecrated ground.

Mr Fowell Buxton saw no reason why a short bill could not be introduced. Mr John Ashby, who had previously rejected the validity of the petition, gave a short speech in support of Mr Sidney Jackson's aims.

Mr Richard Jackson objected to the petition presented by the hon. member, and read aloud a letter from the Prime Minister [who could not be present] which stated his opinion that any further discussion of the matter would be a wilful abuse of both the time and patience of parliamentarians, who had issues of far greater significance to attend to, than the private matter of the burial of a boy who had died at least half a century ago.

Petition Withdrawn.

Births, Marriages & Deaths

Birth – At Bedford Square, 13th Nov, the lady of Mr Harrington, a daughter, Theodora.

Celebration of the Marriage of Sir Walter's Daughter

On the morning of Friday, 3ʳᵈ March, Tumbridge-Wells, the country residence of Sir Walter M Rose, was in a great state of excited bustle and anticipation in the hour preceding the marriage ceremony. The Very Reverend Doctor Miller was first to arrive, shortly followed by the bridegroom Mr Guilielmus Jackson Esq. who was accompanied by his younger brother Mr Sidney Jackson Esq., M.P. and that brother's wife [who is said to expect their first child in late spring] in a chaise and four. The gentlemen wore fashionable suits of crimson and the young wife an elegant emerald gown of Brussels lace.

Half an hour saw significant growth in the crowd outside the church and the arrival of Sir Walter M Rose, Governor Sidney Jackson, Mr Richard Jackson Esq., M.P. and his wife. At exactly eleven o'clock, Miss Rose arrived, carried in a very new and modern chaise [a wedding gift from Governor Jackson], wearing a simple gown of white satin that looked more becoming and elegant upon her person than a more luxurious gown might appear on any other young lady.

At five o'clock, the bride and bridegroom quit the festivities to set off in their new carriage for the gentleman's ancestral home in Windsor, where they will remain for a few days before travelling to their new marital home [Mr Jackson's estate in Surrey]. We are certain our readers will join us in wishing a happy and prosperous marriage to this young couple, who are, in every respect, most equally and suitably matched.

267

A letter to Miss Penny Stuart from Mrs Maria Jackson later that year (early summer):

'I am, thank our Lord and saviour, much recovered and removed from the perils of an evil fever. How I hate being ill, and it was particularly torturous owing to my cousin insisting that I must be kept isolated, not only in another room but another house entirely to my love! Sidney, it seems, in these two weeks, has entirely forgotten me and now has eyes for the rather more ample bosom of the young widow Mrs Fairway who, I hear from Sarah, very quickly took my place at Russell Square. I wrote a scribbled, tear-stained letter to my husband expressing how learning of it had shattered my heart. He replied to say only that Sidney is a baby, and I ought not to take offence at his liking best whoever is the present source of his nourishment.'

'I have a favour to ask of you, my love. Will you speak with my cousin and ask him to talk some reason into Mr Jackson? The man will not visit me here at Gilly's home, insisting that he does not wish to catch this plaguey business and pass it on to little Sidney – which I am all in agreement with, and I understand very well his fear and caution in that respect – but that is not what I wish my cousin to address. It has been at least forty days now since my lying-in, and my husband will not even allow me to TALK of his returning to my apartment once I am home. At first, I had considered that the poor man had been so horrified by the dramatics of the delivery room that I should never be at risk of having a second child.'

'He assures me, in that very elaborate, wonderfully officious way that he writes, that this is not at all the case. And the truth of it is his knowing a young woman in his college days who died of a horrid, convulsive fever entirely brought on by her husband's impatience after the birth of their third child (there is a great deal of difference between five days and five weeks, I told him!). As desirous as he claims himself to be to retake his place in my bed, I have just now a letter that informs me he will not at all endanger my life and intends to remain alone in his own till six months of my good health has elapsed. Six months! Good God! That is half a year! What a sentence is this! I have told Gilly, and he found it all very amusing (till, of course, I began to choke with a flood of tears), and he then reassured me that his brother would very soon give up these over-precautious notions.'

268

'Oh, but you must know Mr Jackson has, since last summer, been so very serious in his worries about my health, and he is very, very stubbornly minded when he is fixed on an idea. I beg you instruct Ralph explain to him that there is no need for such caution. Be pleased to take the man every book on obstetrics in my cousin's possession. Mr Jackson is an avid and quick reader and is far too rational to ignore the opinions of men of science even if he will ignore those of his wife, who ought to know her own body better than any book a man could write. I leave in your capable hands, dear creature, to return sense and reason to the husband of your,

Maria Jackson.'

A letter to Mrs Maria Jackson from Mr James Stuart:

'My sister and her husband, perhaps you have forgotten in your illness, left to collect Eliza four days ago and will be remaining in the country for at least a week. I would not have opened your letter – and upon seeing its contents, I wish I had not – but for your underscoring four times the word 'urgent' on its rear. I am sure your cousin shall attend to this matter with his usual diligence upon his return. Really, I am not perturbed to have stumbled across your letter for I had meant to write to you many days ago, to thank you for the gowns. There was not a name given with the parcel, but I really think only you could and would send such a gift. I have not seen them, but Mrs Stephens is indescribably happy to know she will be married in such a pretty gown, and little Caroline has asked every day if she may wear hers. We hope, very much, that you will be well enough recovered to attend.

Your obedient and faithful friend, James Stuart.'

A letter from Mr Paterson (Maria's Grandfather) addressed to Mr Harrington (written the summer before Maria's fifth birthday):

'The contents of this correspondence are delicate, and I shall not further pain you with indirectness; in the early hours of yesterday morning, Maria's condition deteriorated significantly, resulting in a succession of violent seizures of which I was made aware by frantic and despondent cries from her mother. We had all been in agreement that she suffered of a biley fever. The doctor himself was certain of it. Now, our notions of her ailment are all changed entirely.'

'Her cousin has watched every motion of her sickness fastidiously and had remarked several times at her confusions and paroxysms being worse always at the same times of day, usually a short period after mealtimes. Though the child will rarely eat, so we could not have presumed it anything in the food making her so sick. This morning, after another set of terrifying seizures – which I feared would leave the girl quite dead, and I thank the Lord for us all that they did not – her cousin, finding himself a little thirsty, took a drink of the cordial Maria's mother had brought to her, and which she always brings to her at breakfast, lunch and dinner.'

'The boy had an instant idea of what was wrong with the drink, but being young and unable to entirely trust his own instinct, brought the cordial for me to try; your wife, sir, my daughter moreover, has been, for only God knows how long, feeding dear Maria saltwater disguised beneath fruit cordial! When I recollect my many seafaring years, the symptoms of Maria's illness appear entirely consistent with such a cruel trick. The accused does not deny her maleficence and cries only to say, "An angel made me do it!" – she is far madder than we either had allowed. As soon as she is safe to travel, Maria must be immediately and permanently removed from her mother's presence. Mrs Harrington is, for now, kept locked in her chamber and shall not, I am determined, see her child again.

Your obedient and faithful servant, M. Paterson.'

Nine weeks later, Mr Harrington had granted his wife a walk with her daughter, under the strict supervision of himself and her father. They had been about fifty yards away, deep in conversation, when Mr Paterson had seen his daughter and granddaughter approach the edge of an adjacent river. In another moment, his daughter had thrown herself into the water, and little Maria, recovering to her feet on the riverbank, watched silently as her mother sank ever deeper.

The End.

Postscript: Not quite eleven months after young Sidney Jackson was born, he was joined by a darling little sister.

ABOUT THE AUTHOR

Abigail Ted is the debut author of, *Oh dear, Maria!*, whose love for 18th and 19th-century fiction transformed into her telling the story of a dynamite damsel with precarious sanity.

A PhD History student who specialises in Black-British authors of the abolition era, her obsession with 200-year-old novels and the writers who authored them is perhaps the first thing you'll notice after meeting her.

For over a decade, Abigail has enjoyed reading and writing stories that ironise reality, all while securing her bachelor's in history and education and her master's in theology. Today, she may be found munching inspiration from Richardson, Fielding, Austen, Thackeray et al., or perhaps roaming the wild with her mini-me and her other half.

Printed in Great Britain
by Amazon

26953420R00160